Praise for TURNING THIRTY

'Not just readable, fresh and witty but sophisticated in
_____'
Independent on Sunday

'A lively take on growing older.'
Guardian

'This is a warm, funny romantic comedy.'
Daily Mail

'Delightfully observant nostalgia . . . will strike a chord with
both sexes.'
She (Book of the Month)

'Mike Gayle manages to weave everything together with such
a warm-the-cockles-of-your-heart manner that once you've
finished reading Turning Thirty you want to turn right back to
the beginning and start all over again. It's real life – but better
than we know it.'
B Magazine

'Funny and endearing . . . chuckle-on-the-bus readable.'
Heat

Mike Gayle

Turning Thirty

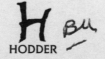

HODDER

First published in Great Britain in 2000 by Hodder & Stoughton
An Hachette UK company

First published in paperback in 2001

This paperback edition published in 2014

1

A CIP catalogue record for this title is available from the British Library.

ISBN 978 1 444 79012 2

Printed and bound by Clays Ltd, St Ives plc

Hodder & Stoughton policy is to use papers that are natural, renewable
and recyclable products and made from wood grown in sustainable forests.
The logging and manufacturing processes are expected to conform to the
environmental regulations of the
country of origin.

Hodder & Stoughton Ltd
338 Euston Road
London NW1 3BH

www.hodder.co.uk

For Jackie Behan and John O'Reilly,
two friends who, like me, are
turning thirty.

Happy birthday to you both.

Acknowledgements

A hearty thank you to all the usual suspects who have helped to get this particular show on the road. As ever a special mention must go to my wife, Claire, without whom you'd have handed over your hard-earned cash to read a couple of hundred pages of blank paper.

To all involved: Live long and prosper.

Acknowledgements

PEOPLE are suffering psychological damage because of society's obsession with 'perma-youth' says an expert . . . Many over-65s seek to prove they are 'young at heart' by rollerblading, taking up aerobics or visiting nightclubs . . . 'Perma-youth' has become the modern 'Holy Grail'. Youthful images in the media, the faces of young TV presenters and the fear of appearing 'past it' at work have all contributed to the trend.

report in the *Birmingham Evening Mail*

'I remember as I turned 30 I said to myself, "I have no more excuses for myself. I've got to figure these things out."'

Brad Pitt, 1999

nostalgia *n.* **1** a yearning for the return of past circumstances, events etc. **2.** the evocation of this emotion, as in book, film, etc. **3.** longing for home or family; homesickness. (Gk. *nostos*, return; *algos*, pain).

Collins English Dictionary

one

Here's the thing: for a long time I, Matt Beckford, had been looking forward to turning thirty. I'd been looking forward to the day when, by the power of thirty, I'd own a wine rack that actually contained wine. Not much of an ambition you might think and you'd probably be right, but then again you're not me. You see, in my world, when a bottle of wine enters it's usually consumed in its entirety in anything from twenty minutes (on a rough day) to twenty-four hours (on a not-so-rough day). This is not because I'm an alcoholic (not quite yet) but is simply due to a liking for wine combined with the fact that I have no self-control whatsoever. So what's my point? Well, the point is this (stay with it): wine racks by their very nature are designed to hold more than one bottle of wine. Some can hold six. Some can hold twelve. It doesn't really matter. What does matter are the big questions raised by the existence and desire for ownership of wine racks:

1) Who can actually afford to buy twelve bottles of wine in one go?
2) Who (assuming that they can afford it) would have twelve bottles of wine in the house, come in from

1

a hard day at work and resist the temptation to consume the lot?

3) Who thinks that wine racks are a good idea anyway?

The answer to 3 – and, for that matter, 2 and 1 – is, of course, thirty-people (as my girlfriend Elaine called them): the thirty-something; the thirty-nothing; the people who used to be twenty and are now . . . well, not so twenty. People like me. We who have scrimped, struggled and saved our way through our twenties precisely because one day in the future we wanted to be able to afford to buy multiple bottles of wine, store them in posh wine racks in our posh kitchens and . . . not drink them. Well, not all at once. We want to be able to show off the fact that finally, after all these years, we have self-control, a taste for the finer things in life, maturity even.

I wanted in. I was ready for it. Ready to embrace this brave new world! I had it all planned out. Right down to the last detail. That's the thing about turning thirty (other than wine racks): before you even get there you already think you know exactly what it will be like. Because it's the big milestone you've been looking forward to all your life that means you've arrived at adulthood. No other birthday has that same power. Thirteen? Pah! Acne and *angst*. Sixteen? More acne, more *angst*. Eighteen? Acne plus *angst* plus really horrible dress sense. Twenty-one? Acne, *angst*, plus a marginally improved dress sense. But thirty? Thirty really is the big one. Somewhere in your parents' house there is a list (or maybe just some random jottings) that you scribbled down when you were, oh . . . say, thirteen, about that near mythical date in the future when you would be turning thirty. In your own inimitable scrawl will be written things like: 'By the time I'm thirty . . . I want to be a [*insert name of flash job here*] and I'd like to be married to [*insert name of whichever person you were obsessed with at the time).'* What's clear from this exercise book is that even at the tender age of thirteen you've realised, like Freud once said, that when it comes to life, 'All that matters is love and work,' a statement that, if you're only thirteen, leads you to ponder two major questions:

1) **What am I going to do with my life?**
2) **Will I ever get a girlfriend?**

What am I going to do with my life?

The answer to the 'What am I going to do with my life?' question was always pretty obvious to me even at thirteen. While my schoolmates wanted to be everything from journalists to actors and lorry drivers through to spacemen, all I ever wanted to do in life was be a computer programmer. And I did just that. I went to university, got a degree in computing and went to work for a company in London called C-Tec that manufactures specially designed software for financial institutions. Okay, so I didn't get to invent the next Space Invaders, Frogger or Pac Man, which definitely was my dream when I was thirteen, but I was at least in the right area. So that was that one ticked off.

Will I ever get a girlfriend?

Of course, the answer to this question was yes (more of which later), but as I grew older it changed into the far deeper question: Is there a perfect woman out there for me, and if so who and where is she? Now, this was a little more difficult for me to answer, not least because, if I recall my more mature entries in the exercise-book correctly, I wrote down Madonna.

I didn't really start thinking about girls until quite late (very late judging by the antics of some of the kids at school) so by the time I'd given the subject any deep consideration my testosterone levels were more or less off the top of the scale. That's where Madonna came in. I remember clearly the first time I saw her on TV. She was on *Top of the Pops* promoting 'Lucky Star', the UK follow-up to 'Holiday', and I was blown away. She wasn't very well known in England at the time, so to my parents she was a mad-looking girl who wore far too much makeup and jewellery, with a penchant for religious imagery. But to me she was gorgeous. Even though I was a teenage boy from Birmingham and she was a twentysomething girl from New York, I was genuinely convinced that one day she'd be my girlfriend. That's the optimism of youth for you. 'Someone's got to be Madonna's boyfriend,' I'd reasoned at the time, 'because if no one thought they could be Madonna's boyfriend then she wouldn't have anyone to snog and Madonna looks to me like someone who needs snogging on a regular basis.'

Thing is, within a few years I'd grown out of my Madonna phase and moved on to real people . . . like Linda Phillips, with the nice smile who sat next to me in Geography, or Bethany Mitchell, a girl in the year above me at school whose tight grey school jumper left little to the imagination. Later still, however, I even outgrew Linda and, rather sadly Bethany, only to move on to *real* real people, the regular ones that you don't have to worship, like Ginny Pascoe, my old on/off girlfriend.

I call Ginny my 'girlfriend' but she was more accurately a girl who was also a friend who I sometimes snogged. We never actually gave what we had a name. It was more of an arrangement between us from the ages of sixteen to twenty-four. At first it wasn't even an arrangement, merely a bad habit. Fuelled by Thunderbird, a potent sweet wine that was then every teenage drinker's tipple of choice, we'd pair off together regularly at sixth-form discos, house parties, and occasionally even at our local, the Kings Arms. However, as soon as Monday morning at school arrived, Ginny and I would always, without fail, feign amnesia, dementia or just plain ignorance of such weekend couplings. This arrangement suited us both as, for a long time, I was in hot pursuit of Amanda Dixon, a girl with whom I had about as much chance of going out as Madonna during her 'Material Girl' phase. In turn, Ginny was in hot pursuit of Nathan Spence, who was not only equally beyond her pulling power but also had a 'reputation', which – in the most bizarre piece of feminine logic I'd come across at that tender age – served only to make him even more desirable. We were never weird about our arrangement (like a lot of odd situations the longer it was around the more normal it became) and, best of all, it never interfered with our friendship. We were friends. And we were sometimes more than friends. And that was that.

As time moved on, so did Ginny and I . . . sort of. She went off to university in Brighton and I departed to university in Hull. Over the next decade or so a steady stream of girls wandered in and out of my life. Each one, I thought, if only for a second, might be the one I'd turn thirty with. For the sake of brevity and embarrassment the list reads like this:

Age: Nineteen
Girls that year: *Ruth Morrell* (a couple of weeks), *Debbie Foley* (a couple of weeks), *Estelle Thompson* (a couple of weeks) and *Anne-Marie Shakir* (a couple of weeks)
Number of times got off with Ginny Pascoe: 8

Age: Twenty
Girls that year: *Faye Hewitt* (eight months), *Vanessa Wright* (on and off for two months)

Number of times got off with Ginny Pascoe: 5

Age: Twenty-one
Girls that year: *Nicky Rowlands* (under a month) and *Maxine Walsh* (nine months)
Number of times got off with Ginny Pascoe: 3

Age: Twenty-two
Girls that year: *Jane Anderson* (two and a bit months) and *Chantelle Stephens* (three months)
Number of times got off with Ginny Pascoe: 10 (a spectacularly bad year for self-control)

Age: Twenty-three
Girls that year: *Harriet 'Harry' Lane* (roughly ten months on and off)
Number of times got off with Ginny Pascoe: 3

Age: Twenty-four
Girls that year: *Natalie Hadleigh* (two months), *Siobhan Mackey* (two months) and *Jennifer Long* (two months)
Number of times got off with Ginny Pascoe: 1

Age: Twenty-five
Girls that year: *Jo Bruton* (a weekend), *Kathryn Fletcher* (nine months-ish), *Becca Caldicott* (one month)
Number of times got off with Ginny Pascoe: 0 (lost contact)

Age: Twenty-six

Girls that year: *Anna O'Hagan* (ten months), *Liz Ward-Smith* (one day), *Dani Scott* (one day), *Eve Chadwick* (a day and a half)
Number of times got off with Ginny Pascoe:
  0 (contact still lost)

Age: Twenty-seven
Girls that year: *Monica Aspel* (nearly but not quite a year)
Number of times got off with Ginny Pascoe:
  0 (contact all but forgotten)

Following the events I will refer to only as 'The Monica Aspel Débâcle', and with no Ginny Pascoe around with whom to find comfort, I decided at the age of twenty-seven that enough was enough and put my name forward for a transfer from the London office of C-Tec to its New York base. After all, I told myself, a change is as good as a rest, and what I needed was a rest from women so that I could concentrate on getting my career to the level at which it should have been. After only two days in the Big Apple, however, I met Elaine Thomas, an attractive, intelligent, slightly 'out there' twenty-year-old student at NYU, who had a passion for bad food, long telephone conversations and Englishmen. We fell in love and following a ridiculously short courtship ended up living together. Finally I allowed myself to relax because, after all this time, after all these girls, I knew which one I would be with when I was thirty.

And it wasn't Madonna.

And it wasn't Ginny Pascoe either.

It was Elaine. My Elaine. And I was happy.

Until it all fell apart.

7

NEW YORK

two

It was a cold, wet day in late September, the day everything fell apart. I'd just come home from work to find that Elaine, as usual, was on the phone. Elaine loved the phone. It was her life. There were times when I'd get home earlier than her, which wasn't that often, and she'd come through the door talking on her mobile, wave hello and kiss me, and while still on the first call dial a second number on our land line and time the end of her first conversation to coincide, to the very second, with the beginning of the second call. I always wondered whether it was just a matter of practice or merely a fluke of nature and I actually asked her once. She flashed me her best smile and said in her most East Coast manner, the one that always made me feel like I was watching TV, 'Bill Gates has a way with computers, Picasso had a way with a paintbrush . . . I have a way with the telephone. It's my gift to the world.'

Depositing my bag on the floor, I kissed her hello and she kissed me back, without breaking her conversation. At a loss as to what to do next, I sat down beside her on the sofa and tried to work out who she was talking to. She seemed to be doing more listening than talking, which was odd for Elaine. In the conversation she was having there were lots of I knows, and so-what-did-you-dos? and Oh-that's-awfuls, and my favourite, 'Hey-ho', which could be translated as 'That's life,' or 'Whatever,' depending on the intonation of her voice. Anyway there were no clues to be had. It might've been any one of Elaine's several million friends. I waited a few minutes for her to finish, but it soon became obvious that that wouldn't be happening for quite a while so I disappeared to the kitchen to see if she'd started dinner.

The kitchen was spotless – just the way I'd left it when I'd cleaned it nine hours earlier before I went to work – and there was no sign of any culinary activity in progress. It wasn't as if I expected Elaine to cook dinner for us because she was a woman (she'd long forced me to give up that idea), no, I expected her to cook dinner for us because it was her turn today. She'd pulled a sickie from work after oversleeping that morning and she'd promised me she was going to do the weekly shop and I hoped – rather optimistically, it seemed – that she might have got in 'something nice'.

In search of evidence of shopping endeavours, I checked all the kitchen cupboards. There was nothing that could be construed as 'something nice', save a bag of pasta twirls, a jar of Marmite my mum had posted to me and two slices of bread so stale that when I accidentally dropped them on the kitchen counter they snapped into pieces. Even a cup of tea was out of the question because the PG Tips tea-bags Mum had also sent (along with the Marmite and a video-tape of two weeks' worth of *EastEnders*) had run out and I absolutely refused to drink any other brand.

Ravenous beyond belief, I returned to the living room chewing a pasta twirl and lodged myself beside my girlfriend once more. She immediately picked up the remote control, pressed the on button and pointed her deftly manicured finger in the TV's direction as if to say, 'Look, pretty lights!'

or, more accurately, 'I'll be off the phone in an hour, amuse yourself.' I ignored her suggestion and bounced up and down on the sofa to annoy her: I didn't want the TV – I wanted her attention and some food. She wasn't having any of it, of course, and did her best to ignore *me*. So I stood up, as if heading towards the window that overlooked our street and pretended to faint before I got there. Lying still on the carpet, barely breathing, I waited patiently for her to respond to her dutiful boyfriend's lack of consciousness. After what felt like several minutes, in which she'd failed to pause for breath let alone end the conversation, I carefully opened an eye but she spotted me immediately and laughed.

'Who is it?' I mouthed silently, from my position on the floor.

'Your mom,' she mouthed back. 'Are you in?'

I shook my head violently mouthing, 'Not in,' repeatedly. It wasn't that I didn't like my mum. I liked her a lot. I loved her even. But with her these days, with me so far from home, there really was no such thing as a quick chat and as I'd already called her this morning at work I reasoned I'd paid my dues. Anyway, I really was hungry now so I mouthed at Elaine, 'Where's my dinner?'

She raised her left eyebrow suggestively, as if to say, 'Ask me for dinner, will you? We'll see about that!' and then she narrowed her eyes like some sort of mischievous imp and said down the line, 'I think I hear Matt coming in, Cynthia,' then paused, waiting for my response, which was to hand her both the menu for the nearest takeaway pizzeria and my credit card.

'No, it wasn't Matt after all,' said Elaine sweetly, into the phone, while miming the swiping of my credit card through an imaginary card reader. 'I must be hearing things. Well, I must be going, Cynthia. I think I hear the door buzzer. 'Bye.'

She moved to put the phone down but was forced to stop half-way as my mother was still talking. 'No, I don't think it'll be Matt, Cynthia,' she said patiently. 'He's been such a good boy recently that I actually let him have his own keys.' With that she hung up.

'You're such a baby, Matt,' she said, rolling her eyes. 'I don't know why you couldn't have suggested getting a takeaway in the first place.'

'It was your turn to cook,' I protested. 'You do know what "your turn" means, don't you?'

'Yes, well . . .' she began, but her retort faded away as she picked up the delivery menu and scanned through it. 'It looks like it's going to be my turn to call the pizza place, doesn't it?' She continued to scan the menu, and every now and again she mouthed the name of a pizza as if rolling the word around her tongue was an experience similar to eating it.

'I'm sure your mom knew I was lying,' she said, her finger hovering above a Hawaiian Meat Feast. 'The last thing in the world I need is for her to not like me. You know how important it is that everyone likes me. I can't sleep if I know there's someone thinking bad thoughts about me – even in England.' She flopped back against the sofa then swivelled round to lay her head on my lap. 'That has got to be the last time I ever lie to Mrs B.'

'Sure,' I responded. 'Just as long as you remember your words of wisdom next time Mama and Papa Thomas ring and you want me to pretend you're in the shower.'

'Well said, my good man,' said Elaine, adopting a pitiful English accent. 'I'll lie for you and you lie for me, that's the deal. But remember, if we get struck down by lightning for lying to our parents in years to come, we'll only have ourselves to blame.'

'How long were you on the phone to her anyway?'

'She was only going to talk for about five minutes because of the cost. So I called her back,' she thought for a moment, 'so all in all that would be about half an hour.'

'To England?'

She rolled her eyes again.

'Do you know how much that'll cost?'

'It's only money, Matt. You're meant to spend it. If you didn't spend it, it wouldn't be money. It would be just pieces of paper that *you* never did anything with.'

'You really believe that, don't you?'

'Every word,' she said, and smiled angelically.

There was no point in arguing with Elaine on this one. At the best of times she had only the most tenuous grasp of the principle of not spending every single dollar she earned, and even then she ignored it.

'What were you two talking about?' I asked.

'Girl stuff.'

'What kind of girl stuff? She wasn't asking you when we're having kids again, was she?' My mum had really been trying to bond with Elaine because she'd made up her mind that she might be the one to give her grandchildren. 'Tell me she wasn't.'

Elaine laughed. 'Nothing so sinister. She just wanted to ask me what you were doing for your thirtieth. And if you're going to spend it in the UK.'

'It's not until the end of March!'

'We girls like to prepare.'

'So what did you say?'

'I said you didn't know.'

'What did she say?'

'She said you should give it some thought.'

'What did you say about my coming home?'

'I said I'd talk you into it because I'd like to see the place you call home for myself. See where you grew up, meet your old school friends, it'd be fun.'

'Hmm,' I said dismissively, even though I quite liked the idea of visiting home for a while. 'What did she say?'

'She said that we can come any time. Oh, and that I should get you to call back.'

'How did she sound?'

Elaine lost patience with me and threw a cushion at my head. 'If you were that interested why didn't you just speak to her?' She took the cushion back, put it underneath her head, picked up the phone and ordered some random takeaway food. This kind of banter was typical of Elaine's and my everyday interaction. It was tiring but always entertaining, although sometimes I felt like we were trapped inside sitcom world – sometimes I wondered why we never had proper conversations like normal couples did.

'I'm going to pick it up,' she said. 'They said it'd be ready in twenty minutes but I figure if I go pick it up myself it'll make them speed up – I'm ravenous.' She went to the bedroom to get her coat. As she checked her pockets to make sure she had enough money she opened the front door then picked up her bag from the table. Suddenly she stopped.

'What's up?' I asked, looking over at her. 'Forget something?'

Leaving the door half open, she walked across the room and sat on the sofa at the opposite end to me. 'I'm sorry, babe,' she said gently, 'I can't not say this any more.'

I didn't understand. 'You can't not say what any more?'

'This,' she said flatly. 'You. Me. Us. I . . . I . . . don't think I love you any more. There I've said it. You can go ahead and hate me now.' Much to Elaine's consternation an uncontrollable urge to laugh came over me and I let it out. 'Are you laughing at me or with me?' she said, staring hard at me.

'I know you're going to think I'm just saying this to get even,' I said, holding her gaze, 'but the truth is, I feel exactly the same way.'

Then eerily, in that couple symmetry that often develops when you spend so much time with someone that you feel you must be them, we both burst into another fit of laughter then simultaneously whispered, 'What a relief.'

three

'So that's that, then?' I said blankly.

It was two in the morning and Elaine and I had been talking about splitting up from seven o'clock the previous evening. There were no tears, no histrionics, just a lot of long silences followed by a few words of bewilderment, followed by some more long silences.

'I guess so,' said Elaine. She accompanied her words with a shrug, an odd sort of stretch and a peculiarly feline yawn. I'd always thought there was something quite cat-like about her, and more so than ever now: she reminded me of a Persian desperate for its belly to be stroked.

'Wasn't this all . . .' I searched around my vocabulary '. . . a bit too easy? A bit too . . . you know?' I finally stumbled across the right word. 'Civilised?'

Elaine tilted her head upwards. 'Yeah, you're right,' she said. 'I guess you're right.'

I looked at her encouragingly because I wanted her to say something, anything, really, because I knew this was wrong – not us splitting up, that was definitely right, but the lack of drama. On the form of previous break-ups I expected a good deal more grieving, if for no other reason than politeness. Our calm and collected so-long-and-thanks-for-the-nice-time attitude troubled me. I wondered whether this was one of the curious by-products of the turning-thirty process. I'd been twenty-nine for just over six months and had long been expecting some sort of change to come upon me now that thirty was just around the corner – the ability to grow a full beard without bald patches, my elusive wine rack, a partner for life, even – but nothing had happened. Maybe this is it, I told myself. This is my thirty-power: the ability to take the end of a relationship on the chin, like a real man.

When I was twenty-seven this sort of thing would have upset me (*see* Monica Aspel). When I was twenty-two this would have had me scurrying to bed with heart failure (*see* Jane Anderson and Chantelle Stephens). But this numbness . . . this ridiculous passivity was new. But at least, if it was the gift of turning thirty, I had an excuse. Elaine, on the other hand, was still only twenty-two.

'Shouldn't there be more . . . wailing and gnashing of teeth?' I said, after a few moments. I passed her the cup of coffee I'd made for her earlier. 'Shouldn't one of us be begging the other to continue the relationship?'

She handed her coffee back to me and got down on her knees. 'Stay with me, Matt! We can't split up! How will I ever live without you?' She attempted to stand up again but was barely able to for laughing. 'You're right. It does feel kinda lame for me to go, "I think we should break up," and for you to go, "Okay." She laughed gently. 'It's not like I don't love you,' she said, looking at me with a mixture of earnestness and irony. 'I do. You know I do. I can't have been with you, made a home with you this last year and a half without loving you – that's just . . . stupid. It's just that, well, you must've felt it like I did these last six months. The passion has gone. We've been more like . . . I don't know . . . brother and sister, really.'

'Peter and Jane,' I suggested.

'Hansel and Gretel,' she retorted.

'Donny and Marie,' I countered.

'Exactly,' she said, taking back her coffee. She took a moment to sip it. 'Recently when I've looked at you I don't so much want to tear your clothes off as give them a good ironing.'

'You're right,' I replied. 'I mean, I love you too, but I have to admit I'm not *in* love with you. It's like I'd see you first thing in the morning getting ready for work, there you'd be, searching desperately through the closet for something to wear and I'd find myself mentally dressing you with my eyes. By the time you've decided what to wear I have you sporting a chunky-knit polo-neck jumper, a knee-length overcoat and a scarf.'

'What do you think this all means?' she asked, as if she genuinely wanted an answer. 'Do you think it's normal to be so civilised?'

I shrugged. 'I don't think so. I mean, every time a relationship finishes for one of my friends at work and I ask both sides what happened they're always like "It was mutual", as if it'll earn them some sort of Brownie points. But I think this is a first – the first mutual break-up in the history of the world.'

'This is spooky,' said Elaine. 'Where did we get this power and why didn't I have it when I really needed it, like when I was fourteen?' She stood up and disappeared into the kitchen to return with a packet of Oreos, which she consumed one after the other. When she was half-way through her fourth she suddenly shouted, 'I've got it!' and waved a partly consumed biscuit and its attendant crumbs over the coffee table.

'You've got what exactly?'

'The answer,' she replied. 'It's biology. Even at a cellular level we're programmed to perpetuate the species, right?'

I nodded.

'And despite your mom's encouragement we have no urge whatsoever to perpetuate with each other, right?'

I nodded again.

'That's why we're not upset. Biology is telling us there's no point in crying over spilt milk.'

four

It was eleven o'clock on the following Saturday morning, and we'd just finished breakfast. Five days had elapsed since our decision to split up and I was now sleeping on the sofa (a.k.a the Sofa from Hell), which explained why my neck was killing me. On Tuesday I'd told Paul Barron, my boss at work, that I wanted a transfer out of New York and preferably out of the USA altogether. While I'd enjoyed my time there and made a few friends, I knew I didn't want to stay now that Elaine and I were over. A move was definitely what I needed. 'Matt,' began my boss, by way of an answer to my request, 'at the kind of level you've attained here, as a software design team leader, the world is your oyster.' Roughly translated, he meant that because I was good at my job, which I was, I had the choice of all of the company's European offices: London, Paris, Milan and Barcelona. 'Thanks, Paul,' I'd replied. 'That's . . . that's nice.' He then asked me where I wanted to go and that was when I looked really stupid. 'I don't know,' I said. 'I just know I want to go.' He'd smiled and told me to think about it and get back to him.

I looked at Elaine across the empty breakfast plates. I hadn't told her that I was planning to transfer yet. I think I was waiting for the right moment, but right now I didn't feel this was it. Elaine was wearing her slob-around-the-apartment garb: a marl grey T-shirt that she used to wear to her yoga class and a pair of brown shorts from the Gap she'd bought the year that brown was the new black. She had nothing on her feet and she was picking at the dark red polish on her toenails. No one seeing her now would've guessed that she worked for one of New York's coolest public-relations companies albeit in the lower echelons. Monday to Friday she did her work uniform of fashionable-yet-stylish very well. Saturday was her day off.

'What are you thinking?' she asked.

I'd obviously been thinking a little too hard about my transfer. 'What brought things to a head for you?' I asked, as a way out of confronting the transfer. 'I mean, was it any one thing or was it lots of things combined?'

'I think it was that film we watched at Sara and Jimmy's last weekend,' she said, still playing with her toes.

'*The English Patient*?'

She nodded. 'It just got me thinking, you know? That poor English guy's wife runs off with that German pilot and that was supposed to be romantic. I mean, affairs they're so . . . sleazy, they're so yuck. By which I suppose I mean that . . . Well, you know Emily?' Emily was one of Elaine's workmates. 'You know she split up with her boyfriend, Jez, because he went all funny 'cause he didn't think he'd done enough with his life?'

'I think you'll find that what Jez wanted to "do" – and, in fact, actually was "doing" – was more women.'

'And she was having a gadzillion affairs with anything that had a hairy chest and a gym membership card.'

'Gadzillions?' I asked, pulling a face.

'Millions of gadzillions,' said Elaine. 'Millions.' She paused. 'It's just so horrible, isn't it? They obviously just got bored of each other but were afraid to call it quits when their time was up and because of that they put themselves through months of misery dragging the whole thing out . . .' She let her sentence hang in mid-air momentarily, then picked it up. 'The thing is, Matt, you've got to have known we were at that stage.'

'Were we?' I tried to catch her eyes but she wouldn't look at me. Instead she was back to playing with her toes.

'Well, maybe not *that* stage exactly. But we were definitely at the stage where we'd start looking at other people – me, the cute motorcycle delivery guy with the dreadlocks who always smiles at me when we share the elevator; you, the girl in the deli with the belly-button ring, who gives you extra filling in your sandwiches because she thinks you look cute.'

'Which deli girl?'

Elaine narrowed her eyes at me. 'You'd better believe I made her up.' She giggled. 'Before either of us would realise, looking would lead to longing, which would inevitably lead to doing, and I'd hate for us to finish that way. Absolutely hate it. We're better than that. This way we keep an element of control. We can split up with dignity.' She went on thoughtfully, 'You know, I never was your dream girl, was I? And you certainly weren't my dream guy. We just sort of drifted together. And you've got to know that if things had stayed the same and my dream guy had turned up—'

'I would've been in the way.'

'And vice versa.'

She'd made a very good point. I'd always thought that Elaine (whose opening gambit to me was, 'Hi, I have a thing for British men') would've been far more suited to someone taller, more manly looking, with big hands, a boarding-school education and perhaps a family connection to a minor member of royalty. As for me, I suppose I looked like I should've been with someone a bit creative, a singer, an artist, a dancer – the kind of woman who's a bit mad. Not barking mad, but Janis Joplin mad. The kind of woman who walks around without shoes on in the summer and attempts suicide on an annual basis. Joking apart, she had a point.

'So you mean to say that if we'd rented *Pride and Prejudice* like Sara wanted instead of *The English Patient* we'd still be together? Now, that's a weird one.'

Elaine laughed like I'd really tickled her. 'No,' she said, when she'd recovered, 'it still would've happened. But instead of all that *English Patient* stuff I would've realised that you were never going to be my Mr Darcy.'

'Or you my Elizabeth Bennet.'

five

'I mean, we've been struggling since the dawn of time,' said Elaine plaintively. 'We do *waaaaay* too many things that annoy each other.'

It was 7.30 a.m. and Elaine and I were walking along the street towards the subway on our way to work. Four weeks had now gone by and my back was considerably better because I was now sleeping in our bed. Elaine, however, had decamped to the Sofa from Hell because she felt guilty about my bad back. Paul Barron had taken me out to lunch earlier in the week to tell me that my transfer request had been confirmed and that I would be free to leave as soon as I told Human Resources where I wanted to go. He even spent an hour trying to persuade me to stay, which was both flattering and embarrassing. I told him I'd let him know where I wanted to go as soon as I'd made up my mind. He gave me a weird kind of shoulder squeeze that I think was meant to say, 'It was good to have a guy like you on the team,' but which came across as a Vulcan death grip. For hours afterwards I had twinges down my back.

'Breaking up is definitely the right thing to do,' I said, as we descended the stairs to the subway entrance.

'Without a doubt,' she replied. 'I was a terrible girlfriend, really. Probably one of the worst in living memory. I don't cook, I don't clean, and I leave my underwear drying on the radiator, which I know drives you insane.'

This was all true, Elaine *was* a terrible girlfriend. Not only did she do all of the things mentioned, she bought exotic items like star anise or kumquats, promising to 'do something' with them. Then she'd put them in a bowl in the kitchen and leave them to rot.

We walked down to the subway platform and waited for the D train. As usual, the platform was crowded above and beyond the call of duty. I took a brief look around. There were people reading newspapers, people trying to read the newspaper of the person standing next to them, people eating Pop Tarts, and people just staring into space. I think we were the only people over-analysing a recently deceased relationship.

'I wasn't perfect either,' I said, taking up our conversation again.

'No, you weren't,' she said quietly. 'But at least you tried. Anyway, now you're free of all that. Free to look for Ms Perfect.'

'What's she like, this Ms P?'

'Hmm, let's see. What type of woman do you like?' She thought for a moment. 'She'll be older than me – more your kind of age – so that she'll get all the references to your jokes without you having to explain them. She'll be British too, for exactly the same reason. She'll dress well but not overly trendy and when you're with her you'll feel comfortable. And when you look into her eyes you'll feel like you've come home.' She paused, then added, 'Oh, and she'll have a pair of puppies so perky you positively won't know what to do with yourself.'

'Interesting,' I replied vaguely. 'Very interesting.'

'And what about my next bloke?' said Elaine, over-pro-nouncing the word 'bloke', on purpose as if to to say, 'I'll miss you and your curious English words.' 'What will my next hunk o' love be like?'

I sniffed, then scratched my chin and did all the other actions you're supposed to do when mulling over a question. 'All right,' I said, once I'd annoyed her with my pantomime. 'He's about twenty-one, maybe even twenty. He's still at college. He's studying drama. He has loads of cool friends who are actors and writers and he DJs at a club downtown at the weekend. And on a Saturday night you'll stay up until Sunday morning just talking. And when he's with you, he'll make you feel like the centre of the universe.'

Elaine arched her left eyebrow. 'Not bad, Mr Beckford, not bad at all. Have you been reading my diary?'

'No,' I said. 'It wasn't that hard. I just tried to think of someone who wasn't me.'

The train arrived and we struggled through the doors before everyone else and got the last two seats next to each other. As we settled ourselves the carriage filled up until everyone seated had their own personal standing passenger leaning into them in rhythm with the train movements. Elaine got out a novel she was reading so I thought perhaps we'd finished talking, but after a few moments she stopped and laid it face down on her lap.

'Matt?' The question in her voice indicated that I was the source of her inability to read her book. 'If you knew things were wrong between us why didn't you say anything?'

'Hmmm.' I stalled. 'Good question.'

I was playing for time because the answer to her question was simple: I was turning thirty. Elaine was supposed to be the one I was going to turn thirty with. I'd had it all planned out. The fact that things hadn't been going well between us wasn't at the top of my agenda. All I knew was that I had to stick to the plan and not be alone. And because of that I'd seen hope where there wasn't any. I'd wanted to try and save that which was well and truly beyond salvation.

'Bees,' I said, eventually as I noted that the middle-aged woman sitting in the seat next to me was no longer concentrating on the comment page of the *New York Post* but instead was straining with every fibre to listen to our conversation. 'Crippled bumble bees, to be exact.'

'Bees?' queried Elaine.

'Yeah, big fat furry ones.' I sighed, turned to *New York Post* Woman and stared at her until she got the message. 'When I was a kid I used to get upset if I ever came across a dying bumble bee in the garden. The logic of my five-year-old brain ran something like this: It's wrong that something so cute and furry, something that makes honey and generally helps out in the garden, should have to come to an end. So whenever I saw a dying bee I'd try to make it better. I'd place it on the edge of a saucer with some sugary water and encourage it to drink in the hope that it would get better.'

'Did they live?'

'No. They always—' I stopped mid-sentence. *New York Post* Woman was back again. I stared at her once more and this time she lifted her newspaper right up. 'What I'm trying to say,' I continued, 'is that I suppose you and me – us – well, our relationship was a crippled bumble bee. And I suppose I was hoping that maybe we'd get better. But when you called it a day I knew it was over. But no matter how inevitable something is it's still a shock when it happens.' I looked over at Elaine, who had tears in her eyes. 'What's the matter?'

'Bees,' she said quietly. 'That's got to be the dumbest analogy I've ever heard.'

six

By the time I was ready to move out three months had gone by since Elaine and I had decided to split. Just before Christmas I'd had another meeting with my boss. I'd been all geared up to tell him that I'd made up my mind and that I wanted to be transferred back to London when he made me an offer I found impossible to refuse. The company was planning to open a new office in Sydney, Australia and they wanted to promote me to design consultant to oversee the setting up of the software team. The contract would be for six months to a year initially, and the money would double overnight. It was my dream thirtysomething job, with dream thirtysomething money to match.

Perfect. Well, nearly. The only problem was that they wouldn't be starting the project for two months and wouldn't require my assistance for another month after that. In short, I'd spend three months in transfer limbo. The initial suggestion was that I stay in New York, but I told him that was out of the question and suggested I went to the London office for a while. However, it seemed that finding me work there for just three months would cause more problems than it solved. Finally, at the end of what turned out to be a three-hour meeting, I came up with a solution: that

I take the three months off as an unpaid sabbatical. And they agreed.

After eight years of working I wanted a rest. I needed a rest. Unlike most of my mates at university I hadn't taken a year off before or after my degree, and since I'd got a job straight from university I'd never had much of a holiday either. I had enough money stashed in savings accounts to last twice the amount of time on offer so there was nothing to stop me.

'What will you do with yourself?' asked my boss, as if reading my mind. 'Go lie on a beach? Travel?'

'No,' I replied, with such conviction that it shocked me. 'I'm going to go home. I'm going home to Birmingham – see my parents, catch up with old friends and celebrate my thirtieth birthday.'

There were, of course, a lot of reasons why my good idea was actually a very bad one and all of them involved my parents. The top three:

1) The knowledge that, without a doubt, my parents would drive me insane if I spent any longer than twenty-four hours under the same roof as them.
2) The simple fact that there isn't a single way in the English language of making the words, 'I'm moving back in with my parents,' sound the slightest bit cool when you're twenty-nine years old.
3) I couldn't think of another one. The first two were already more than enough.

Despite all this – the parent/child clash, the distinct loss of cool – I knew that home was the only place to go. If life was a maze in which we're supposed to find some kind of answer, then my move across the Atlantic and my relationship with

Elaine had been a huge trip down a long, torturous dead end. It seemed fitting then, now that I was momentarily rudderless, to go back to the beginning. So I made the decision. I was going home for a break, not only from work but from life. I was going to live with my folks, let my mum fuss over me, let my dad give me gardening tips. And in three months' time – by the time I had turned thirty – I'd be ready for a new beginning in Australia.

That was my mission.

seven

My final day in New York came faster than I anticipated and the final few hours even faster. I'd been packing all day and was in the middle of putting my last pair of socks and my laptop into a holdall when a fresh-from-work Elaine knocked on the bedroom door and came in. I noticed sadly that she wasn't on the phone as usual. This evening, my final evening, was special.

'Hi,' she said quietly, and put down her bag on the bed.

'Hi,' I replied, almost as quietly. 'How was work?'

'Work was cool,' she replied. 'You know I had that product shoot today? Well, Martha came to the shoot with orange hair.' Martha was another of Elaine's countless friends. 'She dyed it as a bet with her boyfriend.'

'Insane,' I said, with mock disbelief.

She laughed, and as her grin faded to a smile her eyes seemed to sparkle and I could see that she wanted to tell me some more gossip, to share with me more about her day as she usually did. Then her eyes flitted across to my bags on the bed and the smile evaporated. The sparkle disappeared too.

'How was your day?' she asked, sitting on the edge of the bed.

I shrugged.

'Have you got everything you need?' Elaine was now exuding that kind of loose energy people give off when they don't know what to do but are desperate to do something.

'Yeah, I think so,' I replied, even though I wasn't at all sure.

'What about your toothbrush?'

'Yeah, you're right. Good thinking. I haven't got that.' I disappeared into the bathroom and searched high and low for the toothbrush but couldn't find it anywhere. I returned to the bedroom. 'Can't find it.'

'It's on top of the radio in the kitchen,' she said, without looking at me. 'Where you left it.'

I disappeared to find it and returned, seconds later, toothbrush in hand.

'I'll miss that,' she said, as I returned and dropped it into the bag.

'What?'

'Knowing where all the things you think you've lost are. I can't help but feel that without me you're never going to find anything you own ever again.'

The fact that it had always been me who knew where everything was seemed to have escaped her but I could see that she meant well. Now that we were parting she wanted to give the impression that she'd been the kind of girlfriend who was good at that sort of thing. While I checked around to make sure I hadn't left anything important she followed after me handing me things I'd overlooked that were practically essential to my survival. An hour later my soon-to-be ex-girlfriend and I were standing at Passport Control at JFK.

'Matt?'

'Yeah?'

'Call me when you reach England.'

I nodded, then carefully corrected myself. I couldn't really see that happening. Unlike Elaine I wasn't a great fan of telephones. 'I'll e-mail you at work,' I suggested. 'We can be transatlantic pen-pals . . . and this way you can keep your phone bills down to a minimum.'

That seemed to lift her spirits a little so I picked up my bags and turned to leave. That was the moment I questioned what I'd considered to be the truth all this time.

Was this a mutual break-up?

Did this have anything to do with turning thirty?

Or was this me letting the best thing that had ever happened to me go without a fight?

My change of heart must have been obvious because Elaine started to cry the first real tears of the whole of our three-month protracted break-up. But she didn't say, 'Stay,' or 'Don't go,' she just kissed me, a long, slow, passionate kiss and walked away.

BIRMINGHAM

Month One

Date: Jan 9th
Days left until thirtieth birthday: 81
State of mind: Not too bad I suppose.

eight

'Where to, mate?' said the taxi-driver, as I hauled my holdall and suitcase inside the black cab and settled into its shiny cushiony seat.

'Marlborough Road, King's Heath,' I replied carefully. There was something familiar about him that I couldn't quite place.

He pulled off. 'Been on holiday, have you?'

'Nah,' I said. 'I've just come back from New York where I live – sorry, lived.'

'I've got a cousin in Washington DC,' he replied, by way of nothing.

'Really?'

'Yeah.' He glanced at me in his mirror. 'Never liked him very much, though. Always found him a bit stuck-up, if you get my meaning. Mind you, they were all a bit like that on his side of the family.' He flicked the end of his nose in an attempt either to remove a stray bogey or indicate that his cousin's side of the family had upturned noses. He laughed curtly and brushed the end of his fingers against the steering-wheel.

The cabbie remained silent for the rest of the journey, tapping his fingers on the fur-covered steering-wheel in time to the music on the pirate radio station he was listening to.

I had racked my brains but I still couldn't place where I knew him from so I gazed out of the cab window at the cityscape.

Birmingham, like most industry-based cities, was undergoing a face-lift but its metamorphosis had been rapid and forced – I barely recognised it. It was as if its citizens had tired of it being a national joke and told it to smarten up its act. But despite its near-comic status among the rest of the nation I'd always been proud of coming from Birmingham, precisely because it was so funny. It's hard to take yourself too seriously when the whole nation thinks you're there to amuse them.

This was especially the case during my five years in London. The moment anyone there heard me speak they assumed I was bordering on clinical stupidity and would therefore speak v-e-r-y s-l-o-w-l-y or expected me to act like some sort of latterday court jester: they would goad me into saying words like 'actually' (*ack-chur-lie*) 'going' (*gewin'*) and 'Birmingham' (*Bhuuuuur-ming-gum*), thus revealing my accent in its fullest sing-song glory. It got to the stage where I felt I had to justify to everyone I met *why* I came from Birmingham, as if it was some sort of handicap, curse or practical joke taken a step too far. But I didn't care. This was where I was from and there would always be a part of me that would love the city as long as I lived.

'Excuse me, mate,' said the cabbie, interrupting my reverie, 'but is your name Matt Beckford?'

'Yeah,' I replied cautiously. 'It is.'

'I knew it,' he said. 'Ever since I picked you up I've been trying to work out where I know you from.'

'And where do you know me from?'

'You won't remember me,' he said, turning down the radio, 'but I went to the same secondary school as you, King's

Heath Comprehensive.' He turned and offered his hand. 'Tony Goddard.'

The name rang a bell. 'Dave Goddard's little brother?'

'That's the one.'

'Dave Goddard,' I mused. 'Now, there's a name I haven't heard in years.' Back in my schooldays Dave Goddard had always been the boy most likely to become a brain surgeon. 'What's he doing now?'

'He's in Canada,' said the cabbie. 'Toronto, to be exact. Met a girl there on holiday and moved out about five years ago. He's got three kids and a massive house. He's really living the life.'

I couldn't help myself. 'Is he a brain surgeon, then? He was so smart we always reckoned that's what he'd do.'

The cabbie laughed. 'I know what you mean. He was miles smarter than anyone in our family. But no, he's not. He's a lawyer. Specialises in commercial law.'

'And you're his little brother?'

'I was only twelve when you were at King's Heath. You and my brother were at the top end of the school and I was at the bottom.' He chuckled to himself. 'I tell you what, though.'

'What?'

'You were cool in those days, you know. There were some great stories about you.'

'I doubt it,' I said, embarrassed.

To prove his case he cited some of the legendary events in which I'd supposedly been involved in my schooldays, starting with the time I staged a roof-top protest over the inedible state of our school dinners (true: I got suspended for a fortnight), moved on to the time I streaked naked across the school playing-fields for a dare (false: an urban myth) and concluded with when I organised a policewoman kiss-o-gram for Mr Frederick, my form teacher, to celebrate his fortieth birthday (semi-true: I organised it but the school secretary twigged what she was up to and wouldn't let her in). It was weird hearing him describe these events with the sort of reverent tones usually reserved for the first man on the moon or the fall of the Berlin Wall. But I suppose when you're only twelve the kind of once-in-a-lifetime events that you're actually interested in are the ones that involve sex, nudity and roof-top protests.

'They certainly were good days,' I confided, 'probably the best. But I wasn't the most popular kid at school, that's for sure. I was just like everyone else, keeping my head down, trying to survive.'

We talked about the old days, sharing as much as we had in common. I told him about my life and what I'd been up to. He told me about his life and what he'd been up to, and then he told me about a few of the kids from my year at school that he'd heard about through the ex-King's Heath Comprehensive grapevine. The names he mentioned were ones that I had long forgotten. People like Peter Whittacker (then, the boy most likely to become a professional athlete) was now a sales administrator for a double-glazing firm; Gemma Piper (then, the girl most likely to go to Oxford and become the new Kenneth Branagh) had been spotted in a TV ad for washing powder; Lucy Dunn (then, the girl most likely to remain 'nice but dull' all her life), was now a radio producer at BBC Pebble Mill; and Chris Adams (then, the boy who always smelt of wee) was now the manager of a health-food shop.

That was the news.

'Here it is,' I said, as we pulled into my parents' road. 'It's the one with the immaculate, manicured lawn.' He pulled to a halt. 'How much?'

He clicked off his timer. 'Nothing.'

'You can't do that,' I said. It was a nice gesture but I wouldn't have felt comfortable accepting it. I guessed the fare was somewhere around ten pounds so I took a note out of my wallet and handed it to him.

'I can't take that,' he said. 'No way.'

'Well, thanks a lot,' I replied. 'It was a nice way to be welcomed home.'

He insisted on helping me out with my bags, then we shook hands. As he drove off he beeped his horn and waved.

Out of the corner of my eye I noticed the net curtains of both my parents' neighbours twitching like mad. Unlike London where everyone jumps in and out of black cabs all the time, my parents' road was inhabited by people who only ever used them to go to or from the airport before or after a package holiday. My arrival in one when my parents lived so close to the number 50 bus route, the most frequent bus service in Europe no less, was a clear sign of wanton decadence.

Verily, the prodigal son had returned.

nine

As I stood on the doorstep, my finger hovering over the doorbell, it occurred to me that perhaps I should have called my parents to let them know I was coming home for a visit. And not just a little visit but one that would last some three months. I'd thought about telling them when I'd first had the idea but I just couldn't bring myself to do it because it would involve me admitting that Elaine and I were over, the knock-on effect of that news being that their eldest son would not be providing them with any grandchildren in the foreseeable future.

I rang the doorbell and waited. Even through the frosted-glass panel of the porch door I could tell that the figure approaching was that of my dad.

'All right, Dad?' I said brightly, as he opened the door. 'I'm back!'

Standing on the step in his red tartan slippers, holding a small gardening fork, my dad looked me up and down suspiciously. I could see it in his face that my presence here was causing him some consternation. 'Matt's here at home,' his face was saying. 'Why?'

'Matthew?' said my dad eventually, as if checking I wasn't a random impostor.

'Dad?' I replied, mimicking his tone.

'What are you doing here?'

I wasn't too concerned about the abrupt nature of my father's greeting. He was a man who liked to get to the point and work backwards.

'I'm delivering milk,' I replied, and gave him a wink. 'Heard you'd run out. Thought I'd come all the way from America to bring you two pints of semi-skimmed.'

My dad laughed and shook my hand firmly. He wasn't a hugger, not even with women, but he did like to shake hands. Still standing on the doorstep he muttered, 'You've got bags with you.'

I nodded.

'Are you staying for a while, then?'

I nodded again.

There then followed a long pause as we took each other in. I hadn't seen my dad since the previous May when he and my mum had flown to New York to stay with me and Elaine. It was one of the strangest experiences I'd ever had. My mum insisted on putting on her posh accent for the entire time they were there, and my dad asked my permission every time he wanted to turn on the TV. It was as if they were both on their best behaviour trying to impress not just Elaine but me too.

'Are you going to let me in or what?'

'Of course. Of course.' He stepped outside, still in his slippers – a cardinal sin in my mother's eyes – and picked up one of my bags.

'No Elaine, then?' he said.

He said this not as a proper question, because I was quite sure that he didn't think Elaine was going to drop out of the sky, but more as a statement of fact. My dad wasn't the sort of man to put two and two together unless he really had to. He much preferred to point out a two, then another two, and wait for me to say, 'Bloody hell, Dad, four!' which is what I usually did. But I didn't do it this time. It would be easier on both of us in the long term, I reasoned, if we left it just a little while longer.

'She did send her love, though,' I told him.

Which was true. Elaine thought my parents were fantastic. 'They're so *real*,' she'd say, 'unlike mine who are sooooooo *fake*.' Elaine's dad worked in construction and her mum worked in a bank. They lived in New Jersey and we didn't see much of them, not even in the holidays. At Christmas even though we'd split up, Elaine and I spent the whole day alone together in our apartment. Christmas dinner was left-over Chinese and sixteen bottles of Budweiser.

'That's good,' said my dad, visibly cheered. 'She's a good girl, Elaine.'

'Yeah, Dad, she is,' I replied, and we exchanged smiles. 'Now, is there any chance that I can come in?'

As my mum wasn't home yet I was spared having to explain Elaine's absence so I took my bags up to my old bedroom while my dad rustled up a cup of tea. Over that and a chocolate digestive my dad and I summed up what was going on in our lives in exactly four sentences:

Sentence one: How are you?

Sentence two: Not too bad.

Sentence three: And yourself?

Sentence four: Can't complain.

Pleasantries out of the way, the conversation after that centred on the weather, the state of the nation, recent developments in English football and the rest of the Beckford family. At twenty-nine I was the oldest of my siblings. After me were Yvonne and Tony, known in these parts as 'the twins', who were twenty-seven. Yvonne was doing her second degree at Edinburgh University, having decided after five years of medical school that she didn't want to be a doctor after all. Tony was living in Nottingham, cultivating a borderline alcohol problem while occasionally drumming in a band called Left Bank. The baby of the family was Ed. He was twenty-two, taking a year out after university to travel around Thailand before committing himself to the world of work. As a family we weren't exactly close – in the sense that we were all terrible at keeping in regular touch with each other – but we always knew that if any of us ever needed help or support it would be there without question.

ten

'You should've told me you were coming.'

These were the first words my mum said to me when she arrived home mid-afternoon from the supermarket. Not 'Hello'. Not 'How are you?' But 'You should've told me you were coming.' Like my dad, my mum liked to do her share of pointing out the obvious, no matter how annoying. I nodded and smiled because I knew that in her own way this was her biggest, fattest, sloppiest 'I've missed you, son.'

'I know, Mum,' I said remorsefully, and kissed her cheek. 'You're right, I should've told you I was coming.'

'I didn't get any extra food in,' she said indignantly.

I glanced at the four huge shopping-bags on the floor at her feet with a wry smile. 'It's okay, Mum,' I reassured her. 'I don't eat much, these days.'

'*And* I haven't cleaned your room,' she protested.

'The bedroom's spotless, Mum.'

'I suppose it is,' she conceded, secretly pleased. 'Elaine will think we live in a pig-sty.'

'No, she won't, Mum,' I said quietly, 'because she's not here.'

'Where is she?'

'She couldn't make it,' I explained. 'She would've loved to come but she couldn't get the time off.'

'You should be with Elaine,' she said. 'What if she needs you?'

'She'll be fine,' I said. Despite her protests, I could tell mum was over the moon at having her first-born back. She just wanted to make it clear that she liked things done in a certain order.

'How long are you home for?'

This was a tricky one. Unlike my dad, my mum was blessed with an inquisitive, tenacious mind. Having said that, the tenacious side probably held more sway than the inquisitive, but either meant that I wouldn't be able to get by with a shrug or 'Dunno.' I was going to have to tell her something. I took a deep breath then let it go. 'Quite a while?' I posed it as a question to make the whole idea more palatable.

'How long's quite a while?' she asked suspiciously.

'More than a month, less than . . .' My sentence fizzled out as her stern look made it clear that she'd already had enough of chasing me around. 'Three months,' I said finally.

'Three months?' she echoed.

'Give or take,' I replied, adding a small shrug.

'Give or take what?'

'I dunno . . . a few days probably.'

'What about Elaine?'

This was it. I was going to have to tell her. 'We've . . . split up.'

She moved on to question two. 'And what about your job?'

'Now, that,' I said confidently, 'is fine.' And then I steeled my nerves and told her the full story. My mum clearly couldn't believe what she was hearing because she called my dad and forced me to begin my sorry tale again right from the start.

'Can you see what's happening to *your* son?' said my mum to my dad, as I concluded my tale of woe. This was classic my-mum behaviour. As kids, whenever we got into trouble she would berate my dad with the line 'Can you see what's going on with *your* son/daughter?' 'So let me get this right,' she continued. 'You've split up with Elaine, left your home in America to move back here for three months so you can spend quality time with me and your dad, before going off to a job in a country you've never been before?'

Put like that it did sound a bit dramatic. I couldn't quite understand how my life – which had apparently been so simple for the last twenty-nine and a bit years had suddenly become so complicated.

'And see some friends,' I added feebly.

'Right,' said my mum, still finding this all too much to cope with. 'Now you're here I suppose I'd better sort you out something for lunch.'

While most normal people quite reasonably consider food to be an important daily requirement my mum had turned it into the focal point of her existence. When it came to me and my brothers and sisters, nearly everything she did and said was regulated and defined by food. 'Are you hungry?' 'When will you be hungry?' 'You look thirsty.' 'Are you eating properly?' This, of course, was her way of showing that she loved us, but it could also work your nerves a little bit, especially as, unlike most mums who give up on trying to get everyone in the family to eat together once they're past the age of sixteen, mine was a stickler for communal eating at *all* times. Come a quarter past five, my dad was ordered to finish gardening and by half past five dinner (never 'tea', too common, and never 'supper', way too posh) would be presented on laps, except on Sundays, special occasions or when visitors were present. *Then* we would eat at the dining-table in the front kept-for-best-in-the-off-chance-HM-the-Queen-should-ever-drop-by-unannounced-and-be-in-desperate-need-of-a-cup-of-tea room with its doilies, posh china and scary macramé picture of a donkey that my late great-aunt Irene had made. No excuse was accepted for missing a meal. No 'I'm not hungry yet', no 'I don't fancy this tonight', and certainly none of this 'Come on, no one under forty-eight eats their dinner this early in the day.' No: you liked it or lumped it. So when after I'd unpacked my bags and a quarter past five arrived, I should have known that my mum would be calling up the stairs, 'Matthew, your dinner's ready!' That I'd barely finished digesting the chicken salad sandwiches she'd made at lunchtime counted for nothing.

'What's for dinner, then?' I asked carefully, as I entered the living room and sat down.

'Your favourite,' she replied, lowering a tray on to my lap. 'Eat up.' She smiled. 'You look like you haven't had a proper meal in ages.'

As I looked down dolefully at the plate in front of me it occurred to me that really I had only myself to blame. I knew full well that my mum was for ever mixing up my favourite anything with the favourite anythings of my long-flown-the-nest siblings. Not that what was sitting on the plate was any of my brothers' or sister's favourite anything – other than, possibly, their favourite culinary nightmare: two pork chops, three large spoonfuls of mashed potato, gravy so thick you could stand a knife up in it, carrots, peas and . . . sprouts. Boiled into submission, stinking green balls of soggy-leafed affliction sprouts.

My eyes darted feverishly around the living room to see what the only other diner at Stalag 9 thought of the cuisine. My dad was lodged in the armchair he claimed as his king-dom, watching an early news bulletin on TV, while chewing and pausing occasionally to have a go at the newsreader's dress sense. My mum was still hovering in the doorway to the kitchen waiting for me to tuck into my first home-cooked meal in a long while. I looked up at her and smiled. There was a look of contentment on her face. There she was, watching over us, her family, making sure that all our needs had been attended to. It seemed that this made her happy.

'Why don't you sit down, Mum?' I asked needlessly. I don't think I've ever seen my mother sit down to eat a meal, it was as if her knees had locked and made it impossible.

'You haven't started your dinner,' she said. 'Is it salt you want? I'll just go and get it.'

I looked at my plate again and paused before answering because the words on the tip of my tongue were along the lines of: 'Can't you see what's wrong? Can't you see that there are four sprouts on my plate, each the size of a mandarin orange?' But I didn't say anything like that, mainly because I couldn't, not without hurting her feelings, which was the last thing I wanted to do. It was just like being a kid again. When I was about nine I came up with an ingenious system for disposing of sprouts: it involved me slipping them one by one into a handkerchief, then feigning a desperate need to go to the loo, and on the way throwing them behind the back of the fridge. It worked like a dream in theory, but I lacked the foresight to remove them later and give them a proper burial. After six weeks my system fell apart when the stench of decaying greenery overpowered the kitchen and my mum discovered my sprout hideaway. She went mental and I was grounded for what felt like a decade. And now, years later, I was facing the same dilemma.

'Honestly, Mum,' I began, 'I don't think I can manage all these.' I gestured to the sprouts with my fork.

'Nonsense,' she said firmly. 'They're good for you.'

'But I don't like them.'

'Yes, you do,' she replied impatiently.

'No. I've never liked sprouts.'

'You liked sprouts when I cooked your dinners. How has Elaine been cooking them?'

That thought alone made me want to laugh aloud. 'Elaine never cooked sprouts, Mum. Elaine never cooked at all, if she could help it. Anyway, I'm not even sure they have them in America.'

'You used to love sprouts,' piped up my dad. 'D'you remember when you used to ask if you could play marbles with them?'

I looked at my dad in disbelief. 'That was Tony, Dad, and he may have liked playing marbles with them but he didn't like eating them either.'

'No,' said my mum, 'Yvonne used to love sprouts. I think you must be thinking of Yvonne. She definitely had a thing for sprouts.' Yvonne was the smartest member of our family, so it goes without saying that, like me, she didn't like sprouts either.

'Look,' I said, losing my patience, 'Tony never liked sprouts, Yvonne never liked sprouts, Ed never liked sprouts, and I certainly don't like sprouts. And I'm not eating these sprouts. Not now. Not in a little while. Not ever!'

eleven

With the benefit of hindsight it was easy enough to see that I wasn't getting all weird about a few sprouts. I mean, I was twenty-nine, and if I really didn't want to eat them it wasn't as if my mum was in a position to ground me or stop my pocket money. The truth was, I was getting a bit wonky about the circumstances that had led to my life changing so dramatically. Only twenty-four hours earlier everything had been different. Okay, so it hadn't been perfect but at least it had been near enough normal for someone at my stage in life. I'd had my own place *and* I'd had a crumbling relationship – the minimum lifestyle requirements of your basic turning-thirty-year-old, surely? But now what did I have? Nothing. I had no girlfriend, I had the promise of a smart job that wouldn't be starting for quite a while and I was living at my *parents'*.

Entering the kitchen to deliver an apology I was assaulted by the sound of banging pots and pans emanating from the sink, where my mother was furiously distributing soap-suds in the air under the guise of washing up.

'I'm sorry,' I said, closing the kitchen door behind me. 'I shouldn't have said what I said. I feel awful. It's just that – well, I've got a lot on my mind, what with Elaine and everything and, well—'

'It's all right,' she said, turning away from the sink to look at me. 'I knew it had nothing to do with the sprouts. I just worry about you, that's all.' She disappeared into the living room and returned with my plate, which she put into the microwave. Three minutes, forty seconds and a ping later, she re-presented my dinner to me at the kitchen table with a flourish. 'Here you go. Now, eat up before it goes cold again.'

The three of us spent the evening in front of the TV together, watching the best that British TV had on offer: *Coronation Street*, *Des O'Connor Tonight*, the *Nine o'Clock News* and the last half-hour of a made-for-TV movie about a mother with cancer trying to get her kids placed with new foster-families before she died. My mum cried, my dad channel-hopped in the ad breaks and I enjoyed the spectacle. This was how every evening used to be when I was a kid. Continuous telly from seven thirty until bedtime, cups of tea made during the ads and two bars of the gas fire on to take the chill off the room.

'Right, then,' said my mum, just after ten o'clock. 'Your dad and I are off to bed, Matthew.'

'Night, then,' I said cheerfully, as I picked up the remote control and began flicking. My dad hadn't let me anywhere near it all evening.

'Aren't *you* going to bed?' asked my mum, when I hadn't moved.

'Nah,' I said, still not picking up their hint. 'I'm going to stay up for just a bit longer.'

'Are you sure?' said my dad, somewhat shocked. 'Only it is quite late, Matthew.'

Finally it dawned on me that they wanted me to go to bed too. I was disturbing their routines, and if there's one thing in the world my parents like it's routine. Despite their insistence that I must be jet-lagged, cold, and/or tired of watching TV, I remained up and out of trouble until well after midnight absorbed in Lee Marvin's performance in *The Dirty Dozen*. Turning off the TV as the credits rolled I made my way upstairs and into the bathroom. My mum had opened a new toothbrush just for me and left it next to the sink with a fresh towel. The whole scene made me laugh: when I was a kid she was forever telling me that our house wasn't a hotel and all these years later she was paying attention to detail that would make the Ritz feel like a bedsit in Archway.

Lying in my single bed – *How long had it been since I'd slept in a single bed?* – I looked around the room I used to share with my two brothers. It was a large room and we had a corner each with the fourth left vacant to enable us to open the door. We'd tried to customise our own sections of the room and stamp our personality across them. My corner used to be covered in posters of pop bands and Tony's had housed his collection of steam-train posters and paraphernalia, now lodged deep under his bed. As Ed had been only ten his corner was covered in his drawings of comic-book super-heroes and cars. When Tony and I moved out, Ed had had the room to himself. Now all four walls were covered with his personality – posters of his football team, clip frames housing snapshots of him and his mates at various European football matches, and posters of female kids' TV presenters wearing nothing but their underwear and a sultry smile.

But lying there in my old bed, even without my posters adorning the walls, it still felt like home. This was my history. In this room I had grown into what I was and that made me feel good. I've chosen the right place, I told myself, just as I was free-falling into sleep. If I'm going to find an answer to anything then the best place to find it is at home.

twelve

To: mattb@c-tec.national.com
From: crazedelaine@hotpr.com
Subject: How?

Matt

How are you? How was your flight? How is Birmingham? How are your parents? Hooooooooooooowwwwwwww?
I need to know!

love

Elaine xxx

PS After I left you at the airport I just cried and cried until I was a seething mass of saline solution and snot. Very attractive. When I got back to the apartment I was even worse. The place seemed so empty without you. I also have a confession. You know that black T-shirt you couldn't find? I stole it. It's under my pillow. It's just so cheesy (my actions not the T-shirt) I just wanted something that smelt of you until everything stopped hurting. Anyway – that's enough of that.

Bye!

PS Does anyone famous that I might've heard of come from Birmingham? Just wondering. E.

thirteen

'Morning, Matt,' said my dad, from his position on the sofa.

It was one thirty in the afternoon the following day. I'd just got up and come into the living room dressed in the sky blue pyjamas my mother had thoughtfully left on my bed the night before. They had still been in the packet. Only my mum would have an emergency pack of men's pyjamas.

I looked over to my dad and gave him a little wink to acknowledge the lack of subtlety in his particular brand of sarcasm. 'All right, Dad?' I replied, then proceeded to scratch a number of places that usually got a bit itchy when I'd spent so long in a nice, warm bed.

'Yes, thanks, Matthew,' he said pithily. 'Your mother wanted to send out a search party to see if you were still alive. I told her not to bother as you were probably hibernating.'

'Good one,' I replied, I sniffed, coughed and rubbed my head in an attempt to wake myself up a bit. I picked up my dad's copy of the *Sun* from the coffee table, sat down and had a quick glance through the first couple of pages. A quirky story on page three – next to the assets of Gina, 18, from Essex – caught my eye. A man from Cheltenham had been kicked out of the house he shared with his girlfriend because she was fed up with his collection of twelve thousand milk bottles. The last line of the story really made me laugh: 'It goes to show she wasn't the right girl for me. If she loved me she'd love my milk bottles.'

'What are you laughing at?' asked my dad. 'Is it the milk-bottle bloke?' I nodded. 'You've got to admire a man like that. Those milk bottles must make him really happy.'

'Really, really happy,' I replied. It was a crap joke, really, but it amused me and my dad, and we sat there for a good few minutes passing asides about Milk-bottle Man until we'd exhausted every available pun. I was about to continue reading the paper, assuming that my dad was merely sitting down in his chair for a moment's rest from household maintenance – he was always fixing something – when he coughed and moved his shoulders about as if wanting to get down to business.

'So?' he said, in a manner that once again managed to be both a question and a statement of fact.

'So?' I replied, raising my eyebrows.

It suddenly dawned on me that my mum had sent him in on a mission to find out more about me and Elaine splitting up. I think the idea was supposed to be that because my dad was a man and I was now a man he was supposedly the perfect person for me to talk to about problems to do with life. I could tell just from looking at him that he wasn't in total accord with this idea but it was clear, too, that my mum had promised to make his life hell if he didn't comply with her wishes.

'So?' he repeated.

I scratched my head, closed the newspaper and looked at him expectantly. My mum had got it completely wrong if she thought sending him to talk to me was the way to find out how I was feeling. This was a genuine case of the blind leading the blind. My dad never talked about himself if he could help it and neither did I (well, not to them anyhow), and what she'd failed to see was that we liked it that way. I suppose when I was five or six we talked. I remember I'd tell him how I felt about school and my friends, speculating on what I might like to do when I grew up. And I remember he'd talk to me about how he felt about things too and we both seemed to get a lot of satisfaction from such a meeting of minds. But only a few years later, those sort of conversations dried up as my dad gave me the greatest gift known to mankind – silence. I like to think that he taught me you could communicate as much without words as with – that there were more ways to crack an egg than by talking to it. He taught me that sometimes the only thing you can do is just hold it all in until you reach a point where you can deal with it. I'm not saying it was a perfect philosophy – far from it – but it was a useful one to have when your only other option was to dive off the deep end. So this was why, for the majority of our lives, my dad and I had worked on a strictly need-to-know basis. In fact, over the past few years especially, we'd gone out of our way to give the impression that we weren't even vaguely interested in the need-to-know stuff either. This, of course, was all lies and macho posturing because in phone calls home I'd ask my mum without fail how my dad was, and he always asked Elaine how I was when he spoke to her, which was more frequently than he spoke to me. It was a great system. We were both using the women in our lives to translate our silence and surliness into conversation. Of course, now that my translator and I had gone our separate ways my dad and I could both see the truth: he needed to know about me and I needed to know about him.

It was about time for another 'So?' from me, and I obliged as I still had no idea how we were going to get this talking thing going. His response was to pause and take a long, slow sip of his tea. That was another thing about my dad that I liked. All his movements were slow and considered. He'd always been this way. I don't think I had ever seen him run. He wasn't one of life's runners: he was more of a sturdy walker. I, on the other hand, was one of life's wobblers. I'd wobbled, tripped and slouched my way through life in an ungainly fashion, and my lack of cool worried me. I always got the feeling that when it came to the point at which my dad got to look back over his life for one last time he'd be able to say to himself, 'No matter what I did, no matter whether I was right or wrong, I was always cool.' When the time came for my big goodbye, however, I'd get to cower with embarrassment.

'So,' he began carefully, 'how are you, Matt?'

'I'm . . .' I searched around for the right word. I didn't want to lie to him now that he'd had the courage to get things going. 'I'm . . . doing okay.'

He sighed and looked at the TV, which wasn't even on. 'It's not easy, you know, life,' he began.

'Oh,' I said, quietly.

'But it's worth it,' he said, echoing himself.

I nodded. 'Good.'

Then he joined the two sentences together and said, 'It's not easy but it's worth it.' He took another long, slow sip of his tea and waited – my cue, I presumed, to contribute to the conversation but I honestly couldn't think of a single thing to say in response to his words of wisdom. I could see that he had a point, but that was about all.

'Cheers, Dad,' I said.

He looked up from his tea-cup. I suspect the laws of masculine exchange would say that I was supposed to look away when our eyes met but I didn't, so we looked at each other uncomfortably for far too long, though it was probably only a few seconds. He wanted to talk. Strangely even I wanted to talk. I suppose if this had been a couple of million years ago and we'd been cavemen we could have hunted a brontosaurus or two to release the tension of this awkward situation, but as it wasn't, the best alternative was TV.

'I think there'll be some news headlines on soon, Dad,' I said. 'Shall I turn the TV on so that we can catch them?'

He smiled, shrugged and said, 'If you want.' So I turned on the TV, handed him the remote and settled back in the armchair while we both pretended to watch the news.

fourteen

To: mattb@c-tec.national.com
From: crazedelaine@hotpr.com
Subject: Where are yooooooooooooouuuuuuuuu?????

Dear Matt

   Where are yooooooooooooouuuuuuuuu?????

love

Elaine

fifteen

Friends.

I had some in New York.

I had a few living in Spain and a few more in France.

Closer to home I even had them in London, Cardiff and Glasgow.

Here in Birmingham, however, I had one friend, Gershwin Palmer, my oldest friend. There used to be a lot more old friends here, a whole group of us, in fact, who had gone to King's Heath Comprehensive and had stayed friends through sixth-form and beyond. There was Ginny Pascoe, my ex-girlfriend/not girlfriend, tall, very attractive and the queen of bad decisions; Elliot Sykes, built like a rugby player, laughed like a drain, born with a curious ability always to land on his feet; Pete Sweeney, a man whose obsessions were science fiction, music and girls, in that order; Katrina Turner, the most attractive girl in our gang and also the one destined to be the most successful; and finally Bev Moore, the oddball, a Goth who never admitted to being a Goth, a sarky cow with a wicked sense of humour. With Gershwin and me, we formed the magnificent seven, a group of friends who drank together, got thrown out of nightclubs together and who, so rumour had it, got an education together.

We were friends for life. Or so we thought.

But, like friends for life eventually do, when we reached the eighteen–nineteen mark, we left Birmingham one by one and went our separate ways. Ginny went to Brighton to do an art course, because she wanted to be an artist; Elliot moved to London to live with his sister, because he wanted to get into advertising; Pete went to university in Loughborough to do sports science, because he didn't know what else to do; Katrina went to university in Leeds to read media studies, because she wanted to be the next editor of *Vogue*; and Bev got a job in Miss Selfridge, because she wanted to get enough money together to go travelling for a few years. Quite soon the only time we all met up was on Christmas Eve, at the Kings Arms in Moseley, the pub that acted as the unofficial clubhouse for ex-King's Heath Comprehensive pupils. However, as we graduated our way through to our mid-twenties, even Christmas in the Kings Arms fell by the wayside and before we knew it we'd all moved on so far with our lives that we literally didn't know each other any more. All except Gershwin, that is. He didn't move anywhere.

I'd known Gershwin – named after the great composer because his mum liked 'Rhapsody in Blue' – since my first day at secondary school, some eighteen years ago, and in all that time we'd never lost contact. When the majority of us went to university, Gershwin decided he'd had enough of education and got a job working for a local hospital trust. At the time we all thought he was making a huge mistake and told him so. After all, we thought, he's missing out on being a mad student, getting up to all sorts of mad-student antics, and having mad-student fun. That was one way of looking at it. The other way was this: by the time we'd left university, Gershwin was a high-flying junior manager responsible for a budget of hundreds of thousands of pounds, while my highest-flying achievements included assistant deputy editorship of the university magazine's arts page and an ability to watch the same episode of *Neighbours* twice a day and still find it fascinating. Because of this, Gershwin was the first of all of us to tick off all the big ones on the I'm-a-fully-formed-adult checklist. He was the first to have real money, spend real money and own a car that wasn't held together by Sellotape and goodwill. He was the first to get a mortgage, break the elusive two-and-a-half-year barrier in a relationship – with Zoë, the love of his life whom he met in a nightclub – and, at twenty-four, was the first to get married.

The wedding – at which I was best man – was an event I'll never forget. Not least because it was the last time all seven of us dragged ourselves from the various corners of the world to which we'd been flung and got together to party. While at the back of my mind there was the small worry that Gershwin was too young to be getting hitched, I also felt immense pride about it because this was *my* best mate getting married. When everyone I knew (myself included) was doing everything in their power to hang on to the vestiges of their former student lifestyles it felt like Gershwin, venturing into the world of marriages, mortgages, careers and – a year later – kids, was a pioneer – boldly going where none of my peer group had gone before. Even with this turning-thirty thing he was going to get there before me although our birthdays were only separated by a few weeks.

'Matthew Beckford!
  'Gershwin Palmer!'
  'You porky git!'
  'You balding loser!'
  We always greeted each other like that and it made us

laugh. He could call me fat because, in the big scheme of things, I knew that although I was a little bit out of shape I was far from being lardy, and in turn although he was receding slightly at the temples he was still a long way from the Land of Wispy Strands.

I'd called Gershwin up at work to let him know I was back, and he'd insisted that I come into town and meet him for lunch. On seeing each other we engaged in a not-quite-but-nearly hug and laughed a lot to compensate for being pleased to see each other. The last time I'd seen him was about a year ago when I'd had to fly to London on business and I'd made a brief trip up to Birmingham to see my parents. I was in and out in under thirty-six hours but I made time to see him. Since then we'd exchanged e-mails and the occasional postcard but we weren't regular correspondents. Not that it mattered – some friendships remain strong no matter how much you neglect them and mine and Gershwin's was one of those.

Now we stood back and looked at each other. Gershwin was wearing a dark grey suit, white shirt and dark blue tie. He looked every inch the middle manager he was supposed to be and yet, underneath the suit, I knew he was still the same party-trick Gershwin who could drink beer through his nose, knew all the words to Boston's cheesy soft rock anthem 'More Than A Feeling', and made the best bacon and egg sandwiches the world has ever known. I felt immediate relief: if those I've grown up with are still okay, ran my thought processes, then I'll be okay too. And as I looked at Gershwin, checking that he still had two arms, two legs and his sanity, I knew I was okay too.

It was cold and drizzling as we stepped outside. At Gershwin's suggestion we headed for one of the many coffee-bar retail chains that had erupted out of nowhere in the last few years.

As we walked along Corporation Street towards New Street we talked about football and music, knowing that we'd do the So-how's-life-with-you? thing later. When 'later' arrived, I launched into my enquiries about his life before he could launch into his. I wasn't eager to talk about Elaine just yet.

'How's Zoë?'

'She's fine,' said Gershwin. 'She's still nursing. Still at the QE.'

'Enjoying it?'

He shrugged. 'Not really. I think she misses Charlotte. My mum looks after her during the day but . . . you know how it is, she's knackered when she comes in from work and then she feels like she's not giving Charlotte her best and that makes her feel more guilty. But anyway—'

'And how's my lovely goddaughter?' I asked, interrupting before he could get on to me, which was exactly what he had been about to do.

'She's great,' said Gershwin. 'She's nearly four now. She'll be going to school in September.' He laughed. 'She'll be over the moon when she hears you're back. She calls you "Daddy's friend Matt who brings nice presents". She's got her priorities sorted, that girl—'

'And how's work?' I interjected.

'Crap. I'm bored, tired, bored, fed up and bored. Did I say I was bored? But you know how it is, everyone hates their job, don't they, so why bother moaning?'

Following on from that I found out more about his life: yes, his mum and dad were okay; yes, his sister, Andrea, was okay too and, no, the Palmer family cat, Tweety, was not okay – she'd been run over. Just as I suspected it was dawning on him that I was employing the classic my-life's-so-crap-I-don't-want-to-moan-about-it-quite-yet diversionary questioning strategy, we reached our destination.

Even though it was only just after twelve the café was fairly packed, mainly with gaunt-looking student kids whose migratory path from Aston University's campus to the city encompassed it. They all looked a bit ill as if they'd been surviving on nothing more substantial than cigarettes, coffee and exam pressure for some time. While we waited for the coffee to arrive, Gershwin and I exchanged a brief lift of the eyebrows in salute to a random act of senseless beauty clearing the table behind us. She had a mass of hair tied away from her face that threatened to spring into action at any moment, and a detached smile that almost, but not quite, made me want to weep with gratitude that such women still existed. Cups in hand we made our way to the high stools at the front of the café, considerately positioned by the windows to make it easier for people like us – those on the wrong side of twenty-nine – to watch the girls on the right side of twenty-five go by without causing undue stress to our knees.

'So . . .' said Gershwin, getting out a packet of Silk Cut.

'I thought you'd given up?'

'I did. I have. And tomorrow I give up again. But I've got to have something to live for.' He laughed. 'Anyway, never mind my filthy habit. The game's up, Matt. What is it you don't want to talk about?'

I sighed. 'Elaine.'

'I take it she's what's brought you home?'

I nodded.

'For a while?'

I nodded again, and told him the bulk of the details about splitting up with Elaine, and my new job.

'So, you've been in the wars a bit, have you?' he said, sympathetically. 'I can relate to that for sure.' He smiled. 'Congratulations on the job though. It sounds great. But it's a shame about you and Elaine. A real shame.'

I gazed out of the window, my attention wandering as an attractive girl in office-type clothing walked by briskly as if she was late for something important. 'It was a weird situation,' I said. 'It just wasn't working out.' Gershwin joined me in gazing out of the window. 'There were no tears when we split up. No big hoo-hah. Nothing.'

'That doesn't sound right,' said Gershwin. 'Hoo-hah is par for the course at the end of any relationship – even if you hated each other. Without hoo-hah when you're splitting up, well . . . it's not splitting up, is it?'

'Exactly,' I replied. 'My point entirely.'

'So what happened next?'

'I changed my mind.'

'When?'

'At the airport.'

Gershwin shook his head. 'At the airport? Couldn't you have left it until a bit later?'

'So, there I am with my bags,' I said, ignoring his comment, 'a minute and a half from saying goodbye, and I changed my mind.'

'What about your new job?'

'I would've quit it.'

'So what are you doing here?'

'Well, that's the thing. She didn't change hers.'

'Her what?'

'Keep up, will you?' I said, feigning exasperation. 'Her mind. She did not want to continue the relationship.'

'She actually said this?'

'No, I could just see it in her face. She loved me and all that but she didn't feel the same.' I paused and shrugged. 'I can't blame her. I think it was an age thing, too, you know. Elaine's twenty-two to my twenty-nine. I know it's only seven years' difference and not a huge deal but in a lot of ways those seven years are like dog years.' Gershwin nodded. 'I know they say women mature faster than men but I'm not entirely sure about that. I mean, doesn't everyone need that period to, well, not just hang out and be . . .' I lost the thread of what I was saying as I watched a tall, dark-haired girl on the cusp of her twenties slink by in a T-shirt so tight a six-year-old would've struggled to breathe in it. She was accompanied by her young, lithe, fully follicled boyfriend. 'Basically, I think that sometimes she liked being in a proper grown-up relationship and other times quite naturally she just wanted to be twenty-two, single and stupid.'

'Maybe she wanted to sow her proverbial wild oats,' suggested Gershwin, as his eyes followed a group of Spanish girls across the road. 'Like you say, she is only twenty-two.'

'No, it's more than that,' I said. 'It's me. When I was standing there at the airport my whole life flashed before my eyes. I could see myself finding an apartment somewhere in Australia. I could see me filling it with a few men's style-magazine bachelor-pad staples – the wide-screen TV, the chrome CD racks and the black leather couch. I could see me playing squash on Monday nights, five-a-side football on Wednesday nights, going for the occasional drink and a meal out with whoever would come with me on the nights that remain, and I could see that would be the sum total of the rest of my life.'

'No women?'

'Maybe the odd one or two . . . but they wouldn't last.'

Gershwin laughed. He always found my gloomy side amusing. 'Why not?'

'Because ever since I first started going out with girls, way back when, I've been convinced that my life isn't complete without one. The minute I work out life's actually okay without a full-time one around the house, it's all over! I'd give up. I'd fill my life with any old crap rather than compromise. And you know as well as I do that relationships are all about compromise. I think Elaine was my last chance.'

'As mad as it seems you might have a point there,' said Gershwin. 'Sometimes I feel really good that me and Zoë got serious when we were still so young. We've grown up with each other. We've learned from each other. But . . . well, I dunno. Sometimes I think—'

'What?'

'That we might've missed out on something. I don't regret having Charlotte. Not at all. But sometimes I think, well, I've thought . . . what if?'

'I shouldn't do that,' I replied. 'Don't even think about going down that road. See me?' I pointed to myself with my plastic coffee stirrer. 'I'm your "what if?". You'd be me, sitting here having exactly the same sort of conversation about women that we had twelve years ago. It's getting tedious now we're turning thirty.' Gershwin looked thoughtful but didn't say anything. 'Turning thirty is one of those things that will never happen,' I continued. 'You know, like when you're a kid and you try to work out which year in the future will be the one that you'll turn thirty in, and then you work it out and you think it might as well be a billion years away because it's so far in the future. And now suddenly, the future's right here.'

'The world's full of thirty-year-olds,' said Gershwin. The dark cloud of deep thought that had enveloped him had disappeared. 'It's not like in *Logan's Run*, where they're banished to some netherworld the moment they hit the three-oh.'

'I suppose,' I admitted. 'I'm sure we've both got mates that have already been there and they've all lived to tell the tale. So it can't be that bad, can it?'

'I dunno,' said Gershwin, clearly trying to wind me up. 'I

think it all depends on where you are in life. Some people I've known who turned thirty took it well and had a laugh. Some pretended to take it well then went a bit strange weeks later. Some panicked right up until their birthdays then realised nothing had changed, and then there's the small but not insignificant number who went on that whole where-is-my-life-going? trip and never came back again. Which sort are you, then, Matt?'

'Me?' I said innocently, 'I dunno. What about yourself?'

'I dunno,' said Gershwin, 'but I suppose we'll both find out soon enough.'

sixteen

To: crazedelaine@hotpr.com
From: mattb@c-tec.national.com
Subject: Home

Hi Elaine

Sorry I've taken so long to e-mail you. Everything is fine here. Flight was fine. Mum and Dad have been asking about you a lot. I've told them we've split up and though they were disappointed they seem to be fine about it. Also – it's okay about the T-shirt. I have a confession too – I stole some of your underwear. It's draped over the radiator in my bedroom as I speak. (I lie.) What I actually did take was a tape of music I made you – the one you entitled *Music For Losers*, vol. II. I don't know why I took it. I suppose I just wanted a souvenir of us.

I'll talk more soon.

love Matt.

PS For the record, you loon, all of the following world-famous people are from Birmingham:

1) John Taylor from Duran Duran (the only one from the band anyone can remember who wasn't Simon Le Bon).

2) Joan Armatrading (female singer/songwriter. Had a hit in 1976 with 'Love and Affection').

3) Robert Plant from Led Zeppelin (technically he's from Stourbridge, just outside Birmingham, but that's near enough).

4) Kenny Baker – the guy who played R2D2 in *Star Wars*.
5) Ozzy Osbourne from Black Sabbath.
6) At a push I'd include 'cod reggae' band UB40 but I prefer to keep that kind of regional shame to myself.

seventeen

Finding myself at a loose end the day after meeting up with Gershwin, I decided to do something about my clothing situation. The majority of my belongings had been shipped back to England and wouldn't arrive for several weeks. Also the clothes I'd brought with me were dirty because I'd suffered a mental block about using the laundry room in the basement of our apartment in New York, and the idea of bringing a load of washing home for my mum to do seemed strangely comforting.

As I was sorting out the few clean items of clothing I had that morning, it had occurred to me that perhaps my wardrobe was in need of modernisation. Currently my division-one attire (as opposed to division-two attire: *Frankie Says No to War* T-shirts, jeans that no longer fitted me and things to wear while decorating) consisted of the usual shirts, trousers, T-shirts and jumpers, and the one thing they had in common was that they were all dark blue or black. This was part of the problem I had been trying to explain to Gershwin about my increasing inflexibility. My liking for such clothing had developed in my twenties as a genuine affection for the darker end of the colour spectrum but had gradually metamorphosed into a pathological habit I couldn't break.

Just before Christmas, Elaine and I were shopping on the Upper West Side when she tried to persuade me to buy a pair of light grey trousers she had seen in a Banana Republic window. They weren't hideous. They weren't too trendy for a guy like me. There was nothing *wrong* with them at all. But I couldn't even bring myself to go into the shop, let alone try on the trousers. It wasn't my fault. I was built this way.

It was as if from the day I turned nineteen I'd been filling in a mammoth opinion survey on life and sometime after my twenty-seventh birthday the results came in. Suddenly everything fell into place and life wasn't so complicated any more. Finally I understood what I liked and didn't like and I stuck by it rigidly. Favourite Indian meal: Chicken Tikka Masala. Favourite TV programmes: news, sci-fi stuff, sitcoms and reruns of anything I used to watch in the seventies and eighties. Favourite music: female singer-songwriter stuff, seventies and eighties stuff and anything I listened to when I was a student. I'd had exactly the same haircut for the last six years (short all over) and I had three pairs of exactly the same jeans because I was scared that at some point in the future Levi's might stop making them. I knew myself, I knew exactly what I wanted from life and I was happy.

This didn't mean that I didn't like anything new. I did. What it did mean was that the new things I let into my life were mostly variations on the old things that were already in my life – variations on a very strict theme. Elaine used to think it was insane how happy the status quo made me, but as I explained to her, the point of life is to learn from your mistakes and not to go out and see if you can make some new ones. So, after a disastrous flirtation with pastels, beige and even yellow, I finally decided that dark blue/black clothing was my clothing for life. Soon I discovered that it didn't show up food stains and I could put pretty much everything I owned in the same wash without fear of the colours running.

Wandering through the city centre, in search of new clothes that might bolster my confidence for this bold new stage of my life, I saw an alarming number of attractive young women and tried to imagine myself with them. There we are, walking down the street, hand in hand, laughing gaily, her in one of those breezy slip dresses, even though there is a distinct chill in the air, and me in my dark blue/black outfit. Then, in my imaginary scenario, I catch a glimpse of myself in a shop window and the spell is broken. It has nothing to do with the clothes: it is more a look on my face that seems to ask, 'Is this journey *really* necessary?' The reason for this, of course, is the same as the reason for the colour of my clothes: at twenty-nine I knew exactly what kind of woman I wanted.

I wanted one like I'd already had in the past but without the annoying bits.

I wanted someone I already knew – but who didn't know me so well that my imperfections would put her off.

I wanted someone with whom I could just be me.

But, like the elusive item of clothing you create in your mind's eye – the one that's the right colour, the right shade, the right style – the girlfriend in my head wasn't available and that alone made me feel like giving up on shopping for ever.

On a rather reckless impulse – no doubt spurred on by an impending fit of melancholy – I walked into a clothes shop just off New Street that from the outside seemed suitably hip and happening – if 'hip' and 'happening' are still considered hip and happening words by those in the know. Maybe I've got this all wrong, I told myself. Maybe the new isn't so terrifying, after all. Emanating from the shop's speakers was a rumbling bass track from the loudest song I'd ever heard – it was only a notch or two down from making my ears bleed. In the far corner of the shop by the rear door I saw that they actually had a DJ with his decks. This both amused and saddened me: amused, because this guy in his early twenties, with his goatee beard, beanie hat and trainers like the ones I wore for PE when I was eleven, undoubtedly thought he was the epitome of cool even though his core audience was shopping for trousers, shirts and underpants; and saddened, because just a few years ago I, too, would have thought DJing in a clothes shop was a cool way to spend an afternoon.

In a fit of self-chastisement I threw caution and my dark blue/black-only philosophy to the wind and grabbed a couple of brightly coloured shirts that caught my eye. I approached one of the shop's cooler-than-thou assistants who was sneering by the clothing racks. He was about twenty-one, with the body of a stick insect and wearing a shirt like the one that I had in my hands. Now, because intimidation by trendy clothes-shop assistants was a new experience for me (although, from what Elaine had told me, it was a regular occurrence in women's clothes shops), I threw back my shoulders, sucked in my stomach, and asked him where the changing rooms were. He looked at me, his features only a notch or two down from a grimace, then shrugged and pointed me in the right direction.

I closed the curtains gingerly, removed my jacket and T-shirt, slipped on the first shirt and, in the cold light of the shop's three-tier lighting system (position one: simulated daylight; position two: artificial light; position three: a thunderstorm), stared in disbelief at the mirror. For as long as I had known her Elaine had propagated the urban myth that clothes shops had specially designed mirrors that made customers look like beached whales. According to her, it was all part of a campaign by skinny women to take over the world. It was only now as I stood there afraid to move for fear of popping buttons off the shirt like the Incredible Hulk that I realised skinny men had some world domination plans of their own.

'How's it looking?' called the assistant, from outside the cubicle.

I opened the curtain and let him look for himself. Together we stared into the mirror not quite believing our eyes.

'Isn't this a bit tight?'

'It's cut to be close-fitting,' he replied tersely.

There was no answer to his response that didn't involve an expletive and/or a punch in the face, so I thanked him for his time and, clutching what little dignity I had left, disappeared behind the curtain to mourn the passing of my youth.

eighteen

To: crazedelaine@hotpr.com
From: mattb@c-tec.national.com
Subject: Stuff

Dear Elaine

Make sure you remember to water the spider plants in the bathroom – and remember, just holding the shower head over them once a week doesn't count. Also, don't forget to pay off your credit card before they start charging you a small fortune in interest (again).

Matt xxx

To: crazedelaine@hotpr.com
From: mattb@c-tec.national.com
Subject: Not Dad

Dear Elaine

Forget that last e-mail. Who am I? Your dad? Don't bother to water the spider plant. Don't pay off your credit card. Do what you want.

love

Matt xxx

To: mattb@c-tec.national.com
From: crazedelaine@hotpr.com
Subject: Dad!

For the record – I had already watered the spider plant but I admit had forgotten to pay my Visa bill. This is scary stuff, Matt. We've split up and not only do I have to remember to pay my own Visa bill but I have to miss you too. Don't you dare stop moaning at me . . .

much love

Elaine xxx

nineteen

During my first week at home I led a double life. By night I'd hang out with Gershwin – occasionally Zoë and Charlotte too – and by day I spent time with my parents, which was a bizarre experience. I hadn't 'hung out' with my mum and dad since I was in my mid-teens, and during that week I recalled with a perfect clarity of vision why this was so. Overjoyed at having me, their eldest, back under their roof and trying, in their own small way, to help me forget my current circumstances, they determined to entertain me. For the most part this meant taking me out on day trips to places they'd been to a million times before and had enjoyed so much that they saw no reason not to return.

Our first day out was to nearby Stratford-upon-Avon – which, in fact, turned out to be quite good fun. We visited Anne Hathaway's house which my mum thought 'a bit poky', and then we all walked round the shops for a few hours until my dad announced that he wanted to go back to the car to 'check something'. Permission was denied as Mum revealed that 'checking something' was Dad-speak for being bored and wanting a quick nap in the car. In the evening I attempted to treat them to a meal, but failed miserably.

'You're not paying for me,' said my dad.

'Why not?' I asked, not even close to understanding his logic.

'Because you just can't,' said my dad.

'I'd die of shame,' said my mother, with such vehemence that I was sure she was only *this* far (i.e. not very) from pinning me down and wrestling the bill off me. 'You don't want to be spending your hard-earned money on me and your dad. Put your money away. Your dad will get it.'

'It's only twenty-two pounds fifty!' I protested. 'It's not going to break the bank. I'll get it, honestly, it's okay.'

I was determined not to give in on this because when they'd been to stay with Elaine and me they'd insisted on paying for everything to the point where we had nearly fallen out. With a stubbornness that reminded me of my childhood self, I forced them to let me pay. I handed my credit card to the waitress, and while she disappeared to put it through the reader I went to the toilet. I returned to see my dad sweet-talking her into taking his card instead.

A few days later we took our next trip – to the Botanical Gardens in Edgbaston, which my dad enjoyed immensely. On arrival he insisted on buying me a spider plant because, apparently, when I was a kid he'd taken me and the twins there and he'd bought me one then. It was a beautiful day and we walked all round the gardens, then had tea and scones with fresh cream in their olde-worlde Englishe Tea Shoppe. It was while my mum was trying her best to do an impression of HM Queen Elizabeth II eating a crumbling jam-and-cream-laden scone that my dad piped up, 'Do you remember the talking mynah bird they used to have here, Matt?'

I thought hard. 'No.'

'You must remember it,' he said sourly. 'It lived in one of

the hot-houses and said things like "Who's a cheeky boy?" and "Whoops! There goes a sailor!"'

'No, Dad. I think I'd remember something as surreal as a mynah bird that said, "Whoops! There goes a sailor."'

My dad wouldn't have any of it. He kept badgering me about that bloody mynah bird for the rest of the day. Sample conversation:

Him: Surely you must remember it, Matt. It was black with a big yellow beak.
Me: No, Dad, I don't remember any mynah bird. As far as I can recall I've never seen a mynah bird in my life.
Him: (Tersely) You do remember it, you're just being bloody stubborn now!

This, I now see, was the beginning of the end of the family outings, but the final straw came two days later when we attempted to go to the Malvern Hills for the day. To cut a long story short we got lost and ended up heading towards Bristol on the motorway because my dad misheard one of my directions. He insisted that I'd got it wrong and my mum just sat in the back of the car sucking a pear drop and tutting at both of us while we argued. I think that as we returned to Birmingham, sulking in our separate worlds, my parents and I decided unanimously that, although we loved each other a lot, there was such a thing as too much 'quality time'.

twenty

To: crazedelaine@hotpr.com
From: mattb@c-tec.national.com
Subject: Thirty-people (as you call them)

Dear Elaine

  I met up with Gershwin a few days ago. I always feel good when I see him. I always feel more like myself. He turns thirty in a fortnight but I think he'll take it a lot better than me. I think the art of taking it well is being happy with what you've got. Okay, he's not that in love with his job but he has a great relationship with his wife and the cutest little girl. Not bad for a thirty-person I'd say. Speaking of Charlotte, I gave her the Barbie doll you'd bought for her. She loves it and now insists on calling her Elaine. I told her you look nothing like Barbie, but she wouldn't budge. Kids, eh?

Matt xx

PS Any mail arrived at the apartment for me?

To: mattb@c-tec.national.com
From: crazedelaine@hotpr.com
Subject: Thirty-people

Dear Matt

  Why do you do this to yourself? Why do you constantly have to ovaluate/compare and contrast EVERYTHING in your life? I thought it was just a guy thing but I'm wondering whether it's just a you thing. Your life is great! Just chill out, will you?

Elaine xxx

PS Re: The have-you-got-any-mail quip. You are joking. You never got any when you lived here!!!!!

PPS I know I sound happy but I'm not. I still miss you.

PPPS I also note that none of your e-mails so far mentioned you missing me. Which means you owe me two if I'm not going to race ahead in the 'loser ex-girlfriend/ex-boyfriend still wanting reassurance stakes'.

PPPPS That Barbie-Elaine thing is hilarious. Everyone at work has been calling me Barbie all day. Tell Charlotte she's gorgeous.

twenty-one

'There you go, Matthew,' said my mum.

I looked at the fistful of money-off coupons she was putting into my hands. 'What are these?' I asked.

'What do they look like?' she replied, in her no-nonsense manner.

I plucked one from the pile in my hand and said, 'Well, this one's for tenpence off Bachelor's Cup-a-soup new country-style range.'

'That's what it is,' said my mum.

'But no one uses money-off coupons any more, Mum, it's so . . .'

My mum looked at me, daring me to finish the sentence. 'Look after the pennies,' she said, turning me round and pointing me in the direction of the front door, 'and the pounds will look after themselves.'

The reason for this exchange was guilt. Now that day trips were a thing of the past I was reduced to sitting around the house watching my parents work. Although my mum and dad had retired, their Protestant work ethic seemed to have quadrupled. As well as general household maintenance my dad seemed always to be building shelves for my mum. She, meanwhile, seemed always to be making twee country-style baskets of varnished fake bread plaits and flower arrangements to put on the aforementioned Dad-made shelves. They worked all the time. Like some sort of self perpetuating craft-fair industry. Work. Work. Work. This was why in my second week I volunteered to do the supermarket shopping for my mum just so I could be active too. Also I got to use my dad's car – a pristine Vauxhall Nova. My dad loved his car; he washed it every other day, and had a tub of tyre paint that he applied once a month to keep his tyres looking jet black. It was his pride and joy. But as my mother ruled the roost in the Beckford family, even Dad's pride and joy was at her disposal.

'I'll do the weekly shop,' said my dad, clutching his car keys nervously. 'It won't take long.'

'But Matthew's already offered, Jack,' said my mum. 'And remember, you've got those shelves to finish. Anyway, it will do Matthew good to get out of the house and do something useful . . . for a change.'

I had a certain nostalgic fondness for the Safeway on King's Heath high street, which was my destination. When Gershwin, Katrina, Ginny, Elliot, Bev and I were seventeen, every big night out had kicked off with a trip there because when you're on a tight budget supermarket alcohol is the most effective way to replicate the sensation of downing several pints of pub-bought lager. So standing by the automatic doors at the side of the store we'd pool our allowances and Saturday-job money and hand it over to Elliot, because he looked oldest. Once inside he'd buy as many bottles of Thunderbird as we could afford and we'd polish them off on the bus into town.

During my trip to Safeway, I encountered Mrs Brockel, from number sixty-five, whom I'd known since I was six; Mr and Mrs Butler, the owners of Butler's newsagent's; Mr Mahoney, who was married to Mrs Mahoney, who was still my old junior school's lollipop lady; Mrs Bates, a friend of my mum and dad who used to look after me and my brothers and sister after school, and Mrs Smith, who went everywhere in her slippers and used to be a dinner lady at my old secondary school. I wasn't surprised to bump into all these people under one roof. Every single one of them came from a generation who believed in being born, growing up, getting married, having kids, getting old and dying, if not on the same spot then somewhere quite near it. They were precisely the sort of people who, even if they won a million pounds on the lottery, wouldn't move out of the area, instead preferring to install the UPVC double-glazed windows they'd always dreamed of and put away the rest for a nice holiday in the near future. It was only my generation, their sons and daughters, who had come up with the not so smart idea of roaming the country in search of a better life. Having said that, I also bumped into several ex-King's Heath Comprehensive schoolmates from my year: Alex Craven (then, the boy most likely to play cricket for England; now, guitarist and part-time drug dealer); Mark Barratt (then, the boy most likely to be a bricklayer; now, MD of his own building firm and owner of a BMW) and Jane Nicholson (then, the girl most likely to become the most beautiful woman in the world; now, part-time sales assistant in Texas Homecare).

As I left the shop with my heavy load and headed for my dad's car I thought about New York, which now seemed a million miles away.

I thought about my job, which now seemed like it never existed.

And then I thought about Elaine – and I still missed her like it was only yesterday.

twenty-two

To: crazedelaine@hotpr.com
From: mattb@c-tec.national.com
Subject: You

I miss you.

To: crazedelaine@hotpr.com
From: mattb@c-tec.national.com
Subject: You

I miss you.

To: crazedelaine@hotpr.com
From: mattb@c-tec.national.com
Subject: You

I miss you.

To: crazedelaine@hotpr.com
From: mattb@c-tec.national.com
Subject: You

I miss you.

To: crazedelaine@hotpr.com
From: mattb@c-tec.national.com
Subject: You

I miss you.

To: crazedelaine@hotpr.com
From: mattb@c-tec.national.com
Subject: You

I miss you.

To: crazedelaine@hotpr.com
From: mattb@c-tec.national.com
Subject: You

I miss you.

twenty-three

Today was Gershwin's birthday.

Today he was thirty.

Today he reached the day he'd thought would never come.

And how did he want to celebrate the birthday of birthdays? With a once-in-a-lifetime hot-air balloon ride? A bunch of mates to go off to Dublin for the weekend? A surprise party? No. Ever since arriving back in Birmingham, Zoë and I had been putting our heads together to come up with ideas to make Gershwin's thirtieth a special one, but a week after we'd booked him a surprise weekend trip to Dublin, he scuppered our plans.

'This thirtieth birthday thing is just too depressing,' he said on the Monday evening, a week before the planned trip. 'A guy at work, Steve, was just telling me about his thirtieth. He came home from work last Friday night, expecting a night in front of the telly with his girlfriend, and he opened his front door to discover twenty-five of his closest family and friends in his living room, bags packed, ready to whisk him away to Edinburgh for the weekend! He hated every second of it. Not only did he have to pretend to have a good time on this the most nightmarish of birthdays but on top of all that they wanted to drag out the whole experience for an entire weekend.'

'They were doing it to torture him,' said Zoë, laughing, but when Gershwin wasn't looking she flashed a look of horror in my direction. 'Isn't that right, Matt?'

'Definitely a pure hate thing,' I replied. 'We'd never do anything like that to you, Gershwin. We'd do something far more devious.'

'Like a hot-air balloon ride,' said Zoë.

'Or a surprise party,' I suggested.

'Or a weekend in Dublin . . .' said Zoë finally.

'I couldn't think of anything worse,' he said animatedly. 'These days, Dublin at the weekend is full of nightmare stag and hen parties from England. And as for hot-air balloon rides and surprise parties – no way. All I want on my birthday is me, some good mates and a nice pub that's not too crowded.'

Zoë and I exchanged glances once more, and while Gershwin wasn't looking she mouthed despondently, 'Cancel it – I'll do the rest.'

So the pub it was, the only twist in the tale being that the pub we selected at which to spend the evening was the Kings Arms in Moseley, the old stomping-ground of Gershwin's and my youth.

The Kings Arms was reasonably busy, considering it was only Wednesday night and there was quite a lot of decent television on, as my mum had pointed out while I was getting ready to go out. The place had barely changed since I'd last been there on Christmas Eve five years ago – that night the annual get-together had consisted of Gershwin, Zoë, me and, for roughly ten minutes, Pete, because he was spending the majority of Christmas Eve with his girlfriend's parents in Derby. The pub's tastefully nicotine-stained flock wallpaper was still hanging on for dear life, as were most of the bar staff. However, they had added a concrete beer garden since my last visit, and the toilets had had a major refurbishment too. Yet the place still retained the warmth of a proper English pub: it was a place to sit back, relax, and talk to your fellow human beings, rather than being pummelled to death by flashing lights and constant chart hits. In New York Elaine always insisted on dragging me to the kind of drinking establishments that she and her we-work-in-PR mates inhabited, which invariably meant ridiculously hard-to-find bars with overpriced bottled beers, loud music and nowhere to sit. My knees ached just thinking about it.

The lounge at the back of the pub, which in the old days was where the old gang always sat, was occupied by groups of laid-back thirty-people, chatting, smoking and generally being at ease with themselves. Some I even vaguely recognised from the old days, but not enough to talk to them. Right at the back of the lounge, though, in the far corner, were Gershwin, Zoë and the birthday boy's group of friends, most of whom I didn't know. Zoë had managed to get together most of Gershwin's mates, work and otherwise. Over the course of the first half-hour I was introduced to Davina and Tom (friends of Zoë who were now friends of Gershwin), Christina and Joel (Christina was a friend of Gershwin from work), Neil and Sarah (Neil was apparently a friend of Gershwin from five-a-side football) and Dom and Polly (who were friends of Christina and Joel and were now close friends of Zoë and Gershwin). They all seemed nice enough people, really, but I didn't feel relaxed because I was the only single person in the group. It wouldn't have bothered me so much but a couple of times during the evening I tried to interject a reasonably interesting anecdote into the conversation and suddenly the discussion would veer elsewhere. Under normal circumstances – i.e. when you've actually *got* a girlfriend with you – it's possible to continue your anecdote without fear of looking (a) stupid, (b) boring or (c) both, because you know at least one person will be polite enough to listen. But as I sat there, open-mouthed, half-arsed anecdote still dribbling from my lips, I suddenly felt incredibly alone. I wasn't good at talking to new people at the best of times – large groups of new people were my worst nightmare. I think that was one of the things that attracted me to Elaine – the way that she wasn't in the least bit fazed or intimidated by the new: she could go to a party and not know anyone, but within half an hour she'd have a circle of people hanging on her every word. I think that's why I liked the idea of old friends so much – they're the only people who don't turn every conversation into a popularity contest or a marathon of monologues.

I was listening to Christina and Joel, whose anecdote, delivered in couple stereo, was about a mammoth gas bill they'd just received, when I tired of being the odd man out and volunteered to get a round in. I wanted to be alone at the bar to feel sorry for myself. I nudged Gershwin and asked him what he wanted to drink then went round the table.

Leaning against the bar, heavy of heart and trying to recall whether Davina had asked for a gin and tonic or a vodka and tonic, I was tapped on the shoulder. I turned round.

'Matt Beckford?' said a woman.

'Ginny Pascoe?'

'Matt bloody Beckford!' she cried, wrapping her arms around me.

'Ginny bloody Pascoe!' I shouted, hugging her back. 'Wow. This *is* a surprise!'

twenty-four

The last time I'd seen Ginny was at Gershwin's wedding nearly six years ago, and then we hadn't seen each other for about six months. The conversation that took place a little after midnight in the unlit car park of the Grosvenor Country Hotel, Hagley, went something like this:

Me: (Kissing her frantically) This is a really bad idea.

Her: (Kissing me frantically) You're right. The absolute worst.

Me: What are we doing?

Her: Have we no self-control?

Me: It doesn't look like it.

Her: But why? Why are we cursed so?

Me: (Despondently) I don't know. I don't know.

Her: This has been carrying on seven long years.

Me: Depressing, I know.

Her: When was the last time?

Me: It must've been Bev's I'm-leaving-to-go-to-India-(again) goodbye party.

Her: (Shaking her head) Wrong!

Me: It wasn't? Are you sure?

Her: Try three months after that at Elliot's house-warming.

Me: (Remembering) Oh, yeah. This is terrible. It's like some kind of illness, isn't it?

Her: Yeah, but what can we do about it?

Me: (Hesitantly) I suppose we could . . . well, have you ever thought of . . . do you think that we should have a proper . . .

Her: (Panicking) Don't say it! Don't you dare say it!

Me: What?

Her: You were going to say the 'R' word, weren't you?

Me: (Quite obviously lying) No.

Her: You were, you lying git.

Me: So what if I was? It's not a crime.

Her: Yes, it is. It's the world's most heinous crime.

Me: (Nonchalantly) Now you're just being silly.

Her: Okay, so what *are* you suggesting?

Me: I'm not suggesting anything. I am merely throwing around a few ideas. Why don't you throw one in too?

Her: (Laughing) How about some sort of pact?

Me: What kind?

Her: I don't know . . . like, say, for instance, if at some point in the future . . .

Me: . . . if we're both single . . .

Her: . . . and we both haven't . . .

Me: . . . found anything better . . .

Her: . . . then we'll get together when we're . . .

Me: . . . twenty-six . . .

Her: (Indignantly) No way! Are you mad? That's only two years away!

Me: (Indignantly in return) Okay, then, you choose.

Her: (Thinking) Twenty-seven is too close to twenty-six

for comfort, so that's out. (Pause) By the time I'm twenty-eight I'll still be thinking about my career so that's out too. (Another pause) Twenty-nine sounds slightly better . . . but to be on the safe side I think we should hang on until we're thirty.

Me: Thirty? Are you sure?

Her: Definitely. (Breezily) Thirty's like a million years away.

Me: Okay, then. If this is a pact let's shake on it.

Her: (Laughing) Forget shaking hands. (Raises eyebrows suggestively) I can think of a better way of sealing a pact than that . . . Now where were we again?

twenty-five

The first question that sprang to my mind after we'd parted from the hug and she and I were doing a long and intense will-you-look-at-you! look, was – of course – had she changed since I last saw her? Not really. And certainly not as much as I had. Her hair was a little shorter and there were the beginnings of a few lines around her eyes that enhanced rather than detracted from her good looks. The rest of her – the smile, the laugh, the mannerisms – were exactly the same. Clothing-wise, she looked interesting: she was wearing a black cardigan, a tight black top, black knee-length skirt and bright white Nike trainers. All very nice indeed. Did I fancy her? (This of course, was, the second question I asked myself as I stood staring at her.) I didn't know. Yes? No? Maybe? In the split second available to me I ran through every option. Twice. The jury was out.

'How *are* you?' asked Ginny, excitedly. She was still holding on to my waist, not flirtatiously but in a friendly way, and when she asked the question her face was thoughtful, as if she really wanted to know the answer.

'Good,' I replied. 'Fine. Really good.' An old man attempted to squeeze between us to get to the bar, forcing her to release her grip. 'It's been a long—'

'Yes, it has,' she said, finishing my sentence. 'Are you still in London?'

'New York.'

'Wow!' she exclaimed. 'From King's Heath to New York. Not many people do that.'

I shook my head.

'So are you back visiting your mum and dad?'

I nodded.

Ginny paused, wearing a puzzled expression. 'Are you actually going to speak to me or do I have to guess? Like a game of charades, only not quite as exciting.'

I shook my head again instead of answering, mainly because I was still trying to work out if I fancied her or not.

'Sorry,' I said, regaining my wits. 'Yeah, you're right. I've come back for a while to see my folks. You know, spend a bit of quality time at the old familystead.'

'How's it going?' she said, still beaming enthusiastically. 'The spending quality time with Ma and Pa Beckford?'

'Terrible,' I said, holding the palm of my hand to my head in mock anguish. 'They're driving me up the wall. Any time I enter a room they insist on involving me in one of their strange-but-true conversations. So far the topics covered since my arrival have been as wide and varied as London house prices, my auntie Jean's dodgy third husband and which one of my siblings it is who likes sprouts. It's like I've walked into a surrealist nightmare. I love them but . . .' I paused, not wanting to dominate the conversation but she didn't pick up the signal. Her mind was obviously elsewhere now. 'Anyway, how are you?' I prompted. 'I mean . . . I don't know . . . what are *you* doing here?'

'In the Kings Arms?'

'Well, for starters.'

'Oh, you mean here in Birmingham, don't you? Well, as far

as the pub goes I'm here meeting a friend. It's still my local – that is, if I've got a local any more. I always seem to be working these days.'

'Last time I heard anything about your toings and froings you were living it up in Brighton, weren't you?'

She nodded, and momentarily avoided eye-contact. 'Yeah, that was a while ago, though. My mum died, which is why I'm back.'

'I'm sorry,' I said. 'About your mum. That's terrible.'

She smiled softly. 'Don't worry. It's been eighteen months now. The worst of it's over.'

'Your mum, she was a really nice woman,' I said. And I meant it. Ginny's mum was the kind of parent you could always talk to without the conversation sounding fake. 'She'd always offer to make us beans on toast whenever we were round there, whatever time of day it was.'

Ginny smiled. 'Yeah, Mum was good like that.'

'Was it sudden?'

'Not really. It was cancer. She'd been ill for quite a while, in and out of hospital all the time, and then when the doctors said it was serious I packed in my job and came back from Brighton to look after her. Because it's always just been her and me when she died I inherited the house. I thought briefly about selling it and moving on but then I thought, why not stay? So I did just that. I don't think I could have sold the house anyway . . . too many memories.'

'I really don't know what to say, I'm so sorry.'

'These things happen,' she said, and she gave a little shrug accompanied by an awkward half-smile, and somehow we ended up in another short embrace during which neither of us spoke.

'So, how are you?' I asked, when we were just standing and staring again.

'I think we might have been here before, Matt,' she said, arching her left eyebrow sardonically. 'I'm fine now, honest. Really good.' Her eyes flitted briefly across the room to the door. 'You know how it is. You have your ups and downs but today's an up day.' She smiled. 'Anyway, what do you do in New York, you flash git?'

'I work in computers.'

'What? Building them? Using them? Wearing them on your head? You always were hopeless with details.'

'It's really boring,' I said, wanting to get off the subject. 'I promise you.'

'Try me.'

'I design software for banking systems. Very tedious.'

'But essential all the same,' she said agreeably. 'Without people like you I'm sure my wages would take much longer to arrive in my bank account. Obviously that would probably mean I wouldn't spend it quite as quickly as I do. But I think, generally speaking, you're probably more an asset to my life than a hindrance.'

'How about yourself?' I asked quickly. 'What are you up to?'

'I teach art.'

'An art teacher? Respect due. Art teachers are the coolest type to be – floating about with their easels, generally being groovy, encouraging thirteen-year-olds to reach their inner muse.'

She laughed.

'Where do you teach?' I asked.

'Have a guess.'

'Not King's Heath Comp?'

'The very same.'

'How weird is that?'

'Very. On my first day there I walked into the staffroom

and immediately felt like a fraud. Right there, slap bang in front of me, were Mr Collins, Mr Haynes, Mrs Perkins and Mr Thorne.'

'Don't tell me,' I said laughing. 'Let me see – Mr Collins, geography, Mr Haynes, physics, Mrs Perkins, maths, and Mr Thorne, English?'

'Nearly,' she said laughing. 'Mr Haynes teaches history.'

'They must be nearly a million years old now because they were half a million when we were there.'

'I know,' she said, 'and now I'm one of them.'

We halted the conversation to allow me to get the drinks for which Gershwin and his friends must have been desperate by now. It was also at this moment that it occurred to me that Ginny was still waiting for her friend. I wasn't going to ask her if this friend was a man because it would've been too obvious. But Ginny was apparently as curious about me as I was about her because as the barman began my order she asked me questions of a more personal nature.

'Anyone special in your life?' she began. 'Any kids? Any pets?'

'Special people, one ex-girlfriend back in the States. Kids, definitely nil, and, er, pets, nil.' I was relieved to get it over. 'What about yourself?'

She took a deep breath and began. 'Er . . . special people, one boyfriend who is extremely late. Kids, none – that's discounting the hundred or so I teach, of course. Pets, yes, two boy cats – Larry and Sanders.'

There was a break in the conversation again while the barman checked the drinks order with me. I used the time to make a decision. The question was: do I want to see her again? The answer was: yes.

'Listen,' I began, 'how late is your bloke?'

'Put it this way,' she said, 'when he arrives I'm going

to have to have a right strop with him for at least half an hour.'

'Well, feel free to say no, if you want to, but why don't you come over and say hello to Gershwin? He's here as well. It's his thirtieth today. He'd love to see you.'

'Thirty,' she said, 'I had my thirtieth back in December. It was all right, actually. Good fun.' She paused. 'Are you sure?'

'About Gershwin having his thirtieth birthday?'

She stared at me menacingly. 'No, about joining you. I don't want to crash the party.'

'You'd be doing me a huge favour,' I explained. 'It's just me, Gershwin, Zoë and a whole bunch of new Gershwin friends who I don't know and who don't listen to my supposedly amusing anecdotes.' Ginny looked confused. 'I'll explain on the way. Come and join us, or I might be forced to do something really drastic.'

'Like what?'

I raised my eyebrows, grabbed a tray for the drinks and left the question hanging there. Ginny followed behind.

twenty-six

'Gershwin!' I called, as I reached the table. 'Guess who I've just bumped into?'

He looked up and, once his brain had got into gear, practically leapt out of his seat to hug Ginny.

'I haven't seen you since our wedding!' said Zoë, giving her a kiss too. 'Oh, it's great to see you.'

'It's good to see you both too,' said Ginny. 'I should've kept in touch. I'm just really crap at it.'

'I think we all are,' said Gershwin.

'I'm the reason for the delay in your drinks,' Ginny explained, for the benefit of the rest of the table, who didn't know what was going on. 'I bumped into Matt and we were just trying to fill in the last six years or so.' She laughed and looked over at me. 'Gershwin, Matt and I used to go to school together.'

'Everybody, this is Ginny,' said Gershwin, gesturing to the entire table. 'And, Ginny . . .' I could see from his face that he was trying to work out whether it was worth introducing them all individually. He decided against it. '. . . this is everybody.'

Once Gershwin sat down, conversation at the table started up again almost immediately. The first topic of conversation that sprang up was an offshoot of Ginny's arrival: what had

Gershwin been like at school? Out of politeness everyone looked to Ginny to give the first illustration, so she told them the story about when we were thirteen and Gershwin, Pete, Elliot and I went to see *Breakdance – The Movie*. Even though we couldn't dance, let alone spin on our heads to save our lives, we were so worked up by the film that we thought we'd be able to do it right there in the cinema. We thought we looked fantastic in our silky tracksuit bottoms and heavily logoed T-shirts, but all we got for our troubles were carpet burns, headaches and a four-week ban from the cinema. This started off a new round of school-based anecdotes, beginning with Sarah (of Sarah and Neil), then moving on to Polly (of Dom and Polly).

It was at this point that Ginny decided to take the opportunity to go in search of her boyfriend. When she returned five minutes later, with a man in tow, she didn't do an 'Everyone, this is . . .' because that would have been embarrassing. Instead she dragged him to the table, allowed everyone to do that kind of cool raise-of-the-eyebrows acknowledgement, then introduced him properly to our end of the table, which consisted of Zoë and Gershwin and me.

'Ian,' she said, gesturing to her man, 'this is Zoë, her husband – and my old schoolfriend – Gershwin, and Matt, another old schoolfriend.' She paused and gestured to us. 'Everybody, this is Ian.'

Ian wasn't what I had been expecting. Ginny always told me that she had a thing for guys who looked a bit seedy. I remember her once saying that her dream man was of the type whose natural instinct on waking up was to reach for a cigarette and a lighter. Ian wasn't like that at all. He was tall and clean-looking, handsome, in a girlish way, and somewhere about my age.

'So, you guys went to school with Ginny,' said Ian.

'Yeah,' said Gershwin. 'Seems like years ago.'

'That's because it was years ago,' said Zoë, ruffling Gershwin's hair fondly. 'You're an old man now,' she teased. 'Your schooldays are ancient history, mate.'

At the other end of the table a conversation about pro- grammes that were on TV when we were kids gradually enticed Gershwin and Zoë to join in. I would have loved to participate in it so that I could show off my ability to name all the main characters in 'old-skool' cartoons like *Battle Beyond the Planets* (Mark, Jason, Princess, Tiny, Keyop), but I knew I'd never get a look in. Instead I started my own version of the conversation between Ginny, Ian and me. Ian was not only impressed by my *Battle Beyond the Planets* naming skills but he earned my respect and admiration by being able to recite all the words to the theme tune of *Hong Kong Phooey*, even the really difficult bit. That conversation eventually led to an entirely different one about music, and before I knew it we were waxing lyrical about our favourite female singer-songwriters, praising the practicalities of dark blue/black clothing and the importance of having exactly the same haircut every time you go to the barber's.

Of all the new people I'd met that evening Ian was far and away my favourite. Eventually we left our favourite things and got on to the so-tell-me-about-yourself tack.

'I'm a teacher, too, for my sins,' said Ian. 'That's how Ginny and I met. I'm a supply teacher. You know, it pays the bills and all that.'

'You're not just a supply teacher!' said Ginny, reprimanding him jokingly. 'Ian's doing a part-time Ph.D.,' she explained. 'Go on, Ian, tell him.'

He smiled, embarrassed by her maternal enthusiasm. 'Er, yes, well, as Ginny's hinted, I'm doing a part-time Ph.D. in meteorological studies. No use to man or beast, really.

It's just a load of nonsense. I've no idea why I'm doing it.'

'Just ignore him,' said Ginny impatiently. 'He's going to be a lecturer. I have no idea why he puts himself down like that.'

I could see what Ginny found attractive in him. Ian was both charming and funny but there was a shyness about him that bordered on vulnerable. Unlike me, however, he had no fear of meeting new people, and when I returned from a quick trip to the toilet, Ian was holding forth to the table with tale after tale of the I'm-so-crap-honestly variety. Every time he'd finished one story he looked embarrassed for dominating the conversation and tried to encourage someone else to take centre stage. Of course, no one did, because even though they were all bursting with humorous stories of their own, no one wanted to have to follow a class act like his. So that was it. Ian. More Ian. 'You're so funny, Ian.' 'Can I buy you a drink, Ian?' And, at the end of the night, 'We really must swap numbers and meet up again, Ian.' The funny thing was, it didn't annoy me. I genuinely liked Ian too. In a lot of ways he reminded me of Elaine. She had exactly the same ability to hold people's attention and make them her best friend in a second.

twenty-seven

It was ten to eleven and, as if by instinct, the majority of the table – i.e. Gershwin's new friends – began to pull on their coats and jackets ready to go home.

'Right, then,' slurred Gershwin, who by this time was very much the worse for wear. 'Who fancies going to a club?'

A collective look of horror had swept across all their faces – the look that crosses the majority of late-twenties/thirty-people couples when anyone suggests having a proper late night during the week. I could see their minds flashing forward to whatever hour they had to get up at for work. I could see them imagining going in feeling knackered, working all day feeling knackered and coming home feeling knackered. The very thought of being that knackered made them feel ill. I knew this look because I'd worn it myself regularly when Elaine and her friends ever suggested such midweek mayhem.

'I'm in,' I said to Gershwin, secure in the knowledge that I could sleep late tomorrow. 'Definitely.'

'Good,' said Gershwin. 'Who else?'

Apologies/excuses ran thus:

'We'd love to, Gershwin,' said Davina (of Davina and Tom), 'but we've both got to be at work extra early tomorrow.'

'Can't do it tonight, mate,' said Dom (of Dom and Polly). 'I've got a meeting with my boss first thing and Polly's got to be in Cheshire for ten thirty.'

'We couldn't even if we wanted to,' said Christina (of Christina and Joel). 'My sister won't babysit past eleven thirty.'

'No can do, birthday boy,' said Neil (of Neil and Sarah). 'I'm on call at the hospital tomorrow night and Sarah gets really grumpy if she doesn't get enough sleep.'

'I can't either,' said Ian (of Ian and Ginny). 'I'm behind with my Ph.D. as it is.'

I was horrified at this one. 'Come on, Ian, mate!' I said over enthusiastically. 'You can't go home – you're my new best friend.'

'I appreciate your candour,' said Ian, laughing, 'but I can't, honestly.'

Gershwin looked at Zoë hopefully. 'What about you, babe?'

'I'm probably going to regret this,' said Zoë, sighing, 'but as Charlotte's staying at her gran's tonight I can officially be a young person again. I'm up for it.'

'Are you sure?' said Gershwin. 'I know how tired you are.'

Zoë leaned forward until her forehead was resting on his and kissed him. 'Yeah, I'm sure. But I'm so tired I'll probably fall asleep the second we get there.'

Gershwin kissed her back affectionately. 'Right, then, so that's two.' He turned to Ginny. 'What about you, Gin? Other than Matt, you're my oldest friend. I haven't seen you for years. You can't just go home.'

'I can't stay out late on a school night,' said Ginny, embarrassed to hear herself saying it. 'The kids will know what I've been up to if I come in all bleary-eyed.'

I laughed and looked across at her. Our eyes met for just a

second, and I knew, in that instant, that she was on the verge of changing her mind.

'Please!' begged Gershwin.

She exchanged glances with Ian, who smiled and gave her a nod of encouragement as if to say, 'Go on, live a little.'

'I'll just have to wear sunglasses all day!' she said gleefully.

twenty-eight

Standing outside the Kings Arms in the freezing cold, watching our breath rise up into the sky, having said goodbye to Gershwin's friends and Ian, the four of us were at a loss what to do next.

'Shall we just get a taxi into town?' said Ginny.

'Hadn't we better have some sort of game-plan first?' I suggested. 'Where's good to go at . . .' I looked at my watch '. . . ten past eleven on a Wednesday night?'

'We could go to the Dome,' said Zoë. 'I think they have some sort of a student night on a Wednesday.'

'We can't go there!' said Ginny, horrified. 'I know for a fact that some of the kids I teach go there!'

'Where else is there?' I asked Gershwin.

'Dunno, mate,' he said. 'I haven't been out clubbing in years.'

There was a long silence while we all got colder and – if everyone else was thinking like me – contemplated going home.

'Forget going to a club,' said Ginny. 'Let's nip to the off-licence, get some beers, go back to mine and stay up all night.'

It was a clear reference to our youth. Way back when,

staying up for an entire night had seemed like such a grown-up thing to do that we were always trying to do it. But no matter how many times we attempted it we were all such lightweights in the party-animal stakes that we always fell asleep well before dawn. Since then, of course, I had done more than my fair share of all-nighters but not in a while. A very long while.

Gershwin and Zoë looked at me. I looked at Gershwin. Ginny looked at all of us and simultaneously we said, 'Let's do it.'

The journey to Ginny's house brought back floods of memories of the hundreds of times I'd walked Ginny home in the early hours of the morning. Nearly all of the old landmarks I used to count off on the journey from hers back to mine were still there: the post-box on the corner of Ethel Street, the chip shop on Podmore Road and the zebra crossing on King's Heath high street. The only one that was missing was the huge run-down house on Valentine Road, which had been bulldozed and replaced with two new Barratt-type 'executive' homes.

As soon as we'd reached our destination, we all felt incredibly hungry so we raided Ginny's kitchen cupboards and located an industrial-sized pack of tortilla chips and a jar of salsa. With the aid of a microwave and haphazardly grated Cheddar, we had a feast. Once we were sated, Ginny put on some music (Wham!'s *Greatest Hits*) and we sat around swapping stories about the things that had happened to us since we'd last been together, carefully resisting phrases like, 'remember when' and 'whatever happened to . . .' so that Zoë didn't feel excluded. During my time with Elaine I'd sat through enough where-are-they-now? conversations with her old college and high-school friends to know better than to inflict them on someone else.

As I returned from yet another exploratory rummage through Ginny's kitchen cupboards armed with a packet of Hobnobs, a selection box of cheese crackers, a small tub of glacé cherries while singing along to 'Club Tropicana', Gershwin told me to keep the noise down because Zoë, as she'd predicted, had fallen asleep in an armchair. 'My wife is such a lightweight,' he said, laughing.

'Will she be all right there?' asked Ginny. 'She can sleep in my bed, if she wants. If I actually stay awake through the night I'm sure I'll be far too tired to make it up the stairs.' She looked over at me and kicked my foot playfully. 'There's a spare room upstairs for you as well, if you don't think you can make it.'

'I'll be here to the bitter end,' I replied.

'Are you sure about Zoë sleeping upstairs?' said Gershwin. 'I could easily call a mini-cab to drop us home.'

'Don't worry about it,' she said cheerily. 'It's not a problem.'

Gershwin gently roused Zoë. 'Ginny said you can sleep in her bed. Do you want to do that?'

She nodded, without even opening her eyes.

'Are you sure you don't want to go home?'

She mumbled incoherently.

'Right, then,' said Gershwin, picking her up. 'Let's get you to bed.'

'Knackered yet?' I asked Ginny, as Gershwin left the room.

'No way.' She paused. 'Pass the cherries, chump.' I handed her the tub and she consumed several at once. 'These are gorgeous,' she said.

Feeling even more hungry just from watching her eat, I grabbed a cheese cracker. 'So,' I said, crunching, 'Ian's nice.' I'd wanted to say something more dynamic than that, but 'nice' was the word that seemed best to sum him up.

She smiled contentedly. 'Yeah, he is.'

'How long have you been seeing him?'

'About two years.'

'But you don't live together?'

'No, no, *no*,' she said, emphatically. 'He has his place. I have mine.'

'But you've got plans to move in together?'

'I thought you were a software-designer-type blokey not a relationship counsellor,' she said. 'No, Ian and I haven't got any plans to move in together. At least, none that I'm aware of. We like being the way we are, thank you very much. Anyway,' she sighed, 'while I'm grateful for your concern about my love-life, what about your own?'

'What about it?'

'The ex-girlfriend you mentioned in the Kings Arms? Is she American?'

'Her name's Elaine,' I replied, 'and, yeah, she's American.'

'What's she like?'

'She was really cool . . .' I corrected myself. 'She still is really cool.'

'So what went wrong?'

'Familiarity, I think, bred discontent.'

'You were at the Stage,' said Ginny. 'Wandering eyes and all that.'

'We thought it was best to put down our rabid relationship before we started foaming at the mouth.'

'Mmmm,' said Ginny, licking her lips, 'nice metaphor there, Matthew. You should get a job writing the insides of birthday cards.' She paused. 'So, if the relationship was doomed, why do I detect such a heavy sense of loss?'

'Because—' I was interrupted by Gershwin entering the room.

'I haven't disturbed anything, have I?' he asked, smirking.

Ginny and I exchanged glances.

'No,' I said. 'We were just talking about how much weight you've put on around your neck. You look huge, boy.'

'Enough of the jibes,' said Gershwin cheerfully. 'Let's get to business.'

'What business?' said Ginny, feigning ignorance. Suddenly she burst out laughing. 'I know it's crap but I've been *dying* to do it all night. I love talking about old times. I really do.' She tore open the packet of Hobnobs, grabbed one and settled back in her chair. 'Has anyone seen any of the old gang recently?'

Gershwin and I shook our heads.

'I had a postcard from Bev about a million years ago when I was in Brighton,' said Ginny, 'but I was a bit rubbish and forgot to call her for ages. And by the time I did she'd moved house.'

'What was she up to?' asked Gershwin.

'Dunno, she didn't say. Probably saving the whale or something. The postcard was nice, though. It was from New Zealand.'

'You know Pete's younger brother Ray?' began Gershwin. 'He used to go out with that girl with mousy hair when we were teenagers. Well, Zoë and I bumped into her about a year ago in town and she said that she was still in contact with him. I asked her how Pete was and she said he'd got married or something.'

'Pete?' said Ginny. 'Him? Get married? Never.'

'Apparently he's got a kid too.'

'Pete, married with kid?' said Ginny disbelievingly. 'Never. Never. Never.'

'Who have you seen, Matt?'

I grabbed a biscuit and tried to remember the last time I'd seen any of our old friends. 'I think the last person I saw

117

was Elliot, but that was about three years ago when I was in London. He'd got my mobile number from my mum and called me out of the blue because he was in town on some conference and wanted to meet up. I wouldn't have minded but it was about ten to midnight and I was in bed. Half an hour later he picked me up in his flash company car and we had this absolutely mad night out – curry houses, late-night members-only drinking clubs, hotel bars, the lot. I ended up crashing at his hotel room. We exchanged numbers and everything the next day, but then neither of us called.'

'Sounds like typical Elliot to me,' said Ginny.

'What about Katrina?' said Gershwin. 'Has no one heard from her?'

'Last time I spoke to her was at your wedding,' said Ginny. 'She was in London, wasn't she?'

'That's right,' I said. 'She'd moved there because she was going to make it as editor of *Vogue*. She always was more determined than the rest of us. I wonder if she did it?'

Ginny sighed heavily. 'Do you know what?'

'What?' I said, needlessly. I knew exactly what she was going to say.

'I miss all that lot,' she said. 'And I miss those days.'

'Me too,' said Gershwin.

twenty-nine

When I woke up the next morning and found myself face down on the sofa, I thought for a minute that I was back in New York on the Sofa from Hell. Gershwin was asleep on the smaller sofa in the corner of the room and Ginny was curled up in the armchair she'd been sitting in. We must have fallen asleep somewhere after our where-are-they-now conversation because I couldn't remember much else after that . . . apart from the renewing of our pact to stay awake all night by promising to wake each other up if any of us started to nod off.

That whole evening, since the moment I had seen Ginny again, had reminded me what I'd been missing out on by not keeping in touch with my old friends. Talking to them made me feel like I'd known Gershwin and Ginny for ever. They knew the me who had been suspended from school for smashing a stink bomb in an English lesson; they knew the me who had been so drunk at Nadine Baggott's sixteenth birthday party that I'd spent the night asleep in the garden and had to be taken to hospital the next day to be treated for hypothermia. Only they and the rest of the group would remember those times as I did.

Without waking anyone I went to the toilet, grabbed a slice

of bread from the bread-bin in Ginny's kitchen to stave off hunger pangs and slipped out of the front door. I checked my watch: it was just coming up to a quarter to six. There was something glorious about being up at this time of the day, still wearing the previous night's clothes, smelling slightly sour, probably looking a bit rough around the edges. It reminded me of parties of the past, the days when I really could go out clubbing until four in the morning. It reminded me of how things used to be.

Unfortunately, when I got home I had another reminder of the old days waiting for me as I came in through the door.

'Is that you, Matthew?'

My mum was standing at the top of the stairs wearing her nightie, her dressing-gown and an uncompromising frown.

'Yeah, of course,' I replied. My mum knew it was me.

'Where have you been all night? You didn't say anything to me about staying out all night. You didn't ring. You didn't do anything. I can't believe you would be so inconsiderate.'

I found myself breathing deeply – always a sign that I'm trying to be patient. My first instinct, of course, was to explain to my mother that at nearly thirty years of age I'd earned the right to come in at six o'clock in the morning, but that wouldn't have achieved anything. Then it occurred to me that she was right: it had been selfish not to tell her. It wasn't her fault that she worried about me. She worried about me whether I was in New York or right under her roof.

'I'm sorry, Mum,' I said, and tried to placate her by heading upstairs to plant a kiss on her cheek. 'You're right, I should've called you. There's no excuse. You haven't been awake all night waiting for me, have you?'

'You must be joking,' said my mum. 'I'm just a light sleeper, that's all. You'd better get off to bed,' she said. 'You look absolutely terrible.'

thirty

To: mattb@c-tec.national.com
From: crazedelaine@hotpr.com
Subject: **Your last several million e-mails . . .**

Dear Matt

   When I logged on at work today I got all of your 'I miss you' e-mails and I ended up crying so much I had to go and hide in the ladies' restroom. You should've seen me – my mascara had run so much I looked like a panda. I'm such a wuss.

love

Elaine

PS No more miss yous allowed. Okay?

To: crazedelaine@hotpr.com
From: mattb@c-tec.national.com
Subject: **Sorry**

E, I didn't mean to make you cry.
I'm sorry.

Matt xxx

thirty-one

'Matthew, it's the phone for you,' said a voice in my dreams. 'Matthew, it's the phone for you,' it repeated. It wasn't until the third 'Matthew, it's the phone for you,' and my mum banged on the door that I woke up and realised that indeed there was a phone call for me. I looked at my watch, lying on the floor next to the slippers my mum had bought me which I had no intention of wearing. It was one o'clock in the afternoon.

'It's the middle of the night,' I called back to my mum. 'Get them to call back at a decent hour.'

'I'm not your skivvy, you know,' said my mum, teasing me. 'If you will go out until all hours then you get what you deserve.'

Grappling with a dressing-gown, I groped my way downstairs to the phone in the hall. 'Who is it?' I mumbled, picking up the phone while scratching anywhere that itched.

'I'm sorry, Matt, I know it's a bit early.'

It was Ginny.

'No, you're all right,' I said, concentrating on a patch of hair just below my navel. 'I was just about to get up and go for a jog anyway. A few laps of the park and I'd have been right as rain.'

'Yeah, right.' She laughed. 'I'd like to see that.'

'Where are you?' I asked.

'At home,' she said, guiltily.

'Shouldn't you be at work or something?' I said, sitting down on the bottom stair. 'I know a lot of things have changed about the education system since I was last at school but surely teachers aren't allowed to stroll into school as late as the kids.'

'I've pulled a sickie,' she admitted. 'I feel dead guilty but I wouldn't have been any good to them today, the way I'm feeling.'

'You were flat out when I left and that must've been about six.'

'I think I woke up when I heard the sound of the front door. That must have been you going, and I think I even thought about getting up, but I was so comfortable that I must've fallen back to sleep. By the time I'd woken up properly at about seven fifteen I just couldn't be arsed to go in.'

'You art-teacher rebel, you,' I said. 'How are Gershwin and Zoë?'

'Fine. Zoë went off to work about seven thirty this morning and Gershwin's still half asleep on the sofa. Which brings me to my point. Have you seen the sky today? It's absolutely bloody gorgeous!'

'I haven't as it happens. It's pretty hard to see when you're in bed, under a duvet and the curtains are closed.'

'Never mind all that. Go and take a look out of a window.'

I partially opened the front door and peered upwards. The sun was bright, the sky near perfect and it looked warm even though it was only January.

'You're right. It looks like it's going to be great. Is this what you get for going out with a meteorologist?'

'I wish,' she said. 'Listen. Gershwin and I were just talking and as we both appear to have taken the day off, and as you're not doing whatever it is you're not doing, and as it's a nice day – the sort of day that three old friends *should* spend together – we thought we should do exactly that. Are you in?'

I looked at my watch again and wondered if I was still tired. I was. Very. But I still found myself saying, 'Give me time to have a shave and I'll be raring to go.'

thirty-two

'Do you know what this reminds me of?' said Gershwin, passing the bottle of Thunderbird to me.

'The summer we finished our A levels?' I enquired.

'How did you guess?'

'I was thinking exactly the same thing.'

'Me too,' said Ginny. 'Fantastic, isn't it?'

By the time I'd got round to Ginny's a little after two o'clock, she and Gershwin had made a plan for what was left of the day. First, we drove to a Little Chef near Halesowen and partook of a satisfying all-day English breakfast and unlimited toast. Next we stopped at a nearby off-licence to buy a bottle of Thunderbird, for old times' sake, and finally we drove to the nearby Clent Hills, and armed with jackets and coats we climbed a hill, opened the Thunderbird, lay down on the grass and did nothing but talk and stare at the sky.

2.52 pm

'Do you know what I was doing this time last year?'

'What?' asked Ginny.

'I was locked in my office in Manhattan for a month training new recruits. Me, Matt Beckford, from King's Heath, in Manhattan. I was working from five thirty in the morning until ten o'clock at night. I even cultivated a nice stress-related stomach ulcer into the bargain. And now here I am lying in a park, one year later, with beer, fags, friends. What more does a man need?'

'I've often thought about downsizing,' said Ginny. 'Y'know, going part-time and doing something interesting with my life. I mean, what use is money if your life's too busy?' She stopped suddenly, belched, took another sip of the Thunderbird and passed it to me. 'That was a big one.' She giggled, then sighed while gesturing to the air. 'How did we let all of this drift away?'

'It just happens, doesn't it?' said Gershwin. 'Life gets busy. Priorities change. We have only ourselves to blame, really.'

'Too true,' said Ginny. 'We're mad for letting it happen. We get older and don't realise what's happening and it's only when—'

'—you get to our age—' I chipped in.

'—that you realise how important stuff like this is,' said Gershwin.

3.05 pm

'Until I turned twenty-nine I was quite into the idea of thirty,' I said, rolling over on to my front. 'I knew I wasn't about to start swapping vodka shots for Horlicks and, all right, I started to be as interested in the fluctuations of the interest rate as I was in the football results back home but I never wanted to be one of those people who are scared of growing older.' I paused, feeling my mind go off at a tangent. 'D'you know how some people in their thirties feel exactly like they did when they were twenty-four?'

'Yeah.' Ginny nodded vigorously, as if this was a self-knowledge quiz in a women's mag. 'I don't think I've changed since I was about twenty-six. Old enough to feel mature but young enough to still be stupid.' She laughed. 'How about you, Gershwin?'

Gershwin scratched his head vigorously. 'When Charlotte's around I feel about thirty-five. I feel like a dad. It's a nice feeling, though. When she's not around I could be anything from fourteen to twenty-six.'

'I think I've always felt thirty inside,' I said. 'I've always felt that life takes a bit more effort than I've actually got.'

'He's right, you know,' said Ginny to Gershwin. 'Matt's always been the old fart of our gang. Judgemental. Inflexible. Mr Dad.'

'Thank you both kindly,' I said sarcastically. 'It's true, though. I am a bit of a dad sometimes.' I framed a question, then posed it. 'When did you feel that you were actually a fully fledged grown-up?'

'When Charlotte was born,' said Gershwin.

'When Mum died,' said Ginny. 'What about you?'

'I dunno. I think I'm still waiting.'

3.23 pm

'When you think about it, thirty's not a big deal these days, is it?' said Ginny. 'It's like a whole generation got together and decided to delay real life just that little bit longer. These days, you can't really tell the thirty-year-olds from the twenty-year-olds, except that we've usually got more money . . .'

'. . . and less hair . . .' I added.

'. . . and fewer clothes in our wardrobes that we regret buying . . .' said Gershwin.

'Thirty is just like being twenty, probably more so,' said Ginny. 'Forty is the new thirty.' She nudged me with her elbow. 'You've got another ten years before you really have to worry.'

'By which time hopefully forty will be the new something else,' I replied.

'Ahhh,' said Gershwin. 'But what does that make twenty-somethings? The new teenagers?'

None of us could come up with an answer to that one.

3.37 pm

'Hands up, who's got any grey hairs?' said Ginny.

Gershwin and I waved our hands in the air.

'I've only got one,' said Gershwin. 'It's just by my temple. Zoë was going to pluck it out but I told her not to in the vain hope it might make me look distinguished.'

'I haven't got any,' said Ginny. 'But I've been dyeing my hair for so long I have no idea what my real colour is any more. What about you, Matt?'

'Two,' I revealed reluctantly. 'One that pops up every now and again on my chest and one that's . . . well, for the sake of any delicate stomachs round here, let's just say it's one that makes its appearance lower down.'

'Lower than your navel?' said Ginny inquisitively.

'Lower.'

'But higher than, say, your knees?'

'Yes,' I said dolefully.

Ginny let out a scream of laughter.

'No,' said Gershwin incredulously. 'You're having me on?'

'I kid you not,' I replied.

'Can we see it?' asked Ginny, sniggering wildly. 'Go on, please.'

'Never,' I said, trying to maintain my dignity while the others creased up. 'Never in a million years.'

3.55 pm

'So what does thirty mean to you?' said Ginny, addressing Gershwin.

'Nothing much,' he said. 'It means in another ten years

I'll be forty, which seems ancient – but at the same time miles away.'

'Good point,' said Ginny.

'Same question back to you, Gin,' said Gershwin.

'What does thirty mean to me? Thirty means feeling smug about the fact that when my mum was my age she had a kid and very briefly a husband. It also means that for the first time in my life I can feel like a woman and act like a girl.'

'As opposed to?'

'I dunno . . . feeling like a fake woman and acting like a prat. I still feel like a fake woman but sometimes I feel like a proper woman too. I mean, I'm head of the art department! Me, Ginny Pascoe! Every once in a while when I'm holding a departmental meeting I'm struck by the fact that people are listening to what I've got to say. Then, of course, I feel all self-conscious, but for a second or so, I really do feel like I've made it. That's what thirty means to me.'

Ginny and Gershwin both looked at me expectantly. 'Come on then, Matt,' said Ginny. 'Your turn.'

'I dunno.'

'Honestly, Matt, you're hopeless,' said Ginny.

'Okay.' I took a long breath. 'I'll tell you what thirty means to me. Thirty means only going to the pub if there's somewhere to sit down. Thirty means owning at least one classical CD, even if it's *Now That's What I Call Classical Vol 6*. Thirty means calling off the search for the perfect partner because now, after all these years in the wilderness, you've finally found what you've been looking for.' I hesitated. 'Well, that's the way it was supposed to be, anyway.'

4.02 pm

'Getting older's nothing to be ashamed of,' I said comfortingly. 'Who cares if the last time you went to a nightclub you had to shove cotton wool in your ears because it was too loud and then had to be taken to the local Accident and Emergency Department to have it surgically removed because you'd shoved it in too far?'

'You're kidding, right?' said Gershwin, in amazement.

'I wish I was.' I sighed. 'Five hours I had to wait, just for some doctor barely out of short trousers to give me a disparaging look and yank it out with a pair of long tweezers. As I explained how it had happened I could see in his face that he was just dying to say, "Leave clubbing to the kids, Grandpa." Elaine was mortified.'

'Last winter I found myself in Marks and Spencer's lusting after a pair of the biggest pants you've ever seen,' said Ginny. 'It was weird. I was surrounded by all these girls barely out of their teens holding up G-strings and thongs so small you needed a microscope to see them properly and there I was lusting longingly after a pair of neckies.'

'Neckies?'

'Pants so big they cover your navel.' She grabbed Gershwin's arm in mock shame. 'My underwear drawer is no longer a personal armoury in the war of seduction. It is now a haven of peace, tranquillity and warmth. I love my big pants. I used to have an underwear drawer so sexy I got palpitations just opening it. Now I have the underwear drawer of a granny. Practical, practical, practical. Come on, Gershwin, tell us something that'll prove you're just as crap as us.'

Gershwin looked at us both nervously. 'You'll never believe me if I tell you.'

'Try us,' said Ginny.

'I've taken up gardening.'

Ginny and I burst out laughing.

'In case it has escaped your attention, Gershwin,' I began,

'you haven't got a garden to do any gardening in. You live in a second floor flat.'

'Shows what you know,' he replied, with mock petulance. 'There's more to me than meets the eye, you know. I've got an allotment.'

'Never!' exclaimed Ginny.

'I kid you not,' said Gershwin. 'I've had it for about a year and a half now.'

'You, Gershwin Palmer, have an allotment?' I said incredulously. 'You can't have an allotment. You're Gershwin.'

'Still waters run deep,' replied Gershwin sagely.

'How come you never mentioned it until now?'

'Because I knew how you'd react. Which is to say exactly like this. It's great down there, really peaceful. I've got a shed for all my tools and I've even got a scarecrow – I made it with Charlotte. I go down there as often as I can. Granted, it's full of old codgers smoking Woodbines, but they're all right, y'know. They're a good laugh and they give me tips about where to get the right fertiliser and stuff.'

thirty-three

At around five o'clock it began to rain and we made our way back to the car. It was at this point that we realised that we were well over the limit and so, being the resourceful people that we are, we locked up Gershwin's car and called for a taxi.

Back in King's Heath, we dropped Ginny off first. She kissed Gershwin's cheek, then she kissed me and got out of the car.

'Take it easy,' I said, and gave her a little wave.

'Take it easy yourself,' she replied, and walked away.

That was it.

No promises to meet up in the future.

No promises to call soon.

Not even a promise to keep in touch.

All the way back to King's Heath I'd been wondering how we were going to part, and now that I knew, I was pleased, in an odd sort of way. This way we'd had a fantastic time that had just appeared out of nowhere. This way, with no false promises or clumsy lies, the last twenty-four hours had been one of those chance happenings that life throws your way once in a while to remind you how good things can be. As the taxi-driver pulled away from Ginny's house and headed along the Alcester Road, Gershwin turned to me and asked the question I knew he'd been dying to ask all day: 'So, do you still fancy her, then, after all this time?'

Did I fancy her? I didn't know. But for Gershwin's benefit I smiled, gave him a knowing nod and said, 'Maybe.'

thirty-four

To: mattb@c-tec.national.com
From: crazedelaine@hotpr.com
Subject: re: Sorry

Dear Matt

I'm sorry you're sorry. I shouldn't have sent that last e-mail about your last e-mail (????). You know sometimes it's all okay and then sometimes it's not. But I don't want you to be sorry. Okay? I've decided that I need to start going out more. Sara and I are going to some bars after work and are planning a real killer girl's night out and then to top it off we're going dancing! Listen to me, I sound like 'Desperately Seeking Susan' era Madonna!

love Elaine xxx

Month Two

Date: Feb 1st
Days left until thirtieth birthday: 59
State of mind: Positive(ish)

thirty-five

To: crazedelaine@hotpr.com
From: mattb@c-tec.national.com
Subject: Gershwin's birthday

Dear Elaine

Just had the maddest twenty-four hours with Gershwin. We bumped
into Ginny, an old schoolfriend of ours (who we haven't seen in six years).
To cut a long story short Gershwin and I ended up going to Ginny's for an
'all back to mine' and then next day Gershwin and Ginny bunked off work
and we ended up hanging out all day.
Hope you're well,

love

Matt xxx

To: mattb@c-tec.national.com
From: crazedelaine@hotpr.com
Subject: ?????

Dear Matt

Looks like we've both been out on the town. Sara and I went to a
bar uptown and had a great time. Sara's kind of semi moved into the

apartment. The Sofa from Hell is all hers. She's been having major hassles with Johnny lately so I said she could crash here.

love

Elaine

PS I'm glad you're having a good time with your friends in England.

PPS Wish Gershwin a belated happy birthday for me when you see him next.

PPPS '. . . an old schoolfriend of *ours* . . . who *we* haven't seen in six years . . .' Oh, please!!!!! Old high-school girlfriend alert! (Or the UK equivalent.) You are soooooooooo transparent it's quite adorable.

To: **crazedelaine@hotpr.com**
From: **mattb@c-tec.national.com**
Subject: **Old girlfriend paranoia**

Dear Ms Psychic Hot-line
    For your information, Ginny isn't an ex-girlfriend . . . not a proper one anyway. She was more of a friend that's a girl than anything. She has a boyfriend who she's very happy with. Okay?

love

Matt

To: **mattb@c-tec.national.com**
From: **crazedelaine@hotpr.com**
Subject: **Sarcasm**

Dear Matt
    I love it when you get all defensive. What was it like seeing her after all this time? I only ask because when I saw one of my old high-school boyfriends, Vance Erdmann, a while back, I was well and truly disgusted

with myself! He had the worst mullet haircut I've ever seen. He looked like he should've been a WWF wrestler called 'The Disaster Zone.' I guess Ginny wasn't that bad if you and Gershwin hung out with her *all* night. Only kidding.

love Elaine

To: crazedelaine@hotpr.com
From: mattb@c-tec.national.com
Subject: Friends

Dear E

It was good to see Ginny after all this time. But all that romance stuff felt like a million years ago. Put it this way, when the thing I had with Ginny was at its height you were fifteen – probably still 'making out' with Vance whatshisname (who on earth would call their child Vance?!!!!). It's all history. But it's history that makes us who we are . . . which brings me to an idea I've had . . . Seeing Ginny reminded me of the old days when I lived here. Remember I told you there used to be a whole group of us? Well, since I've got time on my hands and nothing better to do with it I think I might look up my old friends Katrina, Bev, Elliot and Pete. I have no idea where they are or what they're up to but I think it would be a laugh to maybe speak to them on the phone or even see them. What do you think? Is this more thirty-people wonky behaviour?

love

Matt xxx

thirty-six

'Oi, mate!' someone yelled. 'Over here! Over here!'

'Man on!' screamed another, at the top of his voice. 'Man *on*!'

'On my head!' shouted another, as if his life depended on it. 'On my head!'

Despite the urgency in their voices, all I could think of in reaction to the verbal hounding of me was:

1) Why on earth did I let Gershwin persuade me to play five-a-side football at half past nine on a Sunday morning?

2) How long until half-time?

3) Oh, no, I think I'm going to vomit.

Gershwin, Tom (of Davina and Tom), Joel (of Christina and Joel), Dom (of Dom and Polly) and I were, apparently, the King's Heath Harriers. They'd been playing together as a team now for two years and were dedicated, if not particularly talented. Usually Neil (of Neil and Sarah) played as well, but he'd been called to the hospital at short notice and had had to cancel, which was why Gershwin had called me at a quarter to eight that morning. I really didn't want to play because the last time I'd tried to exercise – just before August, when Elaine managed to wangle a couple of free weekend passes to a new health club – it had taken me over a week and a half just to stop aching when I breathed in. Gershwin said that if they didn't have enough for a team they'd have to forfeit the match and would effectively lose their shot at winning the league that season. He'd said all of this with such unswerving conviction, as if it really was a matter of life and death, that I'd agreed to do it. How the equivalent of a kick-around in the park had become so serious I wasn't sure. But I soon found out.

The other team, the imaginatively titled Stirchley Wanderers, looked exactly the same as us – a thirty-people team built up of husbands, boyfriends, young fathers and middle managers all throwing themselves recklessly around a sports gym like the last ten years hadn't happened. Actually, Joel (who, it turned out, was only twenty-eight) was quite fit and zippy with the ball. Tom and Gershwin were hard working, if not exactly on tip-top form health and performance wise.

Dom and I, however, were our team's weak point, but even Dom wasn't half as bad as I was. After ten minutes of racing backwards and forwards I thought I was about to pass out through lack of oxygen and throw up from moving around too much. The rest of the team were used to the pace, because although they, too, looked as if they were about an inch and a half away from a coronary, they still managed to play a determined game of football. In the end we lost 2–1 (the Stirchley Wanderers, I suspect, were slightly younger than us) but we did put up a brave fight. And none braver than I, because when the whistle went for full-time, while the others were shaking hands and patting the backs of the Stirchley Wanderers, I was collapsed on the floor in a heap, sweating out of places that I hadn't realised had sweat glands.

I thought I was going to die.

I really did.

Later, in the bar at the gym, as we all sat around drinking manly pints of orange juice, because it was too early for a beer, everyone congratulated me on my performance. And they weren't being sarcastic. In the car, driving back to King's Heath, Gershwin and I talked of nothing but football. We dissected the game, talked strategy and even suggested that it might be a good idea to have mid-week training sessions. It was all talk, of course, but comforting all the same.

'Do you fancy coming to ours for Sunday dinner?' asked Gershwin.

'What are you having?' I asked.

'Normally it would be something exotic like toast so that we could spend the rest of the day on the sofa but Zoë's mum and dad are coming down from Doncaster so we're having the works – chicken, veg, roast spuds, the lot. As I don't much get on with them your company would be appreciated. Are you in?'

'I'd love to, mate, but I promised to make an appearance at the Beckford family dinner table today.'

'They won't mind you missing one Sunday dinner surely? You live there.'

'Yeah, they will,' I replied. 'My mum's got a good memory for these things. Since your birthday and the-staying-out-all-night-without-telling-them episode I've had to walk on eggshells – especially with my mum. Skipping a Sunday dinner would set me back several trips to the supermarket.'

'Fair enough.' He sighed. 'It was a good night, though.'

'Your birthday?'

'Yeah. And the next day up that hill. When I went into work the day after that I had to keep faking a bit of a cough as though I was struggling with pneumonia but had dragged my sorry arse into work because I'm such a martyr. I was brilliant. Utterly convincing. My boss even asked if I was sure I didn't want to go home.'

'Did you?'

'Nah,' said Gershwin despondently. 'The work was piled up high enough as it was without me making things worse.' He stopped as we pulled up outside my parents' house. 'Have you thought any more about Ginny?'

'A bit, I suppose,' I admitted casually. 'I know you'd like to think I was going to get all obsessed with her . . .'

Gershwin laughed. 'So you're not?'

'Far from it, mate. She and Ian seem right loved-up. I doubt very much that she'd want to give it all up for me.' I paused, thinking. 'Still, it was nice to know that we could be friends now that the curse is finally broken.'

'Zoë seemed to think that there was definite electricity between the two of you. I couldn't see it myself but she tends to be quite good on such things.'

I tried not to look pleased but I probably failed. 'Nah,' I said casually. 'It wasn't electricity, it was nostalgia. The two are easy to confuse.'

'If you say so,' said Gershwin, still smirking.

'I've been thinking, though . . .' I continued, '. . . about us, you know, you, me and Ginny. I think my brain's gearing up for my birthday. I get the feeling that I'm going to be one of the where-am-I-going-how-did-I-get-here? turning-thirty types. It's a bit crap that, especially as I was hoping to do the whole thing gracefully. Instead it looks as though I'm going to abandon all dignity and go kicking and screaming all the way. I'm rambling. And I'm pretty sure I'm not making any sense, but seeing you and Ginny – people I've known for years – has kind of helped me put things into some kind of context.'

'I know what you're saying,' said Gershwin. 'It's been good having you back, here, even if you're only back for a bit. It's easy to forget how good the old times were. It's nice to revel in the past every now and again.'

'Exactly,' I said, reaching my point. 'That's why I'm thinking about getting in touch with the others – Katrina, Elliot, Bev and Pete. It's just an idea I had. I'd like to see them all just once, you know, to see if they're still the same people. I've got time on my hands until I move to Sydney and I haven't really got anything better to do. What do you think?'

'I don't know about that,' said Gershwin. 'I mean, you've been lucky with Ginny and me because, well, we're quality stock,' he said. 'Not that the rest of them aren't, but you know what I mean. People change. People can disappoint you. It's easy to do. Take this, for example. Last summer Zoë and I went to the wedding of one of her friends from university. Zoë's old best friend, Michelle, was there too. They'd been really close at university but had lost touch after graduating – you know how it is, it happens on both sides. When Zoë knew her, this girl was a bit of a flaky hippie chick type, but in the three years since they'd met she'd changed into this horrible bitch-monster with a French boyfriend, a flash car and a bad attitude. She blanked Zoë. Didn't even look at her. We got our revenge, though,' he said, smiling slyly. 'She was staying at the hotel where the wedding reception was held, so we found out her room number, pretended it was our room and asked for an alarm call at five-minute intervals from five o'clock onwards because we were such heavy sleepers.'

'The moral being that the things you might've had in common back then might not be enough any more?'

'Exactly,' said Gershwin. 'It's sad, but true. I'm not saying don't do it because I could be wrong. All I'm saying is, don't be surprised.'

'Well,' I said, after a few moments, 'it's just a theory, surely. And, like all theories, the only way to find out for sure is to go and see for yourself.'

thirty-seven

To: mattb@c-tec.national.com
From: crazedelaine@hotpr.com
Subject: re: Walking down Memory Lane

Dear Matt

   Take my advice: do not do this. All that'll happen is that you'll spoil what few great memories you have of these people. You've been lucky with Ginny and Gershwin, but I'd hate to think how you'd react if the people you get in touch with all had changed into the world's biggest assholes. Remember that weekend when I met up with a bunch of girlfriends from my old high school in Brooklyn? How much of a nightmare was that? I hated every single one of them! My old best friend Lucy Buchanan had smoked so much dope in college I couldn't even get her to construct a meaningful sentence; Sheena Deaver couldn't see what was wrong with dating a semi-Nazi old enough to be her father; Stephanie Dolfini couldn't talk about anything apart from her hugely rich paediatrician fiancé; and even poor Yona 'Top of the Class' Hughes was never the same after she had to drop out of Stamford because she'd burned herself out in high school (although that wasn't her fault). My advice – stay clear. The thing about rummaging about in the past is that you never know what you might find.

love

Elaine xxx

PS But at the end of the day you've got to do what you've got to do!

thirty-eight

Bev Turner

(Then, the girl most likely to say: 'I'm not a Goth, I just like dark clothing.' Now: Mrs Bev McCarthy, Senior French Tutor, North Yorkshire Adult Education Language Department, Sheffield.)

Back when I was a teenager every school had its Bev Turner: the girl who, on reaching her fifteenth birthday, dyed her hair black, stopped going out in the sun and started wearing dodgy Goth makeup. Call her a Goth and she'd get really annoyed and swear blind that she wasn't. Point out that she looked like Ally Sheedy in *The Breakfast Club* and she'd probably tell you to get stuffed but would be secretly pleased. But then ask her why, if she wasn't a Goth, she insisted on looking like a Goth, listening to woefully crap Goth music and never going out in the sun, and she'd probably threaten violence. On top of the Goth/not Goth thing, my Bev Turner had the added dysfunction of having parents that seemed to be permanently in the middle of a long divorce.

I loved Bev. I really did. I found her fascinating. Just thinking about her in those days made me laugh because, for as long as I knew her, she was the patron saint of gloom, doom and bad news. She always wore a sardonic smile, listened to the most depressing music on earth and had a thing for celebrities who had died young. Sylvia Plath, of course, was her favourite, followed by James Dean, and Ian Curtis of Joy Division. That sort of teen brooding was incredibly attractive and I always suspected that quite a number of boys at school secretly fancied her because she was such an unknown and unknowable quantity. No one ever went as far as asking her out because she was too scary for any teenage boy – or grown man, for that matter – but the idea was there. And despite her fondness for suicidal celebrities, depression and black clothing, Bev had a wicked sense of humour and never failed to make me laugh.

In the sixth form Bev and I got into the habit of spending our free periods in King's Heath park. I'd eat my sandwiches and she'd chain-smoke until the nicotine rush made her queasy. Then we'd sit and pontificate about life in a way that makes me shudder with embarrassment just thinking about it. When everyone went off to university Bev didn't bother taking up her place at an all-women Oxford college to study Spanish and French but instead took a year out to travel around India. When she came home after five months it was to earn enough money to travel again, this time to Australia. After that she went to the Far East, spent some time in Japan then returned to India. By the time Gershwin got married, which was the last time any of us saw her, her trips back to England were infrequent.

Late on Sunday afternoon, having spent some time letting my mother's sprout-free Sunday dinner digest, I decided to make Bev the first of my old friends with whom I'd get in touch. Finding her current number was easy enough because I had her gran's phone number in Chelmsley Wood. Bev used to stay with her whenever even she felt she was getting too weird and in need of grandparental guidance. Although the old lady was hard of hearing, after a protracted, confused conversation she furnished me with an English phone number for Bev. I thanked her, said goodbye, and hung up. Then I picked up the phone again and dialled.

'Hello?'

It was a woman's voice.

'Hi? I'm looking for a Bev Turner?'

'Yes?'

'Are you her?'

'I might be. Who's this?'

Suddenly I wasn't sure it was her.

'It's Matt Beckford, an old schoolfriend of hers—'

'Matt!' she exclaimed. 'Matt Beckford! It's me, Bev. I didn't have the faintest clue who it was. I thought for a minute you were some sort of dodgy debt collector trying to get me for some misdemeanour of my youth.'

'Got a lot of debts, have we?'

'The odd unpaid credit card,' said Bev. 'Or two. It's all debt left over from my globe-trotting days. Anyway, I think they've all blacklisted me now.' She laughed. 'But that's okay, I just use Jimmy's.'

'And Jimmy is?'

'My bloke – or, more accurately, my husband, as of three months ago.'

'Congrats.'

'Never mind congrats, fella. What on earth made you decide to call me at three thirty on a Sunday afternoon after . . .' she worked it out '. . . nearly six years of no see or hear – not that I'm not pleasantly surprised, of course.'

'Well, to cut a long story shortish, I've been living in New York and I've just been transferred to Sydney and I'm here at home in Brum for a while – and, well, I was out for Gershwin's birthday—'

'You still see Gershwin? How is he?'

'He's fine. Zoë and he have a little girl now, Charlotte. She's four, I think . . . Anyway, we were out for a drink – in the Kings Arms, as it happens – celebrating the young man's thirtieth when we bumped into Ginny and, well, we all got talking and, well, I just wanted to see how everyone is. That's all. I just wanted to see if you're . . . okay.'

'Yeah, I'm okay,' said Bev, thoughtfully. 'Better than okay, in fact, and all the better for hearing from you.'

Over the next twenty minutes or so Bev filled me in with what she'd been up to since I'd last seen her. At the age of twenty-five she had decided after six years' travelling that it might be advisable to get a career on the go. She had worked as everything from a bee-keeper in Australia to the nanny of the child of the Malaysian answer to Cher. She returned to England and settled in Sheffield, where after several training courses she began teaching at an adult-education college and met her husband Jimmy, also a teacher. They fell in love, got married and bought a two-bedroomed cottage in a small village on the outskirts of Sheffield and were now reasonably happy after some bad news at the early part of the previous year. Bev had been to hospital for tests relating to stomach pains she'd been having. The doctors had sorted out the problem but in the process discovered it would be unlikely that she would ever have children. She told me all of this quite matter-of-factly, I suppose because she'd known so long that it had ceased to upset her. I just took it as yet further evidence of how strange life becomes the older we got.

'You should come up and stay with us before you go to Australia,' said Bev, as we wound up the call. 'I'm not just saying that. I really mean it.'

'Thanks,' I said, and then we swapped addresses and promised to keep in touch.

thirty-nine

Katrina Smith
(Then: the girl most likely to end up working for a glossy women's magazine. Now: lifestyle editor of the Staffordshire Evening Herald.*)*

At school Katrina was the sort of girl who was never without a boyfriend. At various points early on in her dating career she had been involved with me (a week and a half when we were fifteen), Gershwin (two and a bit months when we were fourteen), Pete (one Thunderbird-fuelled night of snogging at Katie Lloyd's sixteenth birthday party), and Elliot (a month and a half just before our mock exams). She was pretty in an attention-grabbing sort of way but insecure – hence her addiction to relationships.

Interestingly I remember once discussing with the boys how curious it was that, in all the time we'd known her, Katrina had never been dumped by a bloke. At first we thought it was because she was lucky but as Elliot (whom she'd dumped to go out with Adam Warner) pointed out – rather astutely, I thought, for a sixteen-year-old boy – the real reason she never got dumped was that she always made the careful precaution of only ever going out with boys who were that tiny bit less attractive than any male should have been in her natural field of vision. As soon as he'd said it we knew it made sense. Katrina's tactics were perfect. If she only chose men who were grateful to have such a fantastic-looking girlfriend, they'd never take her for granted and would always worship her like a princess. This isn't to say that Katrina was a scheming bitch, she wasn't – she was smart, funny and a good friend. It was only when you were her boyfriend that the claws came out.

On the Tuesday following my chat with Bev, I decided that Katrina would be the next of my old friends I'd try to get hold of. Although she was kind of an ex-girlfriend she had actually been more Ginny's friend than mine, so it wasn't any wonder that we'd lost contact. The last time I'd spoken to her was a year after Gershwin's wedding, when a few of us had met up for Elliot's house-warming and to celebrate him getting a new job. Then she'd told me she was temporarily shacked up with her latest boyfriend, Greg, in East London, while she looked for a flat of her own. I rooted around in my bedroom and managed to find an old address book with Greg's number in it. Three phone calls later I traced Katrina via her East London ex-boyfriend, to another ex-boyfriend in Leeds, to a more recent ex-boyfriend in Stoke, who explained that she'd moved out a while ago but was still living in the area and gave me her number.

'Hello?'

'Er, hi . . . Can I speak to Katrina Smith?'

There was a long pause. 'Who's this?'

'I can't tell you that,' I said, teasing her. 'That would take all the fun out of guessing.'

'Is it Dave?'

'No.'

'Paul?'

'Wrong again.'

She paused. 'It's not Greg, is it?'

'Not even warm,' I replied. 'Okay, I'll give you a clue. I once had the misfortune to see your mother naked—'

'Matt Beckford!' she shrieked.

I knew that story would jog her memory. We were eighteen and it was three o'clock in the morning. I'd lost my house keys and was too scared to wake up my folks by ringing the front-door bell. Katrina said I could crash on her mum and dad's sofa but didn't bother informing her parents. First thing next morning I got up to go to the loo and was met by Katrina's mum *sans* clothing on her journey to the bathroom for her morning shower. I screamed. She screamed. It was hideously embarrassing for all concerned.

'I can't believe it!' Katrina shrieked again. 'I thought you were one of my old ex-boyfriends for a second.'

'Ex-boyfriend? Which one?'

'Any of them. You were lucky. I was only indulging your guessing games long enough to find my attack alarm in my handbag so I could blast it down the phone!'

Though my call covered the ins and outs of both our lives, it was Katrina's ins and outs that were by far the more interesting of the two. She told me she was working on the *Staffordshire Evening Herald* and I asked her what the lifestyle editor's job entailed. She said, 'Cheesy fashion, cheesy restaurants, cheesy diet advice and anything else the mighty cheeses of the puff PR industry can churn out. Everything the modern woman doesn't need to know.'

'I take it you don't like it?' I asked.

'Hate it. Absolutely hate it,' she said, laughing. 'By the time I was thirty I was supposed to be working for *Vogue*. Not just working for them either, I was supposed to be the editor.'

'Is it too late, then?' I asked, displaying my ignorance of the world of fashion magazines.

'Only by about ten years,' said Katrina. 'You know, my big mistake was going to university. I should've been one of those fantastically talented teenage journalists – a *wunderkind*. At nineteen I could've had my big break and by now it would be "Hello, Ms Katrina Vogue."' She paused, briefly, before continuing what was clearly one of her favourite rants. 'I've got this theory that university impedes your development. I didn't learn anything at Leeds that would've prepared me for the role I was destined for as editor of *Vogue*. That's three years wasted. Three years! If I hadn't spent all that time fannying around in lecture halls I'd be twenty-seven now instead of thirty! Maybe then there'd still be a chance.'

'Does that mean I'd be twenty-six?'

'You're not thirty yet?'

'March the thirty-first. You can send me a card.'

'Never mind the card, Matt. Worry about the days you've got left in your twenties and savour them because, believe me, it's all downhill from here.' She sighed heavily. 'Bet you didn't expect me to be this mad, did you?'

'Not really,' I replied, 'but it's comforting not to be the only one.'

The conversation after that became slightly more sedate. I told her about the world of software design, my life in New York and splitting up with Elaine, and in return I got all her details. When I'd spoken to her at Gershwin's wedding she'd been doing bits of freelance work for magazines, had actually written a few pieces for *Cosmopolitan* and *The Face*, but with a huge rent bill to pay and the sheer cost of living in London, she had applied for a junior reporter's job on the *South Staffordshire Chronicle*. It was only meant to be a temporary measure – six months tops – just to get her out of debt, but a year later she was still there and couldn't face the thought of going back to London to start all over again. So she stayed where she was and eventually was head-hunted by the *Staffordshire Evening Herald*, for half decent but far from fabulous money.

On the love front she was a little more coy. Reading between the lines, it appeared that she had finally allowed herself to fall in love with someone as attractive, if not more so, as herself. He was called Stephen and she hadn't fallen in love so much as crashed uncontrollably. Everything had been fine for the eighteen months they were together until one day he had told her that he wasn't ready to have a serious relationship. I was just about to make some sympathetic noises when she added, 'This is probably the best thing that's ever happened to me.' She finished off by telling me that she'd been single for a year and that, career prospects apart, it had been the best year of her life. I was so surprised by that that I just said, 'Cool.' Then I gave her my mum and dad's telephone number and said I'd see her soon.

forty

Pete Sweeney
(Then, the boy most likely to fill up all available brain space with Star Wars *trivia. Now, proprietor of Comic Dreams and Movie Memorabilia, Manchester.)*

Of all of the friends I was getting in touch with, Pete was the one I wanted to see most. He had always been one of the most laid-back people you could imagine meeting. My favourite Pete story, perhaps the one that best sums him up, happened when we were sixteen, and at the top of the King's Heath Comprehensive food chain. Throughout our entire school careers we'd been waiting for the day when it would snow and we'd have our chance to be kings of the playground is the Great Snowball Fight. (It was an old school tradition: on the first day it snowed the older boys – it was always the boys – took it upon themselves to terrorise the lower school with snowballs.) When it snowed, the responsibility of terrorising sent us wild and, I'm afraid, we became totally power-crazed. Led by Pete, we sent wave after wave of raiding parties to the lower-school playground. It was fantastic: hundreds of kids ran screaming for cover, and we buried anyone we caught under a foot of snow. It was then that the event occurred after which that day became known as White Wednesday. Furious that hordes of lower-school kids were running for cover across the hallowed patch of grass outside the staffroom window, our headmaster, Mr Charles, came outside to reprimand the entire playground. Just as he was coming to the end of his big speech about how the upper school should be setting a better example, Pete threw a Terminator – a hand-crafted pure ice snowball he'd been sculpting for over twenty minutes – which smacked Mr Charles right on the back of his head. It was a classic moment, the Kennedy assassination set in snow. The playground population, some six hundred kids, inhaled sharply with shock. Mr Charles went purple with rage and threatened to put everyone in detention unless the culprit came forward.

Everyone expected Pete to take his punishment like a man, but he hid like the rest of us – an action which I truly admired. A true coward would have caved in to peer-group pressure but Pete didn't, although he knew that the punishment meted out by the teachers would be nothing compared to those from his fellow students. I remember asking him after school, as we were being chased by a mob seeking vengeance for their lost leisure time, why he'd thrown the snowball at Mr Charles in the first place. Echoing the words of Sir Edmund Hillary after he had climbed Everest, Pete replied simply, 'Because he was there.'

I got hold of Pete via his sister. Although he was slightly dumbfounded to hear from me after all this time we spoke on the phone for ages. The rumours about him getting married were true and he had a little boy, Joe, who was now three. What I didn't know was that he and his wife Amy had split up after eighteen months and divorced two years later. On a lighter note, Pete had however managed to fulfil at least one of his ambitions. As a kid he'd been obsessed with comics and sci-fi films and now, at the age of thirty, he was the proud owner of his own shop: Comic Dreams and Movie Memorabilia, in Chorlton, Manchester and he insisted that I came up and visited him.

'Beckford!' yelled Pete, when I entered the shop.

'Sweeney!' I yelled back, in typically blokey fashion, and headed straight for him at the cash desk.

'You fat old loser!' he said, coming out from behind the till to meet me. We shook hands enthusiastically.

'You . . .' I looked him up and down, trying to find a suitable insult, but I couldn't find one. He had lost even more of his hair than Gershwin had – but even I considered that a joke too far. Otherwise he looked in good shape. In the end I had to resort to, 'You sixties reject!' At the age of fifteen Pete had decided that he was going to become a Mod, and here we were, fifteen years later, and he still dressed in exactly the same style: Levi's denim jacket, black polo neck, beige Levi's white tab cords and, of course, his beloved desert boots.

'You must be on to your hundredth pair of those,' I said, pointing at his footwear.

'More like two hundredth.' He grinned widely. 'Journey up all right?' he asked, returning to the till to serve a customer.

'Uneventful, really,' I replied. 'Never mind all that, though, how are you?'

'All right,' he said. 'Could be worse. Still, the store looks great.'

I looked around it for the first time. I was surrounded by multiple rows of science fiction and fantasy magazines, comics, books, posters, videos and action figures.

'This is all yours?'

He nodded enthusiastically. 'I'll show you the new *Star Wars* stuff, man. I nearly cried when it came in last week.'

He noticed a few more customers lingering at the desk. 'Hang on a sec.' He peered over one of the racks of comics and a young guy with a goatee beard and a baseball cap suddenly appeared from the other side. 'Billy,' said Pete, 'this is my mate, Matt Beckford.' Billy nodded sullenly. 'Matt and I have known each other for . . .' He added it up '. . . seventeen years. Precisely the same amount of time you've been alive. We're off up to the flat for a fag and a coffee. Mind the shop and don't be cheeky.'

Billy shuffled behind the till. I followed Pete through a door that had a piece of A4 paper stuck to it with the words 'Keep out – that means YOU!' scrawled on it in marker pen, and up some stairs to his flat.

'Welcome to my abode,' he said.

When Pete said that he was divorced and lived in a flat over his own shop I must admit I'd imagined the worst but what I saw in front of me was bloke heaven. There might not have been the eighties-style black leather and chrome everywhere the way I'd always imagined the perfect bachelor pad to contain, but there was some highly collectable sixties furniture, a state-of-the-art widescreen TV and a hi-fi separates system with speakers the size of small children. Aside from those items, the flat was largely filled with stuff from the shop – film and comic posters, a host of action figures (everything from *Star Wars* to James Bond), and his record, CD and video collection, which spanned two walls making the living room look more like a library.

'So,' I said, as Pete brought in some coffee, 'you've got a lot of videos.'

'It's nice to have them out,' said Pete, looking over at his collection contentedly. 'The whole lot was in the loft when Amy and I were together.' He gestured to a huge sofa by the window. 'Have a seat, mate.'

'Yeah, in a second. I just want to check out your videos. I don't think I've ever seen half of these.'

This was the greatest compliment I could have paid him, or for that matter any of my male friends: sometimes recognition by our peers of a seemingly pointless achievement is all we have to live for. I scanned the titles, which read like an A–Z of the last fifty years of TV sci-fi history. He had entire series of *The Prisoner, Star Trek, Babylon Five, Star Trek – The Next Generation* and *Blake's Seven*, but outnumbering them all was his *Dr Who* collection. 'I've got every single episode ever,' he said, as I lingered by an episode entitled 'Dr Who and the Cybermen'. 'Took me a long time but it was worth it.'

'Every single episode?'

'Well . . . nearly. There's a couple missing – but the BBC in their wisdom wiped the tapes. I couldn't stand having gaps, though, so I made boxes for them.'

'You made boxes for videotapes of programmes that don't exist?'

He looked down sheepishly. 'Don't ask me why. It made me feel better.'

When I left Pete's six hours and several bottles of Budweiser later, I felt good about life, and a whole lot better about turning thirty. Katrina, Bev and Pete might have had their ups and downs but they were okay. Granted, life had been a little rough on Pete, with his divorce, but he seemed happy enough now. With Ginny and Gershwin we were all okay. I don't know why but I convinced myself that if my oldest friends were okay I'd be okay too – I could handle whatever life threw at me. At least, that's what I thought then. What I didn't know, as I made my way back from Manchester to Birmingham on the train, was that our friend Elliot had died.

forty-one

To: crazedelaine@hotpr.com
From: mattb@c-tec.national.com
Subject: ?

Dear Elaine

It's two o'clock in the morning here in Birmingham and I can't sleep. I've just had the weirdest few hours of my entire life. Over this last couple of days I've been doing the catching up with old friends I told you about. I've spoken to Katrina and Bev on the phone and today (well, yesterday now, I suppose), I went to see my old mate Pete up in Manchester. I came home thinking that everything was okay, that my life was sorted.

Anyway, there I am, a little bit drunk, a little bit cheery, when my mum tells me she's got some bad news for me. I can't remember exactly what her words were but the long and short of it was that my friend Elliot was dead . . . or, to be more accurate, had died two years ago. You see, I'd called Elliot's parents' house yesterday morning and left a message on their machine, explaining who I was, and asking them if they'd give me a ring with his number. While I'd been up in Manchester Elliot's mum had returned my call and told my mum the news.

Apparently Elliot had been driving from Leeds to a club in Liverpool two years ago last December when the car he and his girlfriend were in collided head on with a lorry. Elliot's girlfriend had been killed instantly but Elliot didn't die until a week later. They were both twenty-seven. Only close friends and family had been

162

invited to the funeral and, given that none of us had actually seen or spoken to Elliot in a long while, that hadn't included us. I feel weird. I don't know what it is I should be feeling but whatever it is it's not there.

Matt xxx

forty-two

After I e-mailed Elaine, I attempted to go to sleep. But I couldn't drop off. Instead, lying on my bed, looking at the ceiling, I tried to recall the exact point at which we'd all stopped being friends but I couldn't do it because it had never been that clear-cut. After a few moments I tried to recall the point at which we'd all stopped putting the required effort into our various friendships and that was a lot easier. It was the moment we had all moved away from each other. That was the real test of friendship – geography. This made me feel both sad and guilty. The times I'd shared with them all were supposed to have been some of the best of my life and it seemed like a really poor show that we'd given up some of the best friendships we would ever have just because we no longer lived in the same city. Maybe I was wrong. Maybe we'd just outgrown each other. That was pretty much the last thing I can remember thinking that night, apart from, of course, the hours and hours of musings about my own mortality. My thoughts were centred on the three big questions of life: 'Where am I going?', 'What am I doing?' and 'What's it all about, Alfie?' They were hardly original to say the least, and as such, they're probably best left in my head. I did however manage some sleep eventually but woke up at about six thirty to hear the phone ringing. I slipped out of bed, went downstairs and answered it.

'Hello?'

'Matt, it's me.'

It was Elaine.

'Who is it?' whispered my mum, from the top of the stairs. She was in her dressing-gown and had her rollers in.

'It's okay,' I replied. 'It's for me.' I didn't want to tell her it was Elaine. I didn't want to get her hopes up. 'I'll try and keep the noise down, okay?' She disappeared, leaving me alone.

'Hey,' I said softly, into the phone, 'how are you? It must be – what? – one thirty a.m. with you. What are you doing?'

'I was working late at the office when I got your e-mail about your friend Elliot. I wanted to call you straight away but I figured your folks would be in bed and I didn't want to wake them. I remembered they were early risers from the time they came over to stay with us so I came home and waited up so I could speak to you. Anyway, how are you? How are you coping?'

'I'm fine,' I said. 'It feels a little weird but I'm fine.'

'You don't sound fine at all, Matt.'

'Thanks.'

'You know what I mean. Did you sleep okay?'

'No, not really.' I thought for a moment. 'I'm going to say something, but I'm only going to say it to you because I know you'll get it. But the really shocking thing about this is how not shocked I am by the news. Elliot was a good friend. Okay, I hadn't seen him for a long while but surely I should feel something . . . something more.'

'Not necessarily,' said Elaine. 'For you to really feel a loss you need to have a great big hole ripped in your life. A hole so big that no matter what you throw into it, no matter how much you try and fill it up with other stuff, it'll still be a huge hole.

When you were friends and you all hung out together, and you saw each other every day, that's when he would've left a hole and you would've felt something more. But the reality is that you haven't had that kind of friendship in a long time. Which is okay, it happens all the time. The only bad thing is, when things like this happen, you don't miss the person you've lost because you got over losing them a long time ago. What you miss is the hole they should've left.'

Though part of me wanted to shout 'psychobabble' and 'nonsense', I could see that Elaine had a point; the reason why I couldn't feel the loss of my friend was because I had already lost him and hadn't even noticed.

Elaine and I spoke for nearly an hour. I didn't want to talk about Elliot any more and she knew that, so instead we talked about all the other things in our lives: the apartment and my parents' house; US TV and UK TV; Elaine's spider plants and my parents' gardening habits; her Visa bills and my savings accounts; what it was like living with Sara and what it was like living with my parents; life at work and life not working; and, finally, how much she missed me and how much I missed her.

forty-three

'Is this it?' said Gershwin.

'I think so,' said Ginny.

'Right,' I said. 'So what do we do now?'

It was just after midday on the following Sunday morning and the three of us were standing in the middle of Lodge Hill cemetery on the other side of the city. I'd called Gershwin and Ginny as soon as I could after hearing the news about Elliot, which for Gershwin had been just after I'd spoken to Elaine. Although initially shocked he was stoical about it. He asked the details and didn't say a great deal more. Knowing Gershwin as I did, this didn't mean he didn't care. All it meant was that he didn't know what to say and, rather than say something stupid or clichéd, he preferred to keep quiet. I didn't like the idea of calling Ginny at work so I left it until early evening. Her reaction was similar to Gershwin's, in as much as there were no tears and much silence. I also called Bev, Katrina and Pete, who evinced shock and an uncomfortable silence.

My own feelings however changed from minute to minute but I was now certain that Elaine's 'hole' theory had hit the nail on the head. To compensate, I spent a long time thinking of the Elliot I'd known at school as he was the Elliot I knew best, and the one I wanted to miss most. He'd always been a bit of an entrepreneur even when we were kids. He'd do things like get his dad to buy a load of *Return of the Jedi* stickers from a discount club they belonged to and then bring them into school and sell them at a profit. Once he even got his older brother to buy him copies of soft-porn mags like *Men Only*, *Razzle* and *Escort*, which he cut up and sold page by page to boys in the lower years, which earned him far more than he'd paid for them. One year, just after his twelfth birthday, he brought in his favourite present – a hand-held version of the arcade game, Defender, and hired it out at twenty pence a go. That was Elliot.

I agreed to meet Ginny and Gershwin that evening in the Kings Arms, and we spent the whole night talking about how we felt we should do something for Elliot. Eventually we came up with the idea of paying our respects to him at the cemetery, albeit a little late. We thought that would have made him smile a bit – the three of us being three years late for his funeral.

The next day we clubbed together to buy some flowers – it felt a bit churlish to arrive empty-handed, like visiting someone in hospital without a bottle of Lucozade or some grapes – and at the florist's we'd bickered because none of us could decide which flowers Elliot would have liked. For some reason, I wanted to get him something long, purple and sort of velvety-looking. Gershwin wanted roses and Ginny a bunch of yellow and white flowers that had a funny name. In the end Ginny said she didn't mind what we bought because she didn't think the point of this was to argue about flowers, but Gershwin said we weren't arguing about flowers, we were just trying to make ourselves feel crap. In the end we each bought the flowers we liked and had them all bundled together. Then Ginny drove us to the cemetery in her ancient marine blue Fiat Panda.

No one answered me when I asked, 'What do we do now?' Instead we stood around the grey marble headstone and stared, focusing our attention on it. 'This is so very, very weird,' I whispered, breaking the silence.

'I know,' responded Ginny.

'It's hard to believe this has happened,' said Gershwin.

'Why?' asked Ginny. We both looked at her. 'I mean, it happens all the time, every day. What makes us think we're so special that things like this are never going to touch us?'

'I don't think Gershwin was trying to say that we're special,' I said. 'I just think he was trying to say that, well, you always sort of assume that everything's always going to carry on the same. That nothing ever changes, even though you know it does. It's just human nature, I suppose.' I was losing confidence in my big speech. 'Don't you think that's the way it is, Gershwin?'

Gershwin just shrugged and said, 'Let's go to the pub.'

And that's what we did. We left the flowers by the grave, got back in the car, went to the Kings Arms and held an impromptu wake.

forty-four

'What's my favourite Elliot story?' said Gershwin, in response to Ginny's question. 'Give me a few seconds and I'll come up with one.'

We were sitting in the lounge of the Kings Arms, at the same table we'd occupied on Gershwin's birthday – possibly even in the same seats – and we'd been drinking and talking in a random way about nothing much for a couple of hours until Ginny upped the conversational stakes.

'I've got it,' said Gershwin. 'Once when he and I were walking along King's Heath Street a huge kid from another school bumped into him on purpose. Elliot didn't look at him. Then the kid came from behind and pushed him and said something schoolboyish like, "Do you want to fight?" and Elliot just looked at him and said, "Why?" like he really wanted to know the answer. It was a stroke of brilliance. It totally threw this kid. All he wanted to do was show off to his mates how hard he was and Elliot wanted a discussion with him about his motivation towards violence. He still got a punch in the mouth but that moment when the kid looked all confused because Elliot hadn't reacted how he'd wanted was perfect.'

'Okay,' said Ginny. 'My turn. It's not a story as such, it's my favourite image of him. D'you remember that dark pinstripe second-hand suit he bought from Oxfam and insisted on wearing to my eighteenth?'

'That's right,' said Gershwin. 'He used to wear it with his trainers. He thought he looked really cool. We all thought he looked insane.'

I took my turn. 'I remember a time when Elliot and I were in a chemistry lesson, we must've been thirteen or fourteen, and Philip Jones was being his usual pleasant self going round kicking people's bags around the room and he kicked Elliot's.'

'I remember this one,' said Gershwin.

'So Elliot said, "Right, that's it," and he got a fifty-pence piece, put it on the desk, picked it up with a pair of tongs and heated it up in a Bunsen burner flame until it glowed orange and then he dropped it on the floor next to Philip Jones's bench and pretended that he'd lost some money. Jones, being the idiot that he was, yelled, "I'm having that," pushed Elliot away and picked it up. You could smell the singed skin for days afterwards. He was away from school for a week after that. Mind you, he beat the living daylights out of Elliot when he came back.'

'Elliot and I once got *Gremlins II* out on video,' said Gershwin, 'and we both thought it was the best thing ever. For days afterwards we'd just quote bits to each other in class and crack up in hysterics.'

'D'you remember the time we all stayed in my mum's caravan in Wales for the weekend?' said Ginny. 'The first night there you all went off to the woods in the middle of the night to try to scare yourselves witless. Elliot didn't go because he said it was too cold and I didn't go because I thought Mum would find out that boys were staying in the caravan with us. Elliot and I hadn't really talked very much before that but I remember that after we'd drunk half a bottle each of Thunderbird we warmed to each other. I remember at one point we were talking about what we were going to do with the rest of our lives. I told him I was going to go travelling and end up living in Australia with a Mel Gibson lookalike called Brad. And he told me how he was going to be head of an international company and I said something like, "That's so dull," and he didn't say anything, he just looked really hurt. Then he said that if he didn't get to be head of an international company he'd like to be a wing-walker.'

'A *what*?' I asked.

'One of those people who strap themselves to the wings of biplanes that you see at aeronautical events. He said he saw one once when he was a kid and it looked really good fun. And then I looked at him and he looked at me, and then he just burst out laughing and said that he didn't want to be the head of an international company or a wing-walker. He said, and I quote, "To be truthful, Gin, I'll be happy if I'm still me."'

forty-five

It was just coming up to three o'clock in the afternoon when we decided to leave the comfort of the Kings Arms and venture outside again.

'I'll give you a ring during the week,' said Gershwin to me, as the three of us hovered on the pavement outside the entrance. He turned to Ginny. 'And I'll see you . . . whenever, I suppose.'

Ginny gave an awkward half-smile in response and stretched out her arms to give him a hug. 'Look after yourself,' she said, squeezing him tightly.

'You too,' he said, and kissed her cheek lightly.

With that he gave me a short wave and headed off down Moseley high street, leaving Ginny and me standing, wrapped in our own thoughts, for what felt like ages.

'What are you doing now?' asked Ginny, as it began to rain.

'Nothing. What are you up to? Seeing Ian?'

She looked up at me and stared right into my eyes, her face devoid of expression. 'No. I'm doing nothing too.'

'Fancy doing nothing together?' I asked carefully. Even though our moods were sombre I wanted to make it clear that this wasn't a come-on.

'Yeah,' she replied, nodding as if to acknowledge that this was about friendship, nothing more. She even took my arm, which she wouldn't have done if anything else had been on the agenda. 'Right now, Matt, that sounds like the best idea in the world.'

Doing nothing ended up as doing something because Ginny recalled that she hadn't done a weekly shop for over a month due to pressure of work and that the hour left before Safeway closed would be her only opportunity to get some food in for the next few days. Watching her armed with a trolley reminded me of Elaine. They both had the same inefficient shopping habits, like going up and down the same aisle three times, buying frozen items at the start of the trip instead of at the end and throwing things into the trolley because they liked the sound of them. (In this case Ginny bought a bottle of rose water because she thought it sounded nice and those edible silver balls you put on cakes and biscuits even though she said she didn't bake.)

Inevitably during the forty-two minutes we were there we bumped into two former schoolmates: David Kimble (then, the shortest boy in our year at school; now, no doubt the shortest lorry driver in the country) and Elizabeth Cowan (then, the girl most likely to be travel-sick for the rest of her life; now, a stewardess for Aer Lingus). Both were surprised to see me and Ginny together after all this time and, needless to say, both jumped to the wrong conclusion. Ginny and I made such clumsy attempts to deny it that it seemed as though we were still lying about our entanglement after all these years. Later, laden with shopping-bags, we made our way back to Ginny's, and while she did some preparation for school the following day, I rustled up some pasta for us. After that we cracked open a bottle of wine, sat on her back doorstep and looked out into the garden, drinking and talking. We talked about old times, and then we talked about what we'd wanted to do with our lives back then, and we talked about what we were doing right now. Finally we talked about Elliot's death and how it made us feel. It was an honest, frequently blunt conversation, the kind that could only have occurred between two people like us, old friends, former lovers: we had a long, entwined history that stretched so far into the past it seemed to have had no beginning – it just was. The mood now was less sombre, but more intimate, more reflective – exactly the kind of atmosphere in which anything could happen, but I knew nothing would. This wasn't like the old days. Now every action had a consequence, and we knew it.

I turned to Ginny and smiled. 'This is weird, isn't it?' She half smiled. 'You and me, sitting here in your mum's old house, on the doorstep. How many times have we done this in the past?'

'Who knows,' said Ginny. She set her wine-glass on the ground next to her feet and shifted her gaze towards the end of the garden. 'I miss my mum, you know,' she said, after a few moments of silence.

'Of course,' I said. 'It's only natural.'

'Yeah, I know. It's just that, well, I'm not even sure "miss" is the right word, Matt. Without her I feel like something's missing. That part of me has gone.' She picked up her glass again. 'I try to talk to her sometimes. I know it's only in my head but even that's better than nothing. I imagine us sitting at the kitchen table and me telling her about what's going on in my life – about school, about Ian, about how I feel about the world, and she listens. And just the thought of her listening makes me feel better. It's strange, that, isn't it? How just being listened to can make you feel better. Mum was a really good listener. No matter what I was rambling on about,

175

she'd always make me feel like it was the most important thing in the world. And now she's gone I feel like all the good she worked in my life has gone too.' She sighed. 'Sorry,' she said, turning to me. 'I'm getting a bit depressing, aren't I?'

'No,' I said. 'Far from it. I'm just glad you can talk about it with me, that's all.'

Ginny smiled. 'Of course I can talk about it with you.' She looked at me curiously. 'I can see you want to ask me something. Go ahead.'

I laughed. 'You're right. It's not so much a question as . . . I don't know. It's just that, until this week, no one I've known – at least, been really close to – has died. My grandparents died when I was really young and that's just about it, apart from the odd distant family member. When I saw you in the Kings Arms that night, and you told me your mum had died, I had no idea what you must have been through.'

'I know what you mean. Before Mum became ill I would've had no concept of it either. For my entire life it's just been me and her. I've never met my dad and never wanted to either. So, you know, it was just me and Mum against the world, and that would never end – how could it? To me Mum was indestructible, she'd be around for ever – we'd be with each other for ever. So when she told me she was ill, it was a huge shock. At the age of twenty-eight I found out that Mum wasn't indestructible, after all, that the two of us weren't going to go on for ever . . .' Ginny stopped as her voice broke.

'It's okay,' I said. 'Look, I don't want you to get upset.'

'No,' said Ginny, breathing deeply. 'It's okay, Matt.' She smiled. 'You shouldn't be afraid of people getting upset. It's natural. You can't run away or not do something just because it makes you upset.' She laughed. 'You always used to hate it when I cried on you, didn't you?'

'Just a little bit,' I replied quietly. 'Only because I didn't know what to do to make it stop.'

'That's the thing,' she replied. 'Sometimes you just don't want it to stop. Sometimes all you want in the world is someone to share it with.'

'I don't know what I'd do if either of my parents died,' I said. 'I know I go on about them being annoying, the bane of my life and all that, but if they weren't around I'd miss them for the rest of my life.'

'You should tell them that,' said Ginny. 'It's one of the few good things that came out of this thing with Mum – the fact that I could tell her how much I loved her, and that I knew when the time came that she would know how much she meant to me.'

'I've thought about this, y'know,' I began. 'You might not think so but I have. I've tried to imagine telling my parents that I love them and all that but I dunno . . . I don't think they'd understand. I think it's great that you had that with your mum but my folks haven't got the faintest clue what to do with emotions. Yeah, we love each other and all that, but would we ever say it? I don't know . . . I think that at least for us there's a certain security to be had in the things that aren't said. I mean, if you're that kind of person it's cool, but if you're not then it's . . .'

Ginny smiled. 'I know what you're saying. You can't just magic up that kind of communication out of nowhere and I suppose with it always being just me and Mum we were a lot closer than many mothers and daughters.'

'There are times when I think that I've not had a real conversation with Dad since I was small. At least, at that age I remember wanting to talk, and when he wasn't busy at work or in the garden we *would* talk. But mostly what I remember are the companionable silences, where he'd walk with his usual long strides and I would try desperately to keep up with him. Even though it used to wear me out I could see in his eyes that he was pleased I tried.'

'Your dad loves you, you know,' said Ginny.

I nodded.

'And your mum,' she added.

I nodded again.

'You're trying to work out why I'm telling you all this.' I nodded yet again. 'I'm telling you this for one reason and one reason only: no matter how sure you are of someone's love, it's always nice to hear it.'

We stopped talking for a while, enjoying the confined space of the doorstep together. I wondered for the first time what it would be like to kiss Ginny again. I thought about Elliot and how I still couldn't comprehend quite what his death meant. And, finally, I thought about my mum and dad and tried to imagine life without them. A lot of what Ginny had said to me made sense. There is a great deal of comfort to be taken from imagining that your parents are a permanent fixture in your life who will be there for ever. Maybe, I thought, I should look at the world as it is, rather than how I want it to be. But no matter how hard I tried to imagine it without them, no matter how I tried to guess what it would feel like to have a parent-shaped hole in my life, I couldn't imagine a world without my mum and dad.

It was ten past eight when I eventually announced to Ginny that it was time I went home. I helped her clear away the plates, dishes and the rest of the mess I'd made while cooking then made my way to the hall to collect my jacket. 'Right, then,' I said, opening the front door. 'I'd better be off.'

'Okay,' said Ginny. She stepped forward and kissed my cheek. 'Thanks for today, Matt. It was a weird reason for us to get together again but nice all the same.'

I smiled and stepped outside, then headed down the short path to the front gate. When I reached the gate, though, I stopped, turned round and walked back to Ginny.

'I was hoping you'd do that,' she said.

'Then why didn't you say anything?' I asked.

'Insecurity, fear, a smidgen of self-loathing – the usual suspects. I felt it the last time we said goodbye. I should've said something then, but you know how it is. You just don't want to look stupid, do you? But shall I say it now and save you the trouble?' I laughed. 'Matt, I would love it if, for however long you're back home, you consider our friendship resurrected. Feel free to call me for a drink, a moan or just to hang out.'

'Of course I'd be pleased for us to be friends again.'

'I'm not just saying this, Matt,' said Ginny, a distinct edge of seriousness entering her voice. 'I mean it. Proper mates. And not just you, but Gershwin as well.' She put her arms around me and gave me a hug. 'We all should've known better than to just drift apart.' Her voice was unsteady. 'We should've known better.'

forty-six

To: mattb@c-tec.national.com
From: crazedelaine@hotpr.com
Subject: How are things?

Dear Matt

This is just a quick note to find out how you're keeping. I've been really worried about you since your news. I know you don't like me worrying but I can't help it. I just want to know that you're okay. News this side of the pond is pretty mundane. Work is a bit of a bind (but, hey, when isn't it?). Sara is still sleeping on the Sofa from Hell (incidentally she hasn't mentioned how uncomfortable it is, which either means that she's being really polite or has a spine made of steel), and my parents are talking about coming to see me. I broke the news to them that we'd split up and my dad was so happy he was like a game-show contestant. Did I ever tell you the reason why my dad never liked you? It was because you're English. My dad never has anything good to say about the English. He says, and I quote, 'They all act like they've got flagpoles shoved up their butts.' Truth is, he's never liked any of my boyfriends. That's what dads do best, I guess – hate their daughters' boyfriends. Well, gotta go and do some work now (or at least pretend to).

take it easy

love always

Elaine xxx

To: crazedelaine@hotpr.com
From: mattb@c-tec-national.com
Subject: me

Dear Elaine

Glad to hear you're okay, dudette, and that the Sofa from Hell hasn't crippled Sara and that your dad still hates me. All that aside, thanks for the rest of the contents of your last e-mail and for the phone call the other day. I'm honestly okay. Really I am. Gershwin, Ginny and I went to see where Elliot was buried today, which was strange and not in the least bit comforting. I have no idea what we thought we'd achieve by doing it. It's weird how in times of crisis when you're not sure how to act the most natural thing to do is to act like you're in a TV drama! Fortunately we snapped out of it pretty quickly and ended up retiring to the local pub. I feel like today has been a turning-point for the three of us. I think we're going to be proper mates again and this makes me feel good. Anyway, you take it easy yourself and try not to get too stressed when your folks come to stay.

Love

Matt xxx

forty-seven

True to our word, Ginny and I kept in touch. It started out with the odd trip down to the Kings Arms in time for last orders, with Gershwin tagging along whenever he could make it, progressed to trips to the cinema and mid-week meals out before finally moving on to that special point in friendship: the dropping round to each other's house for no reason other than the desire for company, coffee and the occasional cigarette. Sometimes Ian came out with us, sometimes Zoë came too, but for the most part it was just the three of us and, while I hesitate to say it, it really was just like old times.

On the Tuesday evening, nearly three weeks into our newly reinstated friendship, the three of us were in the lounge of the Kings Arms, spending some quality time together (well, actually, I was moaning about living with my parents, Ginny was moaning about work, and Gershwin was moaning about life *and* work) when they announced that 'Rock Around the Pop' – the Kings Arms' regular Tuesday night quiz – was about to begin. This was the second week in a row that we'd been and we loved every second of it. There's something wonderfully comforting about the Great British Pub Pop Quiz. It was cool to be vindicated: to know that there was indeed a point is knowing which year the Sex Pistols had signed their deal with

EMI, and a good reason to be able to name all five members of Musical Youth; It was fantastic to have Ginny and Gershwin look at me in awe in the what-lyric-comes-next round when I could recite not just a line but all of Wham!'s 'Club Tropicana'. It was a real bonding moment for us. My speciality was hits of the eighties, Ginny was spot on almost every time on current music and Gershwin excelled at everything else. We were like a well-oiled pop-music-trivia machine.

Half-way through the quiz, when Gershwin and I were hunched over Ginny's shoulders watching her scribble down the answers in her role as holder of the pencil, Ian turned up unexpectedly. I suddenly felt guilty. From the moment that I'd thought about kissing her on the day when we'd sat on her doorstep, it had become harder and harder to stop thinking about Ginny in 'that way'. This disappointed me because, at the age of nearly thirty, I was hoping that I'd somehow gained control of my 'dark' side, and the thought of being obsessed with another man's girlfriend depressed me. Worse still, I liked the idea that, after all this time, Ginny and I could just be friends without leaping all over each other. Having a platonic friendship with an ex-girlfriend/not girlfriend just seemed the sort of thing a nearly thirty-year-old man should be able to do. It didn't help knowing that it was only me who was battling with temptation either. Although affectionate, Ginny hadn't given me the slightest indication that she wanted anything to happen. And why would she? Unlike me, Ginny was in possession of the turning-thirty Holy Grails: a decent job, her own home and a relationship that had a future.

'Hi,' said Ginny, standing up to kiss him. 'This is a nice surprise.'

'Good,' he said, returning her kiss. He turned and looked at me and Gershwin. 'All right, lads?'

'To what do I owe this pleasure?' asked Ginny, pulling up a chair for Ian.

'Bad news, I'm afraid,' he said, sitting down.

Ginny tutted loudly. It was odd seeing her go into girlfriend mode like that. As she'd always been more friend than girlfriend when I'd been involved with her I'd never had to suffer that with her, and judging by the grim look on her face she did it very well.

'I'm off to the bar,' said Gershwin, as he and I exchanged schoolboy smirks of the I-wouldn't-like-to-be-him-right-now variety. 'Can I get you a drink, Ian?' he asked, as he stood up.

'I'd love one,' said Ian, 'but I can't stay out long – too much work to finish off.'

'Oh, great,' snapped Ginny.

'Look, I'm sorry, babe,' said Ian. 'I'll make it up to you soon.'

'You haven't even told me what the bad news is yet,' said Ginny.

'Er . . .' interrupted Gershwin, embarrassed. 'Same again, Ginny?'

'No, thanks. I'll have a double vodka and tonic, if that's okay.'

She'd been nursing half a cider all night.

'No problem,' replied Gershwin, exiting rapidly.

I stood up and gabbled, 'Better go give the old man a hand with the drinks, eh?' in Ginny's direction, waved at Ian and disappeared after Gershwin.

'What do you think that was about?' I asked my companion, as we reached the safety of the bar.

'Dunno, mate, but whatever it is he's definitely in trouble.'

By the time we returned Ian had gone and Ginny was fuming in a way that only a woman wronged by her boyfriend can.

'Where's Ian?' I asked. 'He can't have gone already?'

'He's gone all right.'

'Lovers' tiff?' asked Gershwin.

'You could say that,' said Ginny tersely. 'Every year my old college friend Adele throws a birthday party in her flat in Belsize Park. It's always really fabulous and everyone who went to college with us turns up.'

'So?' I asked.

'*So*,' began Ginny, throwing a hard stare in my direction, 'every year I go just to meet up with everybody and every year I feel like crap because they've all got these fabulous lives. Adele works in an art gallery and has this semi-delinquent toff boyfriend who's loaded. Her best friend number one, Liz, is an art director at some swanky advertising agency in Soho, has got a boyfriend who's a TV presenter and drives a big black sporty-type car—'

'Ferrari or Porsche?' asked Gershwin, unwisely.

'I don't know!' snapped Ginny. 'That's hardly the point, is it?' She exhaled deeply. 'Sorry, Gershwin. Where was I? Oh, that's it – and then there's Adele's best friend number two, Penny, who's married to a banker, has two gorgeous kids, a house in West London and a cottage in Cornwall, and on top of all that she had a show of her paintings at the Serpentine last summer. Finally there's me.'

'Do you actually like these people?' I asked.

'Can't stand them. Couldn't stand them at university either.'

'So why are you going?'

'Because if I don't it would be like admitting defeat. They're all so bloody patronising. It's like, "Oh, poor Ginny!" and I just want to shove their sympathy right up their—'

'Now, now,' interrupted Gershwin, adopting a vicarly tone. 'That won't do at all.'

'This year was going to be different. For one, I was going to tell them all what I thought of them, and for the other I was going to take my very handsome boyfriend with me to show off. I asked him about this ages ago and he's been promising me that he'd come and then I get his excuses and I have to go on my own.'

'Well, if Ian's got to work, he's got to work, hasn't he?' I said, attempting to be the voice of reason.

Ginny wasn't in the mood for reason and glared at me.

'It's only an idea,' began Gershwin, 'but we could come with you. Y'know, be your escorts for the evening. Matt could pretend to be a mega-famous music producer and could spend the evening name-dropping superstars.'

I interrupted, 'And Gershwin could be an airline pilot.'

Ginny attempted to stifle a smirk but failed miserably. 'I've always quite fancied the idea of a pilot. They're quite sexy, aren't they?'

'Yes, indeedy,' said Gershwin. 'And not only have I always wanted to be sexy but I've always wanted to fly a plane. I could make out that I've done a long haul from Singapore just to attend this party with you.'

'Who would I get to be?' asked Ginny, getting into the mood of our new fantasy-career game. 'I'm still only a teacher.'

'That's the beauty of these lies,' I replied sympathetically. 'You don't get to be anyone but yourself. Gershwin and I are two potential suitors who met you on holiday in Barbados and are vying for your love. It'll be a great laugh. Adele and her trendy mates will be so jealous you've managed to hook up with two eligible young studs like us that she'll hopefully choke with jealousy and die.'

Ginny chuckled and draped her left arm around me, her right around Gershwin. 'Thanks, but no thanks, boys. I think if this is going to work I'm just going to be me. I'd like the company though, but only if we go as ourselves. I'll let her humiliate me in front of all her trendy friends one last time, then I'll head to the bathroom, have a good cry, compose myself, say my goodbyes and never see them again. What do you say? Next weekend, are you up for it?'

'All for one and one for all,' said Gershwin, cheerily.

'I'm there like a rocket,' I added, getting into the spirit of things.

'That's that, then,' said Ginny, holding her untouched vodka up to her eyeline as if about to down it in one. 'London, here we come.'

forty-eight

To: mattb@c-tec.national.com
From: crazedelaine@hotpr.com
Subject: New beginnings

Dear Matt

I have a confession to make. Sara and I had another big night out after work on Friday. We just spent the whole night drinking and laughing – it was really good. Anyway, to cut a long story short, I met a guy. The inevitable happened. I'm not seeing him again.

love

Elaine xxxx

To: mattb@c-tec.national.com
From: crazedelaine@hotpr.com
Subject: Where are U?

Matt

It's been a day and a half since my big news. Where are U?
Mail me back so that I can rest assured that you haven't gone weird on me over this.

Elaine xxx

To: mattb@c-tec.national.com
From: crazedelainc@hotpr.oom
Subject: Where are u 2?

Matt, if you're not e-mailing me because of what I've told you then . . .
then . . . then you're not the person I thought you were.

Elaine xxx

To: mattb@c-tec.national.com
From: crazedelaine@hotpr.com
Subject: Why I've had it with men.

Read . . . my . . . e-mail . . . carefully . . . GET OVER IT, YOU ASSHOLE!

Love

Elaine xxx

forty-nine

We arrived in London early on Saturday morning. For a few days beforehand it was touch and go as to whether Gershwin was going to be able to come to the party because it clashed with a prearranged visit to Zoë's parents' for the weekend. However, he managed to negotiate his way out of it, with a promise to up his contribution to household duties from 20 per cent to the golden 50 per cent of perfect married life and a weekend away for the two of them 'somewhere nice'.

For me, though, the party had become the focal point of my life. The prospect of doing something different that involved new people in new surroundings appealed to me mainly, I suspect, because I'd spent the majority of the week helping my dad clear out the garage, running supermarket errands for my mum and generally dealing with Elaine's e-mailed news that she was moving on and seeing other people. She was right to move on. The more we dragged things out, the worse it would be. Of course, I would have been happier if *I* had moved on (something with Ginny, perhaps?) but that's the way it goes. That's why I decided not to reply to her e-mail right away. I didn't want to say anything stupid that I might regret later.

The first thing we did was check into our hotel, the

Rembrandt Court just off Oxford Street. Ginny's friend Adele had said we could crash on her floor or sofa, but with the memory fresh in my mind of my time on the Sofa from Hell, I put forward the proposal that we stay in a hotel. Ginny, however, didn't like the idea of spending her hard-earned on something as decadent as that. In the end we compromised: Gershwin and I booked a twin room and offered Ginny the sofa, should there be one.

'You are joking?' said Ginny, when we suggested this.

'No,' we'd lied in unison.

Bags unpacked, we raided the mini-bar for ludicrously expensive peanuts and soft drinks, before hitting the streets of London determined to spend the next few hours acting like proper tourists. Although I'd lived in London for a good five years after graduating, I'd never really done any of the touristy things you're supposed to do there and now I decided was as good a time as any. We started off with a walk along the river on the South Bank, where we became tangled up in a gaggle of skate-boarding youths and Gershwin gave a kid a pound for a quick go on his board. Next we had a scout round the National Portrait Gallery, where Ginny bought a postcard of Audrey Hepburn for Ian – who was now back in her good books.

After that we went to Trafalgar Square and ate ice-cream, and Ginny got into conversation with an old homeless guy who insisted that there was a government conspiracy to steal the pigeons. Finally, we ended up near Carnaby Street in a bar that had been my after-work bar of choice. We sat there for hours, drinking vodka, flicking through the weekend papers and laughing at twentysomething trendy student types with stupid haircuts and silly footwear. It was early evening by the time we got back to the hotel and we were all so drunk, unfocused and knackered that, without even discussing it, we collapsed on to the beds and napped like four-year-olds. At eight o'clock we woke up, showered and got ready for Adele's party. By a quarter to nine we were ready to go.

We got as far as the hotel lobby when Ginny stopped suddenly. 'Do you know what? I don't think I can be bothered to go all the way to Belsize Park for a party I know I'll hate just to snub people I already know I don't like and make some point I can't even be bothered to make.'

'I'm so glad you said that,' said Gershwin, 'because I think we should stay here too. I'm still incredibly drunk, I'm so tired I can barely keep my eyes open, and that bed upstairs was really comfortable. Can't we just phone up this Adele person and be rude to her down the phone?'

'Good idea, sir,' I said, content to throw in the towel with the rest of them. 'You're both right. I was hoping to pull at this party in the hope that it would make me feel better about the fact that my ex-girlfriend had started seeing other people. But you know what? I can't be arsed. Let's go back upstairs, order room service, make that rude phone call to Adele and have a party of our own.'

I looked at Gershwin, Gershwin looked at Ginny, and Ginny looked at me. All three of us burst out laughing, we did an about-turn and headed back to our room.

Twenty minutes later we were asleep: Gershwin in his double bed, Ginny in my single and me on the hotel-room Sofa from Hell.

fifty

To: crazedelaine@hotpr.com
From: mattb@c-tec.national.com
Subject: A guy in a bar

Dear Elaine

Thank you for your many erratic and slightly barmy e-mails. For your information I didn't e-mail because I didn't know what to say. I suppose random guys in bars are all part of the moving-on process. Part of me wants to be jealous. I suppose a lot of me. But the rest of me knows that this sort of thing has got to happen, hasn't it?

Matt xxx

To: mattb@c-tec.national.com
From: crazedelaine@hotpr.com
Subject: An old friend

Matt, Your e-mail reminded me of why I fell in love with you. Who else would think like that? You're so sensitive sometimes I think you must be half girl. Just for the record, besides 'the other stuff' (which I know you don't want me to go into) Random Bar Guy was an awful kisser. Remember that time just after we first met when we got caught in the rain on the way back from Alexandra's and we ended up kissing in a doorway while we waited from the rain to stop? That was a 11/10 kiss. This guy was a 2/10 at the very best.

Elaine xxx

fifty-one

'Matthew!' called my mum up the stairs. 'It's the phone for you!'

'Okay,' I called back, from the sanctuary of my bedroom. 'I'll be there in a minute. Who is it?'

'Gershwin!'

'What does he want?' I shouted.

'I have no idea,' yelled my mum. 'But if you don't get your backside down here in a minute, you'll never find out because I'll put the phone down!'

It was the Monday after our London trip and I was in bed, still recovering from the booze and the hotel-room Sofa from Hell. Despite all this I'd had every intention of answering the phone and was merely conducting a long-distance shouty conversation with my mum because I knew, from various episodes of my youth, that holding shouty conversations up the stairs with the fruit of her loins really, really annoyed her.

At the risk of sounding like an ungrateful, selfish human being, I reckoned my mum deserved everything she was getting. I know that sounds a bit harsh, but think about it. Parents, you love them dearly, they bring you into this world, they give you everything you need, and they are usually quite nice to you. But it's these same people, the people who have done all these wonderful things, who know that their past benevolence towards you gives them the Power: the Power to get under your skin like no one else on earth; the Power to locate every single one of the buttons you keep hidden from the world; and the Power to press all of them at once thereby guaranteeing that you will be enraged by the seemingly innocuous. Parents know exactly what they're doing. To them it's like a sport, something to do when they're bored. And the day when annoying your children to the point of mental frenzy becomes an Olympic event will be the day that my mother steps up on to the podium as the National Anthem plays and collects her gold medal.

That's why I was trying to wind her up.

Revenge.

Petty, I know. But I considered it self-defence and, anyway, my dad had told me my mum used to do exactly the same to my Gran when she was alive.

It had started off with minor digs about the general untidiness of my appearance but, as the days passed, her remarks became less and less subtle until one afternoon she had a bit of a hissy fit and the words, 'You're not going out until you smarten up your act *and* tidy up this room,' left her lips. I couldn't believe what I was hearing. My room was spotless. Somehow, through circumstances beyond my control, my life had been reduced to a coming-of-age movie in reverse.

Although I knew she loved me, I think the novelty of having her twenty-nine-year-old son living at home was wearing a little thin. At the back of her mind she was seriously worried that I'd get so comfortable I'd never move out.

As if.

It wasn't for ever.

In fact it would only be six weeks until I'd be going.

But the way things were heading . . .

I got the feeling . . .

That the next six weeks . . .

Were going to be the longest six weeks of my life . . .

That was why I was taking so long to answer Gershwin's call.

'Hello?'

'Er . . . hello,' said Gershwin.

'All right, mate?'

'Yeah, I'm fine. I haven't disturbed you, have I?'

'No,' I replied. 'I was just annoying my mum. That's all.'

'Good,' he said. 'Just checking.'

'So what can I do for you, sir?'

'A favour,' said Gershwin, carefully.

'How big a favour?'

'About thigh high.'

'I have no idea what you're on about,' I replied.

'My mum's just called to say that she's got to go to Norwich to look after my aunt, because she's broken her leg or something. She has no idea how long she'll be down there, which means she won't be able to look after Charlotte. The thing is she goes to a nursery class a couple of sessions a week but tomorrow isn't one of them—'

'You're asking me to look after her?' I asked incredulously.

'You'd be doing me and Zoë a massive favour,' said Gershwin. 'I'll owe you big-time. You just need to get here for eight thirty when Zoë has to go to work. She'll give you a list of instructions and stuff like that and then she'll be back around five.'

I thought about it: a day spent hanging out with a four-year-old versus a day spent winding up my mum. 'No problem,' I said confidently. 'I've got nothing else going on anyway. I could do with the diversion.'

'Are you sure?' asked Gershwin. I think he was feeling a bit guilty. 'I mean, we could book her into a full time nursery if you really don't want to.'

'Don't be ridiculous,' I said. 'I'm nearly thirty, I've got a degree in computer science, I think I can handle looking after my own goddaughter, thank you very much.'

fifty-two

'Hi, Matt,' said Zoë, on opening the door, 'or should I say Dad-for-the-day?' She kissed me hello and led me into the living room.

'Hi, Zoë,' I replied. 'I'm ready for whatever Charlotte can throw at me – cereal, teddy bears . . . whatever.'

'She's very well behaved,' said Zoë. 'She'll be an angel for you, won't you, darling?' Charlotte had wandered in and was looking at me with a distinctly detached air. She looked up at her mum.

'What do you fancy doing today, Charlotte?' I asked.

She shrugged.

'Fair enough,' I said. 'I'll think of something then, okay?'

Zoë knelt down next to her. 'Do you want to go and put your things away in your bedroom, darling?' Charlotte disappeared down the hallway, leaving Zoë and me on our own. 'Right,' she said, handing me a list. 'There's loads of food in the fridge and I've written down the sort of thing she'd probably like for lunch. She does sometimes change her mind but don't let her bully you. I've written down my number at work and my mobile number, and Gershwin's work number just in case.'

I looked down the list. 'Is she allowed to watch TV?'

'Yes, but only for an hour at a time. Otherwise she gets a bit zombified.'

Zoë excused herself and went to finish getting ready for work. Standing in the living room I looked at a photo of Gershwin, Zoë and Charlotte on the wall. It was weird seeing that whole mum-dad-kid thing being acted out by people the same age as me. And it was even more strange to equate the Gershwin in the picture, in his role as father and husband, with the Gershwin I'd known as a kid who would light his farts in class.

'Right, then,' said Zoë, carrying Charlotte to the front door in her arms. She gave her a huge hug and a kiss and set her down on the ground. 'You be a good girl for your uncle Matt, won't you?'

Looking after Charlotte for the first half of the day was easy. At four she was at the kind of age where she pretty much amused herself and all I had to do was deal with the odd request for a drink and make sure she didn't get up to anything too dangerous. I took her to Mum and Dad's for lunch, which both my parents enjoyed – in fact, so much that my mum and I were nearly at peace. When I watched my dad talking to her I was surprised by how at ease he was. After lunch, according to the schedule, it was nap time for Charlotte, so I took her back to Gershwin and Zoë's. When she woke up about an hour later we played a couple of rounds of Hungry Hippo, and watched a bit of TV. At about four o'clock she tired of that, and that was when I realised there was more to this child-raising malarkey than met the eye. Charlotte's attention span had reduced to approximately ten minutes, and when she needed entertaining she needed it badly. I wandered through the house looking for inspiration.

Growing up, Gershwin had been fanatical about music and

had a vinyl record collection of around a thousand albums. Looking through the flat, however, it was nowhere to be seen, even though he still had a turntable on his hi-fi set-up. He had a few CDs but the death of vinyl and his hurtling into adulthood must have coincided with a loss of interest in music because all his CDs were crap. I'd seen this syndrome before in other friends and it was always the same: people who had been fanatical about music in their teens and early twenties suddenly had no time to listen to it because of work. Then they got married or shacked up with a girlfriend and their record collections were either deported to their parents' house or removed to the loft because they didn't fit in with the décor. My guess was that Gershwin had hidden his in the loft because I knew his dad had turned his old bedroom into a study the second that Gershwin had moved out. Realising that this was an opportunity both to educate and entertain Charlotte, I grabbed a chair from Gershwin and Zoë's bedroom, and used it to manoeuvre myself into their loft while keeping a careful eye on Charlotte – which was difficult. As I rummaged around I got covered in dust and dirt but finally my hunch paid off. Among the debris of his youth – an old Commodore 64 computer still in its box, an Atari games console, several old pairs of trainers, his large collection of Second World War books – were his records. They were packed in neatly labelled boxes that evidently hadn't been touched in years. I grabbed a box and took it down to show Charlotte.

'Do you know what these are?' I asked her.

'No,' she said.

'Records,' I replied.

'What do they do?' she asked.

'You know what CDs are?' I asked.

She nodded.

'Well, they're old-fashioned versions of those.'

Intrigued, Charlotte attempted to take an album from the box but she couldn't manage it, so I pulled it out and handed it to her. 'Do you know who that is?' I said, pointing to the cover.

She shook her head.

'Have you heard of Michael Jackson?'

She nodded, but she might have been humouring me.

'Well, this,' I said, looking at the album cover, 'is called *Off the Wall*, and it's Michael Jackson before he went all rubbish. Shall we play it?'

She started yelling excitedly at the top of her voice. As this was the most animated I'd seen her since her mum had left, I took this as a good sign and decided to go with the flow. I was only going to play one song but in the end we listened to the whole of the first side. She was transfixed. When 'Don't Stop 'Til You Get Enough' came on she launched herself off the sofa like a miniature disco diva and made me put it on four times in a row.

In the middle of 'She's Out Of My Life,' the door buzzer went and I turned down the music.

'Is it Mummy?' asked Charlotte. 'Maybe she'll want to dance too.'

I looked at my watch. It was too early for either Zoë or Gershwin. I walked over to the intercom nervously – I was now more than half convinced it was one of the neighbours complaining about the music and the caterwauling four-year-old. 'Hello?' I said as I pressed the button.

'Hi, Matt, it's Ginny. Can I come in?'

'Of course,' I said, and pressed the door release. I spent the remaining moments until she knocked on the door wondering why she'd come and how she knew I was here.

'Hi, come in,' I said, opening the door.

'Cheers.'

'How did you know I was here?'

'I called you at your mum and dad's and they told me what you were up to. I couldn't resist the temptation to see how you were getting on in your first day as a nanny—' She stopped as Charlotte appeared in the hallway.

'Is this Charlotte?' she asked. She walked over to her and knelt down. 'Hello. I'm Ginny. I'm a friend of your mum and dad's.'

'I'm four,' said Charlotte.

'You're gorgeous, aren't you?' said Ginny, then beamed at me as if I were semi-responsible for Charlotte's existence.

'Look what we've been doing,' said Charlotte, dragging Ginny by the hand into the living room. 'Uncle Matt, will you play that record again? The one we were just dancing to?'

I did as I was asked. We listened to it three times in a row, during which Charlotte jumped up and down using the sofa as a trampoline.

The rest of that afternoon until Zoë turned up will go down in my autobiography as one of my all time favourites. The three of us listened to *Guilty* by Barbra Streisand (I think it was Gershwin's mum's), *Sign of the Times* by Prince, missing out 'If I Was Your Girlfriend' because I decided the end bit was too rude for Charlotte, *Breakdance – The Album*, for old times' sake, and two Duran Duran singles, to make her proud of her cultural heritage. When Zoë arrived home just after five, she entered to discover Ginny, Charlotte and me lying on the living-room floor, staring at the ceiling and playing air guitar while contemplating the majesty and splendour that is Jimi Hendrix's version of 'All Along The Watch Tower', from Gershwin's vinyl copy of Hendrix's *Greatest Hits*.

'Have you been doing this all afternoon?' asked Zoë.

'Charlotte's been bonding with Gershwin's record collection,' explained Ginny.

'What have you been listening to?' asked Zoë.

'Cool music!' yelled Charlotte, at the top of her voice.

'Where does she get these words?' I asked.

'Gershwin taught her "cool",' said Zoë. 'He said he wanted our daughter to have good taste. And according to him the best way for her to acquire good taste is to know what is and isn't cool.' She ruffled her daughter's hair. 'So, what's cool music, then, Charlotte?'

Charlotte's face took on a look of considered determination as she tried to recall that afternoon's lesson, but then she shrugged nonchalantly as if to say it wasn't important.

'Cool is Michael Jackson's *Off The Wall*,' I said, on Charlotte's behalf.

'Cool is also Elvis, *The Greatest Hits of Barry White*, Culture Club's first album and Kajagoogoo,' added Ginny.

'So what's not cool?' asked Zoë.

'Daddy,' said Charlotte.

Ginny and I stayed on for a little while then left at about a quarter to six. I desperately didn't want to go home and spend the evening watching TV with my parents.

'Do you fancy a quick drink in the Kings Arms?' I said, as we walked along Wake Green Road towards Moseley high street.

'It'll have to be a quick one,' said Ginny. 'Ian's coming round to mine at about seven. I think he wants to go out for something to eat. You could come if you want to.'

'No, no, no,' I replied, a little too effusively. 'I'll just settle for a drink.'

fifty-three

'So, things getting you down at home?' asked Ginny as we sat down, pints in hand, in the empty lounge of the Kings Arms.

'You could say that,' I replied, and took a sip of my beer. 'I'm thinking about going to Australia early.'

'You're joking, right? Things can't be that bad.'

'Oh, they are,' I said emphatically. I told her the you-can't-go-out-until-you've-tidied-your-room story.

'Never!' said Ginny. 'She said that?'

'Those were her very words,' I confirmed unhappily.

'It's unnatural for a man of your age to be living with his parents,' said Ginny. 'Even for a short time. In fact, I think it might be illegal!' She tried to stifle a snigger. 'But you're not serious about going to Australia now, surely?'

'I'm totally serious. It would only be a few weeks earlier than scheduled. I'm sure they'd put me up in a hotel if I asked them. And, anyway, I can understand my parents getting annoyed – I *am* messing up the place. We've done all the bonding we're ever going to do so maybe I should go while we're still on speaking terms.'

'But what about us?'

'Which us?'

'You, me and Gershwin,' said Ginny. 'I thought we were all mates now. Proper mates. Not fake ones.'

'Yeah, we are,' I said, defensively. 'You can both come over to Australia any time you like. The apartment the company said they're going to rent for me is supposed to be really nice. It'll have plenty of room if you and Ian want to come over.'

'Aren't we having a good time?'

'Yes, but look at me tonight. Gershwin and Zoë are staying in, you're off with Ian . . .'

'I invited you to come out with us,' she said.

'And I turned you down! I'm nobody's third wheel, thank you very much. Nah, it all makes sense. It'll give me a bit of time to get myself settled.'

She smiled softly. 'What would it take for you to stay? A million pounds?'

'Higher.'

'Two million pounds and I'll flash my boobs at you?' Ginny chortled.

'How about two million pounds, and I'll give you back five hundred grand to keep your boobs hidden?'

Ginny laughed. 'How about no money, but you can move into the spare room at my place at no charge?'

There was a long silence.

'You're joking, right?' I asked.

'Deadly serious, sir. Why would I joke? You need somewhere to live, right?'

'Yeah.'

'Well, there you go,' said Ginny succinctly. 'Problem sorted.'

'Are you sure?' I said. 'Or is it just the three mouthfuls of lager talking because you've consumed them on a school night?'

Ginny laughed. 'A bit of both, I suspect. It's weird I bump into you and Gershwin on his birthday. Twenty-four hours later I've bunked the day off work. And now weeks later I'm in the pub with you both nearly every night I like this kind of randomness in my life. It's fun.' She paused and took another sip of her drink. 'Do you remember that one half-term when Bev's mum and dad went away and left her in charge of the house and we all moved in for the week? We said then that at the first opportunity we were going to get a huge house together and spend the rest of our lives living together like an episode of the Monkees. This is that opportunity. Gershwin and Zoë could move in with Charlotte, too.'

'But what about Ian?' I asked.

'*What* about Ian?'

'Won't he mind?'

'Mind what? An old schoolfriend moving into the spare room? Of course not.'

I thought about it. 'You'd let me pay rent, of course?'

'No rent, as I've already made clear,' said Ginny. 'You do the supermarket shopping for the two of us and that can be your contribution, if you like.'

I thought about it once more.

'And you're *sure* you're sure?' I asked.

'Of course I am,' she said reassuringly. 'Ian's, like, the most laid-back man in the world. I could probably move a male stripper into my place and he'd be, like, "Oh, that's nice, babe." Anyway, it's my house and I'll do what I like in it.' She seemed amused by her own forthrightness. 'We'll have to have rules, though,' she added, in a voice that said, 'This is me attempting to be stern.' 'I've had some nightmare house-shares in my youth, *especially* when they've been men.'

'What kind of rules did you have in mind?'

'Basic stuff. Like no washing-up left in the sink longer than twenty-four hours.'

'Done.'

'No leaving just two sheets of loo roll for the next person.'
'Done.'
'No leaving your skanky bloke pants in communal areas.'
'Done.'

Ginny was silent, but I could tell she was trying to think of some more.

'Is that all?' I asked, checking.

'Yeah,' she said, uncertainly. 'I think so.'

'Okay,' I said. 'I've got some too. Well, one, actually.'

'You can't make up rules, you cheeky git. I'm the landlady.' She giggled, yawned, then said, 'Go on. What's this rule you've got?'

'No girl-pants or brassières drying on radiators,' I said clearly. 'That's all I ask. Elaine used to do that and it nearly drove me insane.'

fifty-four

Dear Elaine

   With regard to your recent bout of confession-making I now have one too. Sort of. Things were getting a bit tense with my parents so I was seriously thinking about going to Australia a few weeks early but then Ginny offered me a room at her house. So I'm kind of moving in with her in a purely platonic manner (the spare room will be my domain). Her boyfriend's cool with it. And it's only until I fly to Sydney. That's it, really. No biggy.

love

Matt xxx

Dear Matt
   'Okay.'

Love

Elaine

To: crazedelaine@hotpr.com
From: mattb@c-tec.national.com
Re: Re: Re: Confessions

Dear Elaine

What sort of 'okay' was that? 'Okay' as in 'it's all right'? Or 'okay' as in 'over your dead body'?
Just wondering.

love

Matt

To: mattb@c-tec.national.com
From: crazedelaine@hotpr.com
Re: You have NO idea, do you?

Dear Matt

I meant okay as in: 'Of course it's okay for you to live in close proximity to your old high-school (or whatever the UK equivalent is) girlfriend at this crucial point in your being where you are assessing and reassessing your (nearly) thirty years so far and are assuming that your best days are behind you because obviously there won't be any rekindling of old sparks especially when she's parading around all day in just her underwear.'
That's the sort of 'okay' I mean.

Love

Elaine

fifty-five

Over dinner the following evening – beef mince, potatoes, cabbage and carrots – I announced to my parents that I'd be moving out. It was quite heartening, really, because as soon as I said it, I became number-one son again. Mum tried to persuade me to stay and, at her insistence, my dad tried too but not particularly hard. It wasn't that he wanted to see me out on the streets or anything but, as a man, I think he appreciated that if I was ever going to brush myself off and get back on my horse, it would be more likely to happen in a place where I knew my mum wasn't going to come round every five minutes to ask me if I was okay.

The following evening after I'd left from babysitting Charlotte I moved into Ginny's, with the help of my parents. Although I was only moving twenty minutes away my mum made me promise to visit for dinner at least once a week, and insisted that I take a large cardboard box with me as well. It wasn't until my parents had gone and I'd sorted out my new room that I realised the box contained tinned food, tea-bags and breakfast cereals.

fifty-six

To: crazedelaine@hotpr.com
From: mattb@c-tec.national.com
Re: Re: Okay?

Dear Elaine
  Are we having a row here?

Matt xxx

To: mattb@c-tec.national.com
From: crazedelaine@hotpr.com
Re: Re: Re: Okay

Dear Matt
  OF COURSE WE'RE HAVING A FIGHT. (I DON'T 'ROW' I'M
AMERICAN!!!!!!!)

Elaine xxx

To: crazedelaine@hotpr.com
From: mattb@c-tec.national.com
Re: **Row/fight**

Dear Elaine

  Fair enough. Let's . . . argue. Let me see: you're annoyed with me because even though we've split up I've moved into the spare room of an ex-girlfriend from about fifteen gadzillion (your word) years ago. You, meanwhile, have been 'getting together' with random bar guys . . . and I'm the one in the wrong? I love your complete lack of grasp of the fundamental points of logical thought.

Love

Matt xxx

fifty-seven

On the whole living with Ginny was a less stressful experience than I thought it could be, especially given our history. In the old days this definitely would've been a recipe for disaster given the way we used to flit from being lovers to best friends without even pausing for breath. But with my new turning thirty persona, I could handle it. Of course during the first few days we had to made a few more rules: if you finish a bottle of milk, buy a new one – and no getting round it by leaving a few drops in the bottom; the bath had to be washed immediately after use, and with proper bath-cleaning implements – not just a quick wipe round with a damp towel; and no borrowing of gender specific razors without permission. To be truthful, these were my rules, but Ginny didn't complain too much because being such a neat freak, I tended to do most, if not all, of the cooking and cleaning for both of us. It was a lot like living with Elaine and was strangely comforting and helped to take the edge off the lower moments in life.

fifty-eight

To: mattb@c-tec.national.com
From: crazedelaine@hotpr.com
Re: Arguing

Dear Matt

Let's not argue any more. I can't get any work done when I'm just sitting here waiting for your next e-mail. Having slept on the issue I admit that I might have been a little bit hasty re: you and your ex. I apologise. I promise you I'm not jealous. I just worry about you. I know how you are. Maybe you should date her after all. I think it would be good therapy for you to revisit your past like that.

Love

Elaine xxx

fifty-nine

Ginny and I established our own routines as if we were a genuine happily living-together couple. Every weekday she got up at six-thirty, disappeared into the bathroom for a shower, then back into her bedroom where she'd dry her hair, put on her makeup and get dressed. Then she'd go downstairs, have a bowl of muesli and make her sandwiches for work. The entire process took her an hour and a half and, without fail, she would leave the house late.

My routine was far less sedate. Gershwin's mum was still away so on the days I had to look after Charlotte I'd get up at seven forty-five, race into the shower, nip back into my bedroom, get dressed and be out of the door seconds before Ginny.

It was fun hanging out with a nearly four-year-old and fortunately she seemed to like hanging out with me. To make her laugh all I had to do was make a farty noise on the back of my hand; and to make me laugh all she had to do was laugh at my farty noise. With her love of television, odd combinations of food (try beans on toast with cottage cheese all mixed together) and walking in the park, she made the perfect companion. I suspect I was built to look after children. I really was.

sixty

To: crazedelaine@hotpr.com
From: mattb@c-tec.national.com
Re: your last e-mail

Dear Elaine

   I'm having trouble following your line of thought. Now you want me to go out with her?
Just checking,

love

Matt

To: mattb@c-tec.national.com
From: crazedelaine@hotpr.com
Re: Just checking.

Dear Matt

   First off (I am soooooo going to get fired when they realise that I do nothing here all day except write e-mails to England). Second off, since we broke up (and let's not forget it's been a long time) I've only 'got together' with one guy in a bar! All you've done is move in with an old girlfriend who already has a boyfriend! If you're not going to date her then I think you should date somebody. It's only natural.

love,

Elaine

sixty-one

The only problem I really had was loneliness. On the evenings when Ginny seeing Ian coincided with Gershwin staying in or going out with his other mates, I'd find myself at a loose end. I'm not the kind of person who enjoys their own company very much. I need people to bounce off. I am very much a people-bouncing-off type of person.

sixty-two

To: crazedelaine@hotpr.com
From: mattb@c-tec.national.com
Subject: The dating game

Dear Elaine

Okay, I promise you I will go on a date. I am only doing this because I know that you won't give up until you get your way. It must feel good to know that your power to annoy extends right across the Atlantic. Seriously, though, I think you've got a point. However, I think things may be more difficult for me than you might think. I was looking in the personal ads in the paper on Saturday and women in their thirties (i.e. my new catchment area) always specify that they're looking for a man who:

1) Is financially solvent.

2) Supportive.

3) Has no emotional baggage.

While I'm okay on (1) and (2) I suspect that you may well constitute 'emotional baggage'. Regardless, I shall find a date so we can get on with our lives.

love

Matt 'luggage handler of the lonely' Beckford xxx

sixty-three

'Good night?' asked Ginny.

It was just past half-eleven on Friday night a week after I'd moved into Ginny's. My now slightly merry landlady had just come back from another night out with Ian while my evening had been a simpler affair along the lines of *Weekend Watchdog* followed by *Top of the Pops*, followed by feelings of hunger and self-pity, followed by a call to Domino's Pizza, followed by more self-pity and an intense half-hour of channel surfing, followed by the arrival of my thin-crust Meat Feast pizza, followed by *Friends*, followed by half a tub of ice-cream followed by *Frasier*, followed by half of an unconvincing vampire film followed by the arrival of Ginny.

Terrible,' I replied to Ginny's question, without lifting my head from the arm of the sofa. 'How about yours?'

'Nowhere near as bad as yours, I suspect.' She took off her coat, moved my legs out of the way and slumped on the sofa next to me. 'We went for a drink at a new bar in town and to the Persian restaurant above it.'

'How was it?'

'Fine.' She smiled. 'They make all-right food, you know the Persians.' She gave a little yawn then stretched. 'So come on, Mr Misery, why was tonight so awful for you?'

'No special reason.'

'Hard day with Charlotte?'

'Not in the least. She was brilliant. We went to the art museum this afternoon. I think she quite enjoyed it. Well, she must have done because on the bus on the way home she told me she was going to be an artist when she grew up. Well, either that or an accountant.' Ginny giggled. 'I'm not making it up either. I don't know where she gets these things from, I really don't. Kids' minds are a total enigma to me.'

'So what's wrong, then?'

'I'm bored, I suppose.'

'Oh, poor baby,' said Ginny, and rubbed her eyes. 'Ian was on about going to the cinema tomorrow night. You can come if you want.'

'That's the second time you've invited me to play gooseberry. I have my dignity. I don't need your charity . . . yet.'

'You'll be fine.' Ginny kicked off her shoes and looked at the clock on the far wall. 'What are you doing now? Off to bed?'

'Not this early,' I replied. 'I was toying with watching this week's *ER*. I taped it on Wednesday and I've been waiting for a really low moment in my life to watch it. The way I see it, other people's misery, even fictional other people's misery, is bound to make me feel better about my own life.'

'I've never watched *ER* before,' said Ginny, settling back in the sofa. 'I never really like the idea of all that blood and guts and shouting.'

'You're joking!' I said. 'The shouting's the best bit. I used to be like you, ignorant about such things. In fact, I used to leave the room whenever Elaine started watching it, saying I was going to leave her to her "girls' programmes" but she converted me. It only took about three episodes and I was addicted. You make some coffee, I'll set up the video, and I'll give you a crash course on all of the characters' histories like

Elaine did with me – all the who's sleeping with who, the who's slept with who, the who hates who and the who's pregnant by who. It's just like real life, only it happens in a hospital.'

It was just coming up to a quarter to one in the morning when Ginny and I got our second wind of energy after watching sixty minutes' worth of top-quality hospital drama. In fact, we were so hyperactive that we decided to play *ER live!*, a stupid in-joke of a game invented by Elaine and me that nobody else understood or found remotely funny but that we found hilarious. To play *ER live!* all you had to do was find a willing patient (Elaine and I used one of her mother's embroidered cushions), assign roles (Elaine was always Dr Shula Hobgoblin, a one-armed hot-headed maverick surgeon new to the trauma department, and I was always Staff Nurse Zimmerman, a hard but fair male nurse born on the wrong side of the Austrian Alps). The rest of the game involved trying to deliver as many *ER* clichés as possible in a minute.

Ginny loved the idea because it was so bizarre. She decided she was going to be Dr Elizabeth Hatstand, a brilliant but eccentric second-year surgical resident from London, England. In an attempt not to reawaken too many old memories I decided to be Dr Lance Buttie, a brilliant but acutely miserable trainee surgeon with a chip on his shoulder the size of brick.

'Dr Buttie!' said Ginny, barely able to control her laughter. 'To the trauma room quickly! We've got a gangbanger with a GSW to the head, suffering from anaphylactic shock and – er – other stuff.'

'Here's the patient, Dr Hatstand.' I picked up Ginny's cat Larry (Sanders, smart animal, had made a crafty exit) and settled her in front of the TV with the two of us kneeling on the floor beside him. 'It doesn't look good,' I said. 'It looks like he's lost a lot of blood. He may never bring another dead mouse into the house again.' I thumped the ground in mock anguish. 'Damn these youngsters and their gang warfare. Can't they see this is such a waste of young life?'

Ginny pretended to smack me across the face. 'Dammit, Buttie, you're getting hysterical. Do you know that I've never lost a patient yet? Not even one with whiskers!' She slapped me again. Larry watched the two of us passively, flicked his whiskers and rolled on to his back.

'You're right, Dr Hatstand. I'm sorry. I'm being hysterical. It's just that I've never told you this but I lost my own cat in exactly the same way. It's such a tragedy! I should never have—'

Ginny interrupted with loud beeping noises.

'What is it, Hatstand?'

'The patient's going into anaphylactic shock! Get me two teaspoons full of O-neg, an ECG, a DTP, a CBC, a Chem 7, a BBC1, a BBC2 and maybe even an ITV – oh, and get me the big thing that gives electric shocks too, otherwise this cat is on a one-way trip through that great cat-flap in the sky!'

'But, Dr Hatstand, shouldn't we just intubate? Or perform a cricothyroidoctomy? Or a cordotomy? Or even a lobotomy?'

'Dammit, Dr Buttie!' yelled Ginny, really getting into her role. 'Who's the senior surgeon round here? Me or you, dammit?'

Larry was tired of two humans shouting nonsense over his head: she rolled on to her feet, stretched and wandered off to the kitchen.

'Come back, Larry!' said Ginny, rolling about on the floor with mirth. 'We promise we'll cure you!'

'Ungrateful patient,' I called after him. I crawled back on to the sofa. 'I'm shattered,' I said. 'Who'd want to work in a real *ER*? Computers are far easier to handle.'

Ginny laughed. 'Never mind computers. Let's open a bottle of wine or three, relax and have a good old talk.'

sixty-four

'You miss her, don't you?' said Ginny, handing me what would be the first of several glasses of wine.

'Who?' I said, feigning ignorance.

'Elaine.'

I attempted to work backwards through our conversation to see how she'd gone from computing to Elaine.

'I've been meaning to talk to you about her for a while. When we finished playing *ER live!* you looked so sad – as though you were thinking about her,' Ginny said. 'Maybe you weren't. Maybe you were thinking about next week's *ER*.'

Ginny was right. I had been thinking about Elaine, but only fleetingly. I was thinking about how when we played *ER live!* she'd always go on about a character who neither of us played called Dr Salami. It was the kind of rude, throwaway gag that in the normal world isn't that funny. But it was our joke and nobody else's, and that made it hilarious.

'You're right,' I said. 'I do miss her . . . a lot. It's just the stupid stuff, really. As well as playing *ER* we used to play a game called "Name That Vegetable". We'd take it in turns to hide a vegetable underneath a towel and try to guess what it was.'

'Mmm-hmm,' said Ginny, raising her eyebrows. 'That sounds like very odd behaviour indeed.'

'I know,' I said, laughing. 'But that's not the really stupid thing. The really stupid thing was that it was always a potato.'

'So, are you going to tell me what went wrong with you two? I've been dying to ask you about her for ages and it's only now that I'm trying to get you drunk that I feel able to. All you've said about your relationship with her so far is that it didn't work out.' Ginny pulled a face. 'I mean, you haven't even told me where you two met – and we're supposed to be friends!'

'Are you sure you want to talk about all this?' I asked. 'I mean, it's a bit gloomy, isn't it?'

'No, no, no,' said Ginny keenly. 'Talking about relationships isn't gloomy – it's therapy.'

'Okay.' I took a sip of my wine. 'Are you sitting comfortably? Then I'll begin. Once upon a time there was a handsome financial software designer called Matt. He'd been living in London for five years, was doing well in his job and was going out with a rather smashing girl called Monica Aspel who worked in management consultancy. Now, Matt was proud of his relationship with Monica because at the age of twenty-seven it was the first he'd ever had in which both parties referred to each other as my boy/girlfriend without the use of two-fingered ironical quotation marks. He even thought it would break the twelve-month relationship barrier that he had yet to experience. Unfortunately a month before their one-year anniversary he made the mistake of coming home to their top floor Muswell Hill flat early to discover that his darling management-consultant girlfriend had brought some work home with her and was consulting rather too closely with a manager on their bed . . .'

'Oh, no!' exclaimed Ginny.

'Don't worry,' I replied. 'Matt was okay – in the end. He moved out straight away and made a new home on a workmate's sofa. Anyway, that was when – he – oh, sod it, I can't keep this up.

This was when I heard about an internal job opportunity for a software team leader, a step up the ladder and, best of all, the job was in New York. I had a massive interview, got the job and went over for the first time to meet my new bosses. Before I knew it I was in possession of a green card and on a Virgin Atlantic flight to JFK.'

'All this sounds really exciting,' said Ginny, encouragingly.

'It was, although I was a bit overwhelmed by it all at first. I had all these plans. I was going to buy a Ford Gran Torino, like the one Starsky and Hutch had, I was going to go on long road trips during my vacations and I was going to join a gym and get myself some biceps – I was going to do everything. Instead, during my first week in New York, two days after I'd found my new apartment I went to a party in Greenwich Village and that was where I met Elaine. We got on well. We dated for all of two weeks before she fell out with her room-mates and moved into my apartment on a temporary basis while she looked for somewhere else and, well, she never moved out.'

'Move in together in haste, sleep on the sofa at leisure,' said Ginny sagely.

'That's pretty much it,' I continued. 'It worked for quite a long time, given my relationship track record, and then it suddenly stopped working. We didn't row. In fact we always got on really, really well. We were – in fact, we still are – good friends. I've got my lap-top with me and I e-mail her almost every other day. I could talk to Elaine about anything, but I suppose when I got to asking myself the big question, Can I see myself with this woman in five years from now?, the answer always came back no, and if you'd asked Elaine she'd have said the same thing.' I looked over at Ginny, unsure if I should confess. 'When we split, everything was fine. Neither of us made a big deal out of it. It was over and we were both happy and then . . .'

'What?'

'I changed my mind at the last minute.'

'But that's good, isn't it?'

'No,' I replied. 'It was bad. Everything was only all right when it was the two of us wanting the split. When one wants in and the other wants out it's just, well, desperate.'

'What made you change your mind?'

I looked at Ginny again, checking to see if I could trust the face sitting opposite me. 'Turning thirty,' I replied. 'I know it's sad. I know it's just another birthday. But in that one moment I just thought, I'm tired of this move-in move-out thing. I'm tired of meeting new people, persuading them to like me, spending time with them then realising I'm just wasting my time again. I don't know, I just felt like she was my last chance. Not a terribly dynamic way of seeing the world, but then again I'm not that dynamic.'

Ginny nodded, as if musing on something. 'You were missing that thing.'

'What thing?'

'You and Elaine were missing that thing. The thing you're supposed to have with the person you're in love with – the flash of lightning, the clap of thunder, whatever it is that makes you think you can't carry on another second without this person by your side.'

'I think you're right. We probably even had it once but didn't know it was there. And now, well, I think we've kind of missed it.' I paused for a moment. 'How about you and Ian?'

'What?' said Ginny, pointing to herself in mock innocence. 'Have I got That Thing with Ian? I don't know. Sometimes I think we've got it and then other times I think I couldn't be further from him if he was half a world away. All I know is that I'm a bit like you, I think half the disappointment in my life comes from the fact that when I imagined myself at thirty, this just wasn't what I had in mind.'

I knew exactly what she meant.

'What did you have in mind?' I asked.

Ginny thought. 'When I was about fourteen, I always thought I'd be a lawyer because I used to watch *LA Law* every Thursday night. I even decided I was going to practise criminal law and defend women who had no one else to turn to. I was also going to drive a black BMW convertible, wear sunglasses in my hair, irrespective of the weather, and have a smart, square-jawed boyfriend with strong muscular thighs. He and I would get married and have two children – a boy and a girl – and I'd look after them half the week and spend the other half convicting nasty men. Now look at the reality. I'm a thirty-year-old art teacher, in a reasonably okay school, with a boyfriend who's sometimes wonderful and who's sometimes an arse, but neither of us has any plans to make the relationship more permanent. I own my own house but I can't put up wallpaper. I have two cats, who, without a doubt, are surrogate children and an ex boyfriend/not ex-boyfriend in my spare room. On top of all of that, I'm an orphan.' She smiled sadly. 'Now, how's that for things turning out just the way you planned them?'

We sat in silence for a few minutes.

'What about you, Matt? How did you think things would be for you when you turned thirty?'

'Careerwise, I think things have turned out pretty much the way I always thought they would. As for that partner-for-life thing, who knows? I used to have a thing for Madonna when I was a kid. I suspect she's taken.'

'Who else did you have in mind?'

I thought very hard about the answer to this question and then said, 'You.'

sixty-five

'Is this a good idea, Matt?'

'You're not sure?'

'No,' said Ginny. 'I'm not sure.'

'What aren't you sure about?'

'About you. Me. Here on this sofa. Your . . . left hand up my cardigan.' I withdrew it. 'Do I need to spell it out?'

'No,' I sighed. 'Spelling it out will only drag on this painful interlude. You had to go and wake up your conscience and rouse mine at the same time. Don't you want to do this?'

'Do you?' asked Ginny, running her fingers through her hair in an agitated fashion.

'Yes,' I replied but my voice lacked conviction.

'Are you sure sure? Or are you just sure?'

'I'm sure! I'm sure! In fact I don't think in the history of mankind – and I do mean *man*kind – that any man has ever been more sure of what I want to do as I am right now.'

Ginny laughed, and we resumed kissing only to stop seconds later.

'What now?' I snapped.

'Now that's a nice tone of voice to use in this context.'

I laughed. 'Sorry.'

'Good. Now, say we did do this thing we're about to do,

how will we be afterwards? What I mean to say – and I know this is forward planning of the most extreme kind and not at all passionate but I don't want us to get all . . . y'know.'

I exhaled heavily and folded my arms defensively. 'Okay, let's not do it.'

'Hang on,' said Ginny, surprised. 'Let's not be hasty. I'm just looking out for our friendship, that's all. I would've thought that's a good thing, surely?' I nodded. She did have a point. 'Now, stop sulking and let's discuss this like the adults we are. Okay? Let's agree right now that we're not going to get all weird about this.'

'Agreed. Anything else?'

Ginny thought for a moment. 'No.'

'Good.'

We resumed kissing until once again she stopped mid snog.

'What about if one of us changes our mind?'

'Are you going to change your mind?' I said shifting positions on the sofa. Ginny's leg was currently resting on mine and sending it to sleep.

'Not necessarily,' she said, 'but you might.'

'Believe me, Ginny, I strongly doubt that I'm going to change my mind . . .'

'So we're agreed?'

'Totally. Anything else?'

'No.'

'Are you sure?'

'Yes.'

'Good.'

'Well there is . . .'

'What?'

'Nothing. Just ignore me.'

'What?'

'It's nothing. Honestly. Come on.' She kissed my neck in an attempt to encourage me but it was too late. Her 'nothing' was 'something' and despite my best attempts my conscience wouldn't let me carry on while there was a 'nothing' that was 'something' lingering in the air.

'What is it?' I pleaded.

Ginny laughed. 'I'm sorry, Matt, I am. This is the last thing, I promise, okay? I just want to make sure that if we do actually do what we're about to do we should make sure this is a one off. As in never again. As in not to be repeated in this or any other lifetime.'

'Why?'

'Other than the fact that I'm in a relationship with Ian and you're getting over your ex-girlfriend and moving to Australia quite soon?'

'Yeah,' I replied. 'Other than that.'

'Well for one thing, it could result in an extended period of repeated procedures which you know would lead to trouble. Because you know what the other word for repeated procedures is, don't you?'

'A nightmare?'

'Bingo,' replied Ginny. 'And, well . . . we're not seventeen any more.'

'Actions do have consequences,' I added.

'Exactly. So maybe we should leave it after all.'

'Yeah,' I said, uncoiling myself from her arms sadly. 'Perhaps we should.' I sighed and kissed her on the cheek. 'No harm done, eh?'

'All we did was kiss,' said Ginny.

'It was a moment of madness,' I added.

'It didn't mean anything. It was just . . . nostalgia.'

'A trip down Memory Lane.'

There was a long pause.

'And it shouldn't happen again.' I added, carefully.

'Yeah,' said Ginny. 'You're right. It should never happen again.'

sixty-six

To: crazedelaine@hotpr.com
From: mattb@c-tec.national.com
Subject: Well spotted

Dear Elaine

Q: What do you get if you take one ex-boyfriend/not ex-boyfriend/ lodger and an ex-girlfriend/not ex-girlfriend, add a few bottles of wine and leave in a confined space? Yes . . . sadly, my life is that predictable. Just as you said, Ginny and I have indeed ended up snogging but fortunately it stopped before we went too far. It's funny, we sort of made a joke out of it but I actually feel really bad about it. I mean, she's got a boyfriend and for the most part they seem happy. We haven't gone into analysis overtime with this yet because we've taken the other option and decided to pretend it didn't happen. I know this is going to sound like a huuuuuuuuuuge excuse but I've been working on the theory that it was just curiosity about the past. We'd been talking about relationships and stuff and, yeah, we had been drinking but the urge to kiss her at that particular moment wasn't about lust or passion so much as I-wonder-what-it-would-be-like-to-kiss-this-person-who-I-haven't-kissed-since-I-was-twenty-four? I don't know what I expected it to be like but it definitely wasn't like those from the past. To be truthful it was more like . . . well . . . comfort food. Mashed potato loaded with forkfuls of butter; an ice cold beer and a cigarette; a fried English breakfast and a cup of lukewarm tea.

Poetic, huh? Anyway, as passionless as it was, it's over, we're back to normal and I for one am glad.
Write soon,

love

Matt xxx

To: **mattb@c-tec.national.com**
From: **crazedelaine@hotpr.com**
Re: **Re: Well spotted**

Dear Matt
Listen very carefully: I TOLD YOU SO!!!!!!!!!!!!!!! It's not even like I had to use my special woman powers to work that one out. It's been written all over your e-mails! Listen, you want my advice? Stay clear. You're leaving next month and, like you say, she seems happy enough with this Ian guy. In spite of myself I actually do understand your weird comfort-food analogy. I guess if you were sleeping on the Sofa from Hell instead of Sara (who, incidentally, is being the biggest pain in the ass with her non-washing of my crockery) and I'd just come in from a crappy day at work (which, by the way, I have), I think I'd want some Matt-Beckford-style comfort food too – something handy, familiar and immediately satisfying!!!! I guess for now I'll just have to rely on the two-day-old cold pizza that's in the refrigerator for my comfort kicks.
Take it easy,

big love

Elaine xxx

PS I know it was a mistake, Matt, but I really do think you shouldn't let it happen again. I know that if it was me in Ian's shoes and I found out I'd be devastated. You know me. Honesty is everything.

sixty-seven

Thursday. Mid-afternoon. Three o'clock to be exact.

The reason I was thinking about the time of day was because it struck me as I walked up the high street to the supermarket, with Charlotte holding my hand, that only two months ago at this time of day I would have been sitting in a design-strategy meeting, or possibly a client briefing, or a client proposal meeting, or a design presentation, or a team-strategy meeting, or a team-design-strategy briefing, the difference between the last two being invisible to the naked eye. And now I was on my way to Safeway, in Birmingham, babysitting a friend's four-year-old, about to do the weekly food shop for my former girlfriend/not girlfriend who was now also my landlady (of sorts).

Life's weird like that.

When we got to the trolley-park, or whatever the place is called where shopping trolleys congregate, Charlotte insisted that she rode in the 'child goes here' section in one of the mammoth shopping trolleys only ever piloted by housewives with Volvo estates. I thought about saying no, because I found that sort of trolley emasculating, but Charlotte and I had already had one altercation that day (I had not allowed her to draw with her mother's lipstick) and I didn't see the reason to have another one just because I didn't want to look girly. So, pushing the huge trolley with a beaming Charlotte at the helm, I made my way through the automatic doors and began shopping in earnest from the list that Ginny had made up for me. If anybody had been watching, which I hope they weren't, I'm sure I must have looked like a paragon of reconstructed masculinity: a twenty-nine-year-old man with tampons in his trolley and a nearly four-year-old in his charge. The fact that neither the child nor the tampons (or, indeed, the woman the tampons were for) was mine only served to make me more self-conscious.

Needless to say, I bumped into yet more people I used to go to school with: Adam Heller (then, boy most likely to become a drug dealer; now, a fully qualified dentist); Lionel Orton, whose sister Janine was in my year (then, the boy most likely to be befriended by older boys who wanted to go out with his sister; now, a library assistant at the university); and Faye Jones (then, the girl most likely to become a hairdresser; now, a hairdresser). With each encounter, even if they didn't enquire, I felt compelled to explain that neither Charlotte nor the tampons were mine, and they all gave me an oh-yeah-pull-the-other-one look of disbelief. What was I afraid of? I asked myself. Word getting around the ex-King's Heath Comprehensive grapevine that Matt Beckford was a house-husband? Am I really that petty? Just as my subconscious came back with the answer 'Yes! You are that petty!' I bumped into Ian, who was standing in the booze aisle reading the label on a bottle of red wine.

'All right?' I called out. 'How are you, mate?'

'Matt . . .' said Ian, distractedly.

'I would've thought a man like you would've had one of the sportier numbers,' I said, indicating his large trolley.

'What?' he said, not quite getting it.

'You know,' I continued, 'one of those smaller, more stylish shopping trolleys. The one's designed for trendy non-cohabiting people like you. Just big enough to carry a couple of packets of fresh pasta, some pesto sauce and a copy of the *Guardian*.'

He laughed nervously and looked around him. 'Oh, right, yeah. I get you.'

I looked into his trolley surreptitiously. Ian's inner child was obviously incredibly hungry because I spied eight packets of pickled onion Monster Munch, three packets of Coco-Pops and a large bottle of lemonade among the usual assembly of fresh fruit and vegetables. I thought about letting it go – I knew there was nothing more embarrassing than people making small-talk about your supermarket shopping choices – but I couldn't.

'Very nutritious,' I commented heartily, waving at his trolley. 'I haven't had a packet of Monster Munch in years. Gershwin used to eat them in class all the time at school. The moment he opened the packet he stank the place out.'

'Er . . . yes,' he mumbled. 'I . . . er . . .'

Ian didn't have a chance to finish his sentence because he was interrupted by a young woman brandishing two bottles of white wine. 'Which do you think? The Hungarian we had last time or this Italian number with fifty pence knocked off?'

'I don't mind,' he said blankly.

She sighed heavily. 'You would say that.' She looked at me, then at him, then looked embarrassed. 'Oh, I'm so sorry, Ian, you were in the middle of a conversation.'

'Er . . . yeah,' said Ian.

She gave me a little wave. 'Hello,' she said cheerily. 'I don't think we've met before, have we?'

'Hi,' I said, wishing for all the world that there was another supermarket in King's Heath that was not quite so popular with people I knew. I shook her hand. 'I'm Matt Beckford.'

'I'm Susanna, Ian's other half.'

Ian looked at me guiltily, like a small boy caught doing something naughty by his parents. Then his face flashed sheer panic but returned to normal just as Susanna turned to look at him for an introduction. 'Matt's a friend of a friend at one of the schools I've worked at,' he explained. 'We met a while ago when I went for a drink after work.'

'Yeah, that's right,' I said absentmindedly, 'in the pub after work—'

I didn't finish my sentence as the final surprise of this travesty interrupted. 'Daddy,' yelled a small child, holding an older woman's hand, 'Jammy Dodgers or chocolate-chip cookies?'

'Neither,' he called. 'We don't want your teeth to fall out, now, do we? Go and put them back, there's a good boy.'

'We've just bumped into a friend of Ian's,' said Susanna to the older woman, who, at a guess, was her mother. 'This is Matt Beckford.'

'Hello,' she said. 'Can't stop. I've got to catch a three-year-old grandson with biscuits on his mind.'

Susanna picked up the conversation. 'I'm quite sure you've never mentioned Matt to me before,' she said, then cupped her hand beside her mouth and said to me in a stage-whisper, 'Ian doesn't tell me anything. I'm always the last to find out anything new. What is it about men that they find communication so difficult?'

I laughed, maybe a little too loudly because I was now well beyond nervous and really didn't know what to do with myself. I laughed so hard that Ian had to join in to stop me looking like an idiot. Susanna just stood there, looking at the two of us, clearly aware that her joke hadn't been that funny.

'Is this your little girl?' she said, smiling at Charlotte. 'Hello, sweetheart.'

Charlotte looked at her blankly, chewed her lip then looked at me.

'She's a bit quiet,' I explained, 'but no, she's not mine, and neither are these tampons.'

'Tampons?' said Susanna.

Damn. She hadn't noticed.

'Now, there's a real man,' she said. 'Buys his partner's tampons. Ian would have a heart-attack if I sent him out for some.'

'They're not my partner's,' I explained – but that sounded worse, as if I was about to declare they were mine. 'They're Ginny my housemate's.'

'Ginny who Ian used to work with?'

My tongue nearly seized up. 'Er . . . yes.'

'I didn't realise *she* was the friend, Ian. You should've said. Ginny's lovely. I've only met her a few times when Ian was working at King's Heath Comp. She was really nice. It was so sad for her when her mother died. I remember Ian telling me about it. She was distraught.'

'I know,' I said.

'Well,' said Susanna, trying to lighten the tone, 'you and Ginny should come round for dinner sometime. I'd love to see her again.'

'Mmmm, yeah,' I said. 'That'd be great, but I know she's up to her eyeballs in work at the moment so . . .'

'I know what you mean. Well, anyway, just get her to give Ian a call when she's come through the other side.'

'I will,' I said, then looked at my watch. 'Will you look at the time? I really do have to be getting off.'

'Yeah, of course,' said Ian. 'It was good to see you again, Matt.'

'Yeah,' I said. 'It was good to see you.' I stopped and looked at Susanna. 'And it was nice to meet you too.' I smiled. 'See you soon.'

'And don't forget to give us a call,' said Susanna.

'Of course,' I replied, relieved to be out of the madness. 'I'll get Ginny to ring you soon,' and then I did that stupid thumb-pointing-up-little-finger-pointing-down international sign language for 'I'll call you and I'm not just saying that,' and left.

sixty-eight

It was half past five by the time I'd dropped Charlotte at home and reached Ginny's. I shouted for her the second I came through the front door: I'd made up my mind to tell her. Knowing her as well as I did I knew she'd be devastated and would more than likely react by shooting the messenger and then shouting a stream of abuse in the general direction of the corpse. But I knew I had no other option. There was no way I was going to contemplate keeping this to myself because I'd seen it happen to people before and knew that there was nothing more soul-destroying than dealing with the shock coupled with the fact that all your friends knew before you did.

I really missed Elaine – she was good at handling extremes of emotion in people and I felt like I was bound to say the wrong thing, which would upset Ginny even more. I didn't have any idea how I was going to tell her. What was the etiquette here? Was I supposed to ask her how her day had been then slip in a quick 'Oh, and by the way your boyfriend's got a wife and kids.' Or was I supposed to go for the dramatic soap-opera option of handing her a stiff drink and insisting she sit down before delivering the punchline? Then, of course, there was the good-news bad-news option.

'First the good news: not long until pay-day, eh? Now the bad news: your boyfriend's a lying toss-bag.'

This wasn't going to be easy.

There was no sign of Ginny but I could hear music coming from her CD player upstairs and the sound of running water emanating from the bathroom. She was listening to Mahler's third symphony and had it turned up incredibly loud. This, combined with a bath so early in the evening, meant she was trying to cancel out the effects of a really bad day at work.

'Hello?' I yelled up the stairs, trying to make myself heard above the music. 'Ginny!'

'I'm in the bath!' came a muffled voice from behind the bathroom door. 'Leave me alone until I'm human!'

'I was just . . .' I tried to work out what to say next. 'I was just making sure you were all right.'

'I'm fine,' she yelled back. 'Long, terrible, torturous day. I'll tell you about it later.'

I left her to it and dropped off the shopping in the kitchen. As I walked through the living room for the second time it occurred to me to check the answerphone in case Ian had called. Sure enough there was a message for her from an agitated Ian asking her to call him urgently on his mobile. He was evidently trying to make sure that he got in his side of the story before I presented mine. I erased the message, put away the shopping, made two mugs of tea and headed upstairs. Ginny was out of the bath and was now in her bedroom drying her hair.

I knocked on her bedroom door. 'Are you decent?'

'As I'll ever be,' she said. 'Come in.'

I pushed open the door with my shoulder. Ginny was sitting on the edge of her bed in her dressing-gown, hair-dryer in hand. 'What can I do for you, Mr Beckford?'

'Cup of tea for you, m'lady,' I said. 'No sugar. No milk. Not too strong. Not too weak.'

'Just how I like it,' she said, then looked puzzled. 'What's this in aid of?'

'Nothing,' I told her. 'It's just a cup of tea.' I paused. 'Maybe it's in aid of having such a nice landlady.'

Ginny narrowed her eyes at me. 'You want to borrow some money, don't you?'

'No,' I replied. 'Although if you're giving it away, I'll have some. No, I was just thinking how nice it is when someone does stuff like this. I can stop if you like and be a miserable arse like your good self, if you want.'

Ginny laughed. 'No, I like this considerate-Matt persona. Is he staying for long?'

'Dunno. I'm not sure how much mileage there is in being nice.' I took a sip of my tea.

'I don't know how Elaine ever let you out of her grip, you know.'

I smiled. 'Did the phone ring while you were in the bath?'

'No,' said Ginny, rubbing her head with a towel. She stopped and thought again. 'Actually, come to think of it, yeah, it did. I was so exhausted that there was no way I was getting out to answer it. Was it something important?'

'No,' I lied. I just wanted to check whether she'd heard from Ian. 'It was just a message for me. My parents. I just wondered what time they'd called. No one else phoned?'

'Not to my knowledge,' she said. 'Anyway, enough of telephone messages. Ask me how my day was.'

'How was it?'

'The worst. Everything that could go wrong did go wrong.' She sighed heavily. 'I'm thinking about running away.'

'Where to?'

'Somewhere where life is easier.'

'Somewhere with a beach, maybe?'

'Definitely. Somewhere in the Caribbean. I could sit on a beach all day and teach art to the local kids.'

'You could make collages using shells and seaweed,' I suggested.

'Excellent.' She smiled. 'I'd like that. Are you going to come with me?'

'To your Caribbean island? What for?'

Ginny laughed. 'Even in Paradise you need your mates with you.'

'Does that mean we've got to take Gershwin too?'

'It'd be mean not to.'

We laughed again and there was a moment's silence when I knew I should have told her. But I didn't. Or, rather, I couldn't. 'What are you up to tonight?' I asked.

'Ian's busy as usual. How about you?'

'Nothing much.'

She looked at me thoughtfully. 'You've got the I-want-to-go-back-to-America blues again, haven't you? I can tell.'

I pulled a face, signalling that this was still something of a sore point. 'Are you hungry?' I asked.

'Is that an offer to cook?'

'It might be,' I said. 'What do you fancy?'

'Comfort food,' she said.

'You want comfort food?' I repeated.

Ginny looked puzzled. 'That's not such a strange request, Matt, really. What I'd love right now would be potato products like frozen waffles or hash brown or Alphabites, beans and a fried egg. With a dash of tomato ketchup.'

'That's all?'

'And someone to slob out in front of the TV with for the rest of the evening so that I don't feel alone in loserdom.'

'Okay,' I said, relieved. 'I'll sort out your potato products and baked beans and a fried egg.'

'What about the someone to watch TV with?'
'Will I do?'
'Definitely.'
'And can we play *ER live!* again?'
'Of course.'

sixty-nine

It was now eleven thirty in the evening. Ginny and I had eaten our stodgy dinner. We'd watched endless crap TV. Played *ER live!* And I still hadn't got round to telling her what I knew. So it wasn't until she yawned and said, 'Right, I'm off to bed,' that I decided to speak.

'I saw Ian in Safeway this afternoon.'

'You see everyone in Safeway,' said Ginny. 'Did you say hello?'

'He was with a woman,' I replied.

There was a barely detectable pause and then she bounced back, 'Don't tell me Ian's got his own supermarket stalker,' and laughed. But by then it was too late. As brief as the pause had been it made everything click into place.

'You already know, don't you?'

'About Ian being in the supermarket?' she bluffed.

I looked into her eyes and I could see I was right. 'You already know he's married, don't you?'

'I've always known,' she said, then bit her lip as tears filled her eyes.

I put my arms around her and gave her a hug. Neither of us said another word until her tears had subsided. When they eventually did, I stood up and got both our coats from the hallway.

'Let's go,' I said, handing her her denim jacket.

'Where to?'

I smiled, took her hand and kissed the top of her head. 'We're running away.'

seventy

'Parks are weird at night,' said Ginny, 'but weird in a good kind of way.'

'I know what you mean,' I replied. 'It's like the whole place is here just for us.'

As if on autopilot we'd walked from Ginny's house to King's Heath park, which, although it was past midnight, was still inviting. As soon as we got there Ginny said, 'Let's go to our bench,' and I thought that was a good idea. The bench was an old wooden one overlooking the fountain in the centre of the park. Back when we were exam-stressed teenagers the seven of us had met up there for a break between revision. It was hard to believe it was still here after all this time. I would have bet good money on vandals having had their evil way with it a long time ago, but although it had suffered the ravages of schoolkids armed with marker pens and knives, it hadn't suffered too badly.

'So are you going to tell me how all this happened?' I asked, after a few moments had passed. 'You don't have to if you don't want to. We can just sit here if you like. But if you do want to talk then, well, I can listen.'

She was quiet for quite a long time. All the time we had been walking, mainly in silence, I'd been thinking about

Ginny's situation and how it must be affecting her. It was obvious that she had probably been holding back the tears since they'd had first begun the relationship.

'It's like I said,' she replied numbly. 'It's all my fault.'

'What do you mean?' I asked.

'It's the way I am. I've got friends who, when they see a good-looking bloke, think, I'll have some of that! I always feel like a fake when I join in because you could put a naked, greased-up male go-go dancer in front of me and, frankly, I'd be more interested in whether he could make a decent cup of tea. It's my fault I'm like this. I don't find strangers attractive. Not at all. They do nothing for me. If I don't know anything about a guy I'm not interested.' She stopped and glanced at me. I met her eyes briefly and then she looked away. 'Anyway, I'd been single for a while. I think I just got tired of putting all that energy into relationships when I knew right from the start that they weren't going anywhere. So I focused on my friends and I focused on work and I focused on Mum . . .'

'And then?'

She looked up at me again. 'And then Ian started supply teaching at King's Heath.'

'In the geography department?'

'You know that,' she replied, and gave me a half-smile acknowledging that I was teasing her. 'I couldn't stand him at first. I'd have a conversation with him and would come away feeling like he was playing games with me. I can't explain it, really. But whether it was out of curiosity or persistence, he grew on me and we started going for drinks after work. Then we built up a real friendship – a solid friendship. A friendship that continued after he moved to a different school. He was a really good friend to me when Mum died. I was finding it hard to cope with things, and he always seemed to be there at the right time to pick up the pieces. He sort of made himself indispensable – filling in all the gaps in my life. Nothing had happened between us at that point, but I knew I was falling in love with him. Then, one evening last summer, we were round at mine sitting in the garden, and the sun was going down and I looked at him and at that moment I knew he was it – and, well, here we are now.'

'When did you find out he was married?'

Her voice became smaller, quieter. 'He told me that night. I know this is going to sound pathetic but he told me right after the first kiss.'

'And?'

'And by then it was too late.'

'What do you mean too late?'

'I'd fallen in love,' she replied unsteadily.

I put my arms round her. 'It's all right,' I said, holding her tightly. 'It's all right.'

'It's not all right,' she said, between sobs. 'It's not all right at all. I know I sound really flippant about all this but I'm not. I can't begin to tell you how much this hurts. I've tried to end it a million times but I can't. I love him. It's so stupid. It's so pointless.' She stopped and allowed herself the benefit of a really good cry. 'I hate how this makes me feel. I feel like a right bitch and I'm not. I'm not. *I* don't do these kinds of things. That's why I haven't told anyone else. The only reason I even introduced him as my boyfriend when you and I bumped into each other on Gershwin's birthday was because I thought I wouldn't see you again after that night. I can't stand to have people think of me like that. I can't stand to have *you* think of me like that.'

'It's okay,' I said. 'I don't think of you like that at all, I promise.'

'Why am I doing this? He's got a kid, you know – a little boy.'

'I take it his wife – Susanna – doesn't know?'

She shook her head. 'No. I've met her – which is worse. Ian used to tell her he was working with me on a project for the lower school as an excuse for us to meet. Then one day she suggested that he invite me round for dinner and Ian couldn't say no without it looking suspicious. It was horrible, one of the worst nights of my life.'

'So where does Ian tell her he is when he's with you?'

'Out with his mates, playing five-a-side, working on his Ph.D. at the library. You name it – he's probably used the excuse.'

'Is he going to leave her?'

'No. He made that clear from the start. He says he loves her in his own way, and he loves his little boy, Jake, more than anything. He's not going to mess that up for me, no matter how much he loves me.'

'And he does love you?' I didn't want to ask this question, but I needed to be sure.

'Yeah, he does,' she said. 'When I've tried to end it before he's been in tears trying to get me to stay with him.' She paused. 'It's funny, but I only told him about you and me being not-quite-but-nearly-exes last week and I was surprised. He was actually jealous, even though it was years ago.'

We carried on talking for the next quarter of an hour or so. I didn't say much, just the odd comment here and there, but she must have realised that I was being quiet so she asked me the one question I really didn't want to answer.

'What do you think I should do?'

When friends ask that question they never want you to tell them what *you* think they should do, they want you to tell them that the decision they've already made is the right one. It's only natural. It'd be exactly the same for me. But if I'd learned anything from the time I'd been with Elaine it was this: what you *want* to hear is rarely, if ever, what's good for you. That's why if I ever asked Elaine that question she'd always give me her honest opinion, even if it hurt. It was one of the qualities I most admired about her.

'You know you've got to stop seeing him, don't you?' I said.

'It's not that simple,' she replied.

'I know,' I conceded. 'Nothing is any more.' A broad smile spread across my face as a thought entered my head.

'What?'

'I'll sound insane.'

'What's new?'

'Okay,' I began. 'I was just thinking that it's like somewhere between the ages of eighteen and thirty you enter the soap-opera era.'

'You're rambling, Matt,' said Ginny. 'You've lost me.'

'Life becomes a soap opera, a never-ending stream of twists, turns and unbelievable scenarios. You know how it is: when you're young life is just so much more obvious. Your little corner of the world is so free of ups and downs that you practically have to invent stuff to worry about. That's why teenagers are so moody – it's got nothing to do with raging hormones, and everything to do with the fact that there's nothing going on in their lives. I look at you, me and Gershwin back then and everything was so simple. Yet here we are, years later and look at us. Gershwin's married with a kid and bored, you're having an affair with a married man, and I'm trying to work out if my ex-girlfriend in the States is the one for me. That's what I mean by being in a soap opera.'

'I've got a friend back in Brighton,' said Ginny, 'who doesn't know that his girlfriend is sleeping with his best mate.'

'You see what I mean?' I said. 'That could be a plot from either *The Bold and The Beautiful* or *Brookside*.' I thought for a moment. 'How about this? Just before I left New York some friends of Elaine's found out that they won't be able to have kids even with IVF treatment.'

'I think I saw something similar on *Home and Away* only last week,' said Ginny, visibly perking up. 'Okay, here's another one. A friend of mine living in Keele found out last year that her mum had had an affair twenty-eight years ago and her dad isn't her real dad.'

'That's a classic *Dallas* episode,' I said, and Ginny laughed and seemed like her old self for a moment. 'Now do you see what I'm saying?' I continued. 'These are all soap-opera staples: the childless couples, the betrayals of best friends, the he's-not-your-real-dad-this-man-is scenario and they're happening to real people. Now tell me, how did this happen?'

'I don't want my life to be *EastEnders*,' said Ginny quietly. 'I just want everything to be normal. I want to be normal.' She pulled herself closer to me.

'Me too,' I said, as I wrapped my arms around her again. 'Maybe we should get some better scriptwriters.'

Half an hour later we were back at the house, wandering in and out of the bathroom doing our regular getting-ready-for-bed routine.

'Are you going to be okay?' I asked, as Ginny came out of the bathroom in her dressing-gown.

'Yeah, I'll be fine,' she said, and then leant forward to kiss me. Her breath smelt of toothpaste. 'Thanks for looking after me.'

'Sleep well. And I'll see you in the morning.'

Ginny was half-way towards her bedroom when she stopped and turned round. 'Matt?'

'What?'

'Nothing.'

'What?' I repeated.

'Nothing.'

'Do you want to stand here on the landing all night?'

She smiled. 'It's nothing. I was just going to ramble, really. I know you're going to think this is a load of New Age nonsense but I believe that things happen for a reason. I think you're back here at home for a reason. I think that you, me and Gershwin are back together to help each other. I really do. I know things look bleak for both of us at the moment but I honestly believe that we'll be okay, because . . . well, when you've got your mates in your corner shouting for you, anything's possible.'

seventy-one

To: crazedelaine@hotpr.com
From: mattb@c-tec.national.com
Subject: Life, eh?

Dear Elaine

Life is getting really weird round here. I discovered last night that Ginny's perfect boyfriend is married. With a kid. She hadn't told anyone at all. I only found out because I bumped into him and his wife by accident. I could just tell from talking to Ginny that, deep inside, she wants to get out of the relationship. She even said that she's accepted that he's never going to leave his wife. She knows there's no future in it. She never gets to see him and yet she won't or rather can't let go. I'm not one to get on my moral high horse (or even a moral low pony if there's one going spare) but this has got to be wrong, surely. Or am I just being an old fart? The worst is that I know he's fine in all this. He gets everything and Ginny gets nothing. I have considered going round to have a 'talk' with him but Ian's quite a big bloke so I don't fancy my chances much. I did decide, however, that if I were in the Mafia I'd have a contract put out on him and get someone to – as they say in gangster parlance – 'put a cap in his ass'. I think it's only fair. I'm off to watch *Godfather II* as I'm now in the mood. Let me know how NYC life is, dudette.

love

Matt xxx

To: mattb@c-tec.national.com
From: crazedelaine@hotpr.com
Subject: The world is full of married men!!!

Dear Matt

I'm sorry to hear about the situation Ginny has got into. You remember Melissa, my friend from college? You always said there was something weird about her and I said it's because she over-plucks her eyebrows and you said that's why she always looks so surprised. Well, anyway, she was seeing this guy Danny, and he was married too. He completely broke her heart as expected. But the thing about it was that she did it all over again a few years later and that ended badly too. Eventually her mom paid for a therapist for her because she said it would be cheaper than all the long-distance calls she had to make every time Melissa fell apart. Anyway, to cut a long story into a snappy soundbite, the therapist told her she was addicted to bad relationships. When she told me I pretty much agreed straight away because in college she was like a magnet for every loser in town. Knowing this hasn't done her any good, though. I talked to her only last week. She's living with a guy who has cheated on her twice and she's forgiven him both times. I'm not saying it's her fault. But it is sad. On a lighter note, you'll be pleased to know I got a tattoo of the Japanese symbol for love done at the top of my ass. Don't ask me why because I couldn't tell you. It just seemed like the right thing to do.

Take it easy,

Elaine xxx

PS This thing with your friend. I know you want to fix it because that's the kind of guy you are. But you can't fix everything. So just try being there for her. If she's half the person you say she is she'll sort it out herself.

seventy-two

To: crazedelaine@hotpr.com
From: mattb@c-tec.national.com
Subject: Tattooed ladies

Dear Elaine

You scare me sometimes. I take it for granted that you have the scattiest brain on the planet and then you come out with Oprah-sized nuggets of wisdom like that. Ginny said that when you've got your mates shouting for you in your corner anything's possible. She might've been a bit optimistic about what the power of friends can do – needless to say Ian's still in the picture – but she's right to assume that at least friends do have a power of some description. The time I've spent with Ginny and Gershwin since I've been back home has been the best thing in the world for me. I don't mean that as a slur against you – I'm just trying to say that these people are my history. So I'm going to take your advice – I'm not going to fix!!! But I am going to sort out a surprise for Ginny. Just to let her know that . . . well . . . I'm on her side.

Love

Matt xxx

PS I always tried to fix things with you. Didn't I?

To: mattb@c-tec.national.com
From: crazedelaine@hotpr.com
Subject: You

Dear Matt

   A surprise is always a great idea. She'll love it.

love

Elaine xxx

PS Yes you did try to fix things but always for the right reasons.

Month Three

Date: March 1st
Days left until thirtieth birthday: 31
State of mind: Reasonably okay.
(All things considered)

seventy-three

It was a quarter to nine on the following Friday evening, and Ginny and I were standing in her living room discussing her clothing. She had been travelling to and from her room, showing me various combinations of her wardrobe for over half an hour.

'What do you think of this one?' she asked.

'Brilliant,' I said, encouragingly, of a long-sleeved black top and black trousers.

'Better or worse than the last one?'

I couldn't remember the last one. 'Better,' I pronounced shamelessly.

'Hmmm,' said Ginny thoughtfully. 'So it's a casual place that we're going to?'

'You could say that.'

She looked me up and down. I was wearing my dark blue combat trousers, a dark blue hooded top and black trainers. 'You're dressed casually.'

'Am I?' I said, unhelpfully.

'You know you are,' she said, squinting at me menacingly. She looked me up and down once again. 'I think this'll be okay,' she mused, '*if* where we're going is casual.'

'Fine, then. That's sorted. We're ready to go.'

'I'll just be a minute,' she said, then disappeared back upstairs to her bedroom only to reappear at the living-room door five minutes later wearing a sheer black shirt and a pair of jeans. 'What about this?'

'I can't believe you've changed again.'

She ignored me. 'Better or worse than the one before?'

'Better,' I enthused.

She looked down at her naked feet. 'Trainers or shoes?'

'Shoes,' I replied. She flashed me an immediate look of disdain. 'No, trainers definitely.'

She disappeared once more and, as I expected, returned minutes later wearing another different outfit: a long-sleeved white cotton top, oatmeal-coloured (never let it be said I hadn't learnt anything of the female colour spectrum from Elaine) wide-legged trousers and her Birkenstocks.

'Good choice,' I said, with as much enthusiasm as I could muster, which by now wasn't much.

'Thanks,' she said. 'Now all I've got to work out is whether I need a jacket.' She twirled around in front of me. 'Jacket or no jacket?'

'Jacket,' I replied.

'But we're getting a taxi, aren't we, so I could go without the jacket? That is, unless where we're going is outside.'

'It's inside,' I said patiently. 'So no jacket.'

Ginny's forehead was creased with concentration. I could see that she was wavering. 'You're right, I don't need a jacket.'

'Great! Now we're all done.'

'But don't you think the jacket goes with the Birkenstocks? I think the Birkenstocks *need* the jacket.' She said it as though her footwear was going to suffer from severe depression without the jacket.

'No.'

'I think you're right. Has anyone ever told you that you'd make a good woman?'

'Not this week.'

'Well, they should've,' she said, as she walked back into the hallway. 'Every woman should have one of you.'

seventy-four

The plan for the evening had been quite straightforward until Ginny got involved. All I had to do was get her to an Indian restaurant in nearby Sparkbrook called King of the Baltis for nine thirty. The only problem was that by the time we arrived, having had to rush back to her house when she decided that she wanted her jacket after all, it was a quarter to ten and we were late.

'So this is where we're going,' said Ginny, as the taxi dropped us off at the door to the restaurant. 'For a curry. Why the secrecy for a simple curry?'

I opened the door for her. 'You'll see.'

She smiled. 'You're really enjoying keeping me in the dark, aren't you? You think it makes you appear mysterious, like you're some sort of James Bond figure. Well—' She stopped mid-sentence as the table reserved for 'the Beckford party of six', which so far seated Bev, Pete, Katrina, Gershwin, stood and cheered at our entrance. 'I don't know what to say,' she said, beaming. 'This is so fantastic, Matt. It's been so long since we've all been back together like this – it's amazing. Bev, Pete and Katrina all here. And you organised it.'

I shrugged dismissively. 'It's like you said,' I began, as I recalled the words of our conversation little over a week ago.

'"When you've got your mates shouting for you in your corner, anything's possible." I just wanted you to know that you don't need someone like Ian, not when you've got people around you who . . .' I was overwhelmed by self-consciousness. It all sounded far too cheesy.

'People who what?' she prompted, when it became clear I wasn't going to finish my sentence.

'Nothing.'

'Nothing?' She studied me thoughtfully, then standing on tiptoe she whispered in my ear, 'Liar,' and kissed me. Unlike our previous kiss this had little to do with curiosity or comfort and more to do with passion. Most importantly, it was a kiss of the moment, so when the moment passed, and we noticed that everyone at the table was looking at us, the kiss passed with it and all that was left was the pleasant feeling that it might happen again soon. Then two waiters brought over a couple of bottles of champagne, popped them open and began pouring.

Ginny nudged me. 'Go on, Matt, say something – make a toast.'

'No, thanks,' I said. 'I'm crap at that sort of thing. Why don't you? It's your night, after all.'

'I couldn't,' she said. 'I'm crap at these things too. But it would mean a lot if you did.'

'Come on,' yelled Gershwin. 'One of you make a toast before this stuff goes flat, will you?'

'To absent friends,' I said, raising my glass. 'And for old friends right here, right now.'

The next hour sped by as we caught up with each other's news. I chatted to Bev for ages. It was weird seeing her in person after having spoken to her on the phone. When I'd pictured her at the other end of the line I'd imagined her still in the Goth-style clothes of her teenage years, but her old black uniform had metamorphosed into a beaded, tie-dyed hippie style. Like most of us she, too, had put on a little weight, but she was still pretty and still wore her trademark sardonic smile. Best of all, her manner was unchanged: in a world in which everyone I knew of around thirty was giving up everything that was bad for them, it was heartening to watch her chain-smoke Silk Cut Ultras as if her life depended on it. Katrina, on the other hand, had changed immensely: in our youth she had been attractive but now she was stunning, so much so that Pete had barely taken his eyes off her all evening. Somehow, in the intervening years, her dark brown eyes had become even more beguiling, her manner more flirtatious and self-deprecating, and her dress sense more sophisticated. Of us all she seemed the most adult, the one who had grown best into her new thirtysomething skin.

During my conversation with Katrina, I disappeared to the toilet, and when I returned she was talking to Pete. I looked round at the rest of the table: Ginny was talking with Gershwin and Bev, so I was out of the conversational loop. Here were six people, who, up to a few months ago, had all but forgotten each other. And now we were together again. Well, nearly. Although no one had talked about Elliot's death directly it was clear to me that we all felt his absence. That there were only six of us made the familiar seem unfamiliar, unbalanced.

However, the evening went extremely well. I knew it was going to be a good one because usually when I was in a restaurant I always saw other tables who seemed to be having a better time than anyone else. For the first time in my life the 'good-time table' was the one that I was at. I had worried that maybe the whole weekend would be a disaster. What if we didn't like each other? What if we'd never really liked each other? What if we ran out of things to say? But it was clear from the way everyone acted that we were still comfortable in each other's company. The stories from way back confirmed that the good times had always been good times. And, like I said, the fact that we were the loudest table in the place proved that we still had plenty to talk about.

seventy-five

It was now a quarter past eleven. We'd all eaten, had drunk several bottles of wine between us and we were in that shouty confident mood that large groups get into at that time of the night. I was listening to Bev who was telling me how she had met her husband when Katrina yelled, 'Matt!'

'What?' I bellowed back.

'Pete and I want to do the big Where-are-they-now conversation.'

We used to have the where-are-they-now conversation every Christmas Eve in the Kings Arms back in the days when everyone came home for the festive season. It was just the seven of us, sitting round the table pooling news about people we knew from school.

'Oh, do we have to do this?' said Ginny, in a whiny voice. She looked over at me as if I was the leader of this disjointed rabble. 'I always think it's tempting fate somehow,' she continued. 'Like, it means that somewhere in the world there's a different group of ex-King's Heath Comprehensive people sitting round the table saying, "Oooh, you know who my mum saw recently? Ginny Pascoe! Dresses like a bag-lady, teaches at our old school and has Matt Beckford stashed away in a spare room!" It's too horrible for words. I don't want the

270

world knowing I'm a loser. I'd much prefer to keep that sort of information to myself.'

'Ginny's got a point,' I admitted. 'I'd hate it if someone out there was saying, "Oh, I spotted Matt Beckford in Safeway buying tampons."' Everyone turned to get a better look at me. 'It's a long story,' I explained. 'My suggestion is that if we're going to do this, let's just keep to the unusual – the I-never-thought-*they*'d-be-doing-that-in-a-million-years ones.'

'Okay,' said Katrina. 'I'll go first because I've got a brilliant one. I was at a club in East London about a year and a half ago with an ex of mine and guess who was working the door as a bouncer?'

'Angela Murphy!' screamed Bev, dementedly. Back in our schooldays Angela Murphy was probably *the* girl most likely to end up as a bouncer, a wrestler or a shot-putter.

'Colin Birch!' said Katrina. Colin Birch was probably the weediest kid at our school. It was Andrew Sasky's (then, our year's obligatory bully/psychopath) favourite game to remove Colin's trousers and hide them. While some of us had felt sorry for Colin, I suspect that the majority were glad he existed: he kept Andrew Sasky entertained so prevented him from torturing the rest of us.

'He was absolutely huge,' continued Katrina. 'A bit sexy too.'

'Colin Birch, sexy?' said Pete disbelievingly.

'I must admit,' said Ginny, 'I find that a little hard to believe.'

'He was,' protested Katrina. 'Really strong-looking broad shoulders.'

'Did you say hello?' asked Gershwin, in a way that made me think he was fishing for something.

'Nah,' said Katrina, running her fingers through her hair. 'He looked like he was too busy . . .'

Gershwin burst out laughing. 'You lie,' he said, pointing at

Katrina. 'I reckon you asked him out or flirted with him or something, and he blew you out!'

'Oh, the shame of it,' said Katrina, laughing. 'How did you know?'

'After all these years, Kat,' said Gershwin, 'you still play with your hair when you lie!'

'I've got a better one than Colin Birch,' said Pete. 'I'm on the train going down to my mum's with my ex and my little boy for the weekend when I look up and guess who's sitting in the seat across from us?'

'Where did they get on?' asked Gershwin.

'What do you mean where did they get on?' said Pete. 'What does that matter?'

'It might be a clue,' said Gershwin.

'Right,' said Pete. 'This *person* got on at Wolverhampton.'

I couldn't think of anyone we went to school with who had a Wolverhampton connection. 'Dunno,' I said eventually, on behalf of all the bemused faces around the table.

'David Coote!' said Katrina.

David Coote was the poshest kid at our school (his dad owned Coote Wine cabins – a chain of high-street off-licences) and the person least likely to have *heard* of Wolverhampton, let alone to have been there.

'I've always wondered what happened to him,' said Bev. 'I got off with him at Ruth Hennassey's sixteenth. He was quite dishy as I remember.'

'Dishy?' said Ginny indignantly. 'David Coote? *Never!* Didn't you hear the rumour about him? The one about his third nipple?'

'David Coote did not have a third nipple,' I protested.

'And do you know that for a fact?' asked Ginny.

'Bev, help me out here,' I said, in exasperation. 'David Coote didn't have a third nipple, did he?'

'How should I know?' said Bev. 'I only snogged him for about ten minutes, during which time he attempted to give me a love-bite and then was violently sick. Before you say anything, it had nothing to do with me and everything to do with the bottle of Coke he brought with him.'

'Coke made him throw up?' asked Katrina, puzzled.

'The Coke didn't make him throw up,' replied Bev, smirking. 'But the half bottle of his dad's whisky might've had something to do with it.'

'Er . . . hello?' called Pete. 'I think you'll find that I was talking. Anyway as I was saying before I was so rudely interrupted, there I am on the train and opposite me is . . . Faye Chambers!'

There was a long silence as we all looked at one another trying to recall the name.

'Short girl with blonde hair?' suggested Katrina. 'Used to hang about with Liz Maher?'

'You're thinking of Annette Roloson,' said Bev. 'Incidentally, I bumped into Nick Hall – red-faced kid who used to eat his sandwiches in class – at a petrol station just outside Sheffield. Anyway, his sister went to university with Annette and she's apparently a nurse or a doctor – or a doctor's receptionist. Something to do with sick people . . . or animals.' She paused, embarrassed to have everyone's attention for such a terrible story. 'Over to you, Pete.'

'Thanks,' he said tersely. 'Faye Chambers was the girl in our year who was really good at maths – remember she won the maths prize three years in a row?'

'I thought that was Jamie Manning,' I said, deliberately trying to wind him up.

'Watch yourself, Beckford,' warned Pete. 'Remember I've got a black belt in wedgies.'

At the mere mention of 'wedgies' all the men around

the table winced as we recalled Pete's schoolboy knack of grabbing the elasticated waistband of your underpants then yanking them up so sharply that you'd be guaranteed to be picking Y-front out of your bum crack for anything up to an hour afterwards.

'You have my total attention, Pete,' I said, laughing.

Pete recommenced his tale. 'Faye had dark brown hair, was painfully skinny and didn't really have any friends.'

'No-mate-stick girl!' said Ginny, Katrina and Bev, in unison.

'It's chilling how cruel prepubescent girls can be,' commented Gershwin.

'We didn't call her that,' said Ginny, in the girls' defence. 'Shelley Heath did.'

'Shelley Heath,' said Katrina. 'Now she really was an evil piece of work . . . Do you know that she once bit my arm because—'

'Tell us your story, Pete,' interrupted Ginny, 'before you blow a fuse or something. What's Faye doing now, then?'

'*Glamour* modelling,' said Pete smugly.

'No!' said Bev.

'Never!' said Ginny.

'Get *out* of here!' said Katrina.

'You're joking!' said Gershwin.

When it came to my turn to let out an exclamation I couldn't because I was lost for words.

'I asked her what she was up to,' continued Pete, 'and she told me just like that. Not even the faintest hint of embarrassment.'

'Is she pretty?' asked Bev.

'*Very*,' acknowledged Pete.

'Is that just your opinion as a bloke?' asked Katrina. 'What did your ex think?'

'Amy thought she was stunning too.'

The game didn't have the same sort of fizz after that revelation as everyone left knew that their own what-are-they-up-to-now? wouldn't be anywhere near as good as Pete's. Katrina, however, revealed that her old flatmate's brother used to go out with Douglas Burton (then, the boy most likely to be on Prozac; now, a radio journalist in Cardiff). Gershwin said that he'd bumped into some guys in a pub in town who used to be in the year below us at school and they'd told him about Adrian Shearer from our year (then, the boy most likely to rob a post-office with a sawn-off shot-gun; now, doing a ten-year stretch for armed robbery in HMP Strangeways). Ginny revealed that she'd been parking her car at the UCI cinema in town when she'd seen Stephanie Tucker (then, the girl most likely to be average for ever) drive past in a Mercedes convertible. Finally, I divulged that Lara Reid (then, the girl most likely to have a hundred notches on her bedpost before her sixteenth birthday) was now managing a Christian bookshop in King's Heath.

'Who'd have thought it?' said Pete quietly. 'Who'd have thought any of it in a million years?'

seventy-six

It was now one o'clock in the morning and we were all sitting in Ginny's living room. Ginny was screaming, 'Noooooooooo!' at the top of her voice, while the rest of us laughed so hard we were on the verge of being sick. Katrina and Pete were lodged on the sofa; Bev was draped across the armchair next to the hi-fi (we allowed her to act as official DJ as long as she promised not to play any of that Goth nonsense); Gershwin was lying in front of the TV with the remote control in his hand and the sound turned right down, Ginny was next to him on the floor and I was lounging next to her.

What had started out as a few beers before going to bed was now a more rowdy affair with us poring over a load of old photographs that Bev had brought up with her from Sheffield. The one that was causing Ginny so much consternation was an incredibly out-of-focus picture of herself running along a beach in a swimming costume. It looked innocuous at a glance but then you saw that her left breast was on show.

'I blame you, Gershwin!' said Ginny, trying to wrestle the snapshot from my hands. 'You took the photograph!'

Gershwin shrugged. 'Why blame me? It was your bap on the loose. You should've had more control over it.'

The picture had been taken the summer we'd all finished

our exams and were looking forward to doing our A levels. None of us was even the faintest bit inclined to get jobs over the summer despite being so poor that the only drink we could afford in the Kings Arms was a half-pint of blackcurrant and soda water. Knowing how poor we were and how hard we'd worked during our exams, Elliot's parents had said we could all stay at their holiday cottage in St Ives. On our third day there, as we were all lying on the beach, an over-energetic Ginny challenged the lads to a race and demanded a huge head start. Gershwin, too lazy to join in, nominated himself the race judge and, to make sure everything was fair, he borrowed Bev's camera to photograph the finish. The race got off to a good start but descended into farce soon after the words 'On your marks, get set, go.' Suffice it to say, it was not the best of ideas for a 'fairly perky' sixteen-year-old girl to be sprinting in a poorly tied halterneck bikini top. As she crossed the line, beating Elliot and me by some considerable distance, her left breast made its break for freedom and was preserved on film by Gershwin in all its glory.

Gershwin stood up, plucked the photo from my hands and handed it to her.

'What are you doing?' I exclaimed. 'She'll tear it up!'

Ginny perked up. 'I take back what I said about you, Gershwin. You're a hero. An absolute gentleman.' She looked at me and pulled a face. 'I think I'm going to keep this photo,' she said. 'I mean, how many women have photos of their boobs in peak condition?'

seventy-seven

It was just coming up to half past three in the morning and we were all in exactly the same position we'd been in two hours earlier. Bev had stopped DJing; Ginny had stopped looking at her left-breast photograph; Pete and Katrina had been deep in conversation for most of the night but were now quiet; Gershwin was on the verge of falling asleep; and I was looking at Ginny thinking of how, right now, I wanted nothing more in the world than to kiss her again.

'I hope you're not falling asleep, Matt,' said Ginny, nudging me.

'I'm totally awake,' I replied, nudging her back.

'I think we should try to stay up all night again,' said Ginny.

'Okay.' I yawned, even though I would rather have shoved strips of bamboo under my fingernails. 'What about every-one else?'

'Definitely,' mumbled Bev.

'Absolutely,' sighed Pete.

'Yeah,' groaned Katrina.

'Without a doubt,' muttered Gershwin.

seventy-eight

When I woke up next morning, bursting to go to the loo, I was less than surprised that we'd failed to stay up all night yet again. I had no idea what we were trying to prove (that we were still young? That we didn't need sleep? That we could still talk rubbish at four o'clock in the morning?) but whatever it was I suspected our constant failure was proving the opposite. The last thing I remembered was Ginny and I going upstairs to bring down duvets and sleeping-bags in order to make our vigil more 'comfortable'. Clearly a little too 'comfortable'. Everyone was dotted around Ginny's living room in various states of unconsciousness. Katrina and Pete were swaddled in one duvet. Bev was curled up in an armchair in the bright yellow sleeping-bag Ginny had owned since she had joined the Brownies. Gershwin was on the sofa beneath his coat and Ginny and I were on the floor in front of the sofa underneath the duvet from my bedroom.

I sneaked out of the room and upstairs to the toilet. On my way back to the living room I heard sounds in the kitchen and ventured in to see who was up. It was Katrina.

'Morning,' she said brightly, as she filled the kettle.

'Morning,' I returned. 'Sleep well?'

'No. Terrible. You?'

'Terrible too.'

'Guess what?' she whispered.

I looked at her blankly. I couldn't have guessed what if my life depended on it. 'I haven't the faintest clue.'

'I can see that from your face,' she said. 'I think I'd better tell you but you'll never believe me.'

Her last sentence piqued my curiosity. 'When did whatever it is happen?'

'Last night.'

'Where?'

'In there.' She pointed to the living room.

'Right,' I said, mystified. 'You've got my attention. What could you possibly have done in a room full of people that's worthy of whispering . . .'

It suddenly hit me. 'Are you trying to tell me that you . . .'

'Not that!' said Katrina, with displeasure. 'Less than that.'

'Who with?'

'There were only two single men in the room last night and you were one of them.'

'You mean, you and Pete were snogging in the living room while all of us were asleep? That's so teenagery. How did it happen?'

'I don't know,' she said. 'One second everyone's saying let's stay up all night and the next everyone but Pete and I are out like lights. A bomb exploding wouldn't have woken you up and, well, we got talking. We'd been at it all night – the talking, that is. He'd been telling me about his divorce and how he missed his son, and I was telling him about my own bad luck with relationships and, well, we just ended up . . . kissing and then we fell asleep.'

'You and Pete. That's so . . . I don't know.'

'He said he's going to come down to Stoke to see me next weekend.'

'What? You're going to make a r-e-l-a-t-i-o-n-s-h-i-p out of it?'

She nodded enthusiastically. 'I know I shouldn't say this only a few hours after we got together but I've got this feeling. This really good feeling. That everything's going to be all right'

'Hmm,' I said.

'What does that mean?'

'I just don't think you should take it so seriously. You'll have forgotten all about him by the time you've gone back to your lifestyle editing on *the Staffordshire* whatever-it's-called, and he'll go back to his comic-book empire. It's been good being back together but I think it's easy to get carried away. But you don't want me to say all this, do you?'

'It's a bit cynical, isn't it?'

'I prefer to call it realistic.'

Katrina raised an eyebrow suggestively. 'Sounds more like you're talking from experience.' Her eyes flitted over to the open living-room door where a Ginny shaped duvet was clearly visible.

The kettle came to the boil and Katrina made two mugs of tea.

'We're just friends,' I said, emphatically, as Katrina handed me a mug. She raised her eyebrows again but remained silent. 'She's already in love with someone,' I added.

'Who?' asked Katrina.

'It's a long story.'

'And what about you?'

'And *what* about me?'

'Who are you in love with?'

I didn't answer.

So she grabbed her tea and disappeared into the living room.

seventy-nine

When everyone else woke up at around eleven, looking somewhat the worse for wear, we made a unanimous decision to go out for breakfast. Pete suggested that we got to British Home Stores in town because they did a full English breakfast for £1.80 but then he remembered they stopped serving at eleven so that was out. Katrina sniffed at BHS straight away and put forward Café Rouge because apparently they did a very nice scrambled eggs and smoked salmon. I was in the middle of pointing out that there was quite a reasonable McDonald's in King's Heath, when Ginny suggested a nearby motorway service station – yet another trip down Memory Lane. When Pete had first passed his driving test his parents bought him an ancient Triumph Dolomite, which became our official chariot. Whenever we could we'd all climb into it, drive to that motorway service station and spend entire evenings hunched over a cup of coffee and a single plate of chips between us. There was no rhyme or reason to our madness – we just did it because we could.

Two hours and several all-day breakfasts later, we were all feeling up to doing something with the day. Again, opinions were diverse, and stretched from shopping to finding a decent pub in which to vegetate. We took the latter option. On the Saturday evening we had a barbecue. Pete, Gershwin, Katrina and I did the cooking, while Ginny and Bev sat inside watching the *Brookside* omnibus, taking a break every now and again to ask us whether we were insane because it was freezing cold, windy and threatening to rain. After we'd eaten we spent the rest of the evening talking, drinking and playing board games (Trivial Pursuit, Monopoly and Mousetrap) until the early hours.

When we woke up the next day, Ginny and Bev went out to a corner shop and purchased the ingredients for a fried breakfast to end all fried breakfasts, which Gershwin, Katrina and I cooked, while Pete volunteered to do the washing-up afterwards, secure in the knowledge that Katrina would take pity on him and give him a hand. Later we descended on the Kings Arms, and spent the afternoon drinking. Somewhere around eight o'clock that evening it became clear that, even though we didn't want it to, the weekend was going to have to end quite soon.

'I'd better be going,' said Bev, finishing her drink. 'The trains to Sheffield are always crap on a Sunday.'

'I'd love to stay a bit longer,' said Pete, his eyes meeting Katrina's, 'but I've got to get off too.'

'And me,' said Katrina.

'You can't go just yet,' said Ginny. 'We haven't organised the next time we're all meeting up.'

'You mean there's got to be a next time?' I said. 'I thought once every six years was enough for us.'

'Very funny,' said Ginny. 'And just for that, the next time we're going to get together will be for your birthday, Matt.'

'I shouldn't bother,' I replied. 'I've decided I'm going to do a Gershwin – just go down the pub, have a few drinks and then go home.'

'You wish,' said Gershwin. 'You've got no choice in the matter. Ginny and I planned the whole thing yesterday.'

I glanced over at Ginny. Our eyes met and she looked away guiltily. 'So,' I said, 'you've been conspiring to surprise me, have you?'

'Oh, get lost!' said Ginny. 'I just wanted to get you back for this weekend.'

'So what have you got planned?' asked Bev.

'Well,' said Gershwin, 'we talked about having a surprise birthday party for Matt, but we were afraid he'd plan something else for the big day.'

'So we're going to do the next best thing,' continued Ginny, 'which is to have a surprise birthday party that he knows about.'

'That won't be much of a surprise, then?' said Pete.

'No matter,' said Ginny, excitedly. 'He'll love it anyway.'

'Definitely,' said Gershwin.

'And you're sure you're not going to tell me what it is?' I asked.

'Definitely not,' said Ginny. 'But what I will say to everyone here is this: keep four Saturdays from now clear so you can bring your wives, husbands, boyfriends and girlfriends or even just yourselves to the best thirtieth birthday party you will ever witness.'

And that was that. Half an hour later we were all at Ginny's saying goodbye. Bev started crying and saying how much she loved everyone: Pete and Katrina decided they could no longer keep their new-found love a secret and were kissing frantically on the doorstep; Gershwin was bemused by all that was going on, and Ginny looked happier than I'd seen her in quite a while.

And that was that.

Katrina went back to Stoke.

Bev went back to Sheffield.

Pete went back to Manchester.

Gershwin went home to Zoë and Charlotte.

And suddenly, after being surrounded by old friends the whole weekend, we were alone.

On the sofa.

Alone.

eighty

'Is this a good idea, Ginny?' I said, still grappling with her bra strap.

'I think we've had this conversation before, Matt,' she said, still unbuttoning my shirt. 'You're not sure again, are you?'

'What do you mean I'm not sure? You weren't sure last time, were you?'

'Well, it's me asking the question this time. So what's your answer?'

'Okay,' I admitted, 'I'm not sure.'

'What aren't you sure about?'

'About you. Me. Here on the living-room floor. Your . . .' I hesitated, getting it right '. . . your *right* hand unbuttoning my shirt, your left underneath the aforementioned shirt.' She withdrew her wandering fingertips. 'Do I need to spell it out?'

At this point we both laughed, looked into each other's eyes and finally unleashed the teenagers within.

eighty-one

To: crazedelaine@hotpr.com
From: mattb@c-tec.national.com
re: Stuff

Dear Elaine

Sorry I haven't been in touch for a while. How are you? How's work? How's life sharing with Sara? How's the spider plant? As for me, I'm fine. The weekend get-together went really well. It was the best time I've had in . . . well, ages. You'll be pleased to know that as the days go by the whole turning-thirty thing is becoming less of a trial. Maybe I'm tempting fate talking like this but right now it feels like just another birthday. Anyway, hope you're well and everything. Take care of yourself.

Love

Matt xxx

eighty-two

To: crazedelaine@hotpr.com
From: mattb@c-tec.national.com
re: **My last attempt at honesty**

Dear Elaine

I'm writing this e-mail all of six seconds after I wrote that last one (which I now give you permission to ignore . . . well, actually don't . . . you can keep it and call it exhibit A should I ever accuse you of cowardice). Three seconds after I pressed SEND I was overwhelmed with guilt. I mean really overwhelmed (the sweaty palms, the hot flushes, that tight feeling in your stomach like you're going to throw up at any second). In as roundabout a way as possible this is me telling you that I have some news — news that I'm not sure how you're going to react to. So here goes: Ginny and I got together as in 'got together'. Obviously things are still complicated. We haven't even had a chance to talk about it yet — she went to work this morning without waking me up but I guess we'll try and sort things out tonight.

I know this probably isn't what you want to hear (mainly because if the tables were turned this is the last thing I'd want to hear myself) but if I don't tell you then everything we ever had is going to fall apart. And if there's one thing I've learnt about turning thirty it's this: good friends are hard to come by

so when you've found a few it's a good idea to keep hold
of them.
That's pretty much it.
Mail me back soon?

love as always,

Matt xxx

eighty-three

Although I'd told Elaine that I thought Ginny and I would have The Talk, as the day wore on and Ginny didn't call, I became less convinced we would. I realised I was right to be sceptical. Not only did we not talk about it that evening but we didn't mention it the evening after that. Or the evening after that. Or the evening after that. It was like being in the sixth form again, only this time without having to pretend we didn't fancy each other. We behaved as if we were together – by which I mean that we were all over each other every night when she came home from work. She took to ignoring Ian's calls, which was deeply satisfying, and we spent every single second we could together, but we didn't talk – or, at least, we didn't have The Talk. We couldn't. Instead every day while she went out to work I went into analysis overdrive. Along the lines of:

Question: Am I happy?

Answer: A resounding yes, followed by a brief furrow of the eyebrows and the question: but what is happy? If happy is feeling carefree then I suspect I'm far from happy. But if happy is laughing so hard at your new girlfriend/not girlfriend's very poor jokes that your sides hurt, if happy is looking into your girlfriend/not girlfriend's eyes and seeing the very something that you'd thought you'd lost a long time ago, if happy is these things then I am indeed happy. But if it isn't, then: no.

This would inevitably lead me to:

Question: Can I allow myself to enjoy this happiness given that it's only a transitory set of emotions providing a brief respite from the knowledge that:

(a) I'm supposed to be moving to Australia in less than three weeks?

(b) My new girlfriend/not girlfriend is still currently in a relationship with a married man?

(c) I suspect that I'm still rebounding from Elaine?

(d) I'm turning thirty?

Answer: no.

Despite all these questions to which I had no real answers, that week Ginny and I had a fantastic time. If our lives had been a film then the week that began with the kiss on Sunday evening would be represented by a cheesy montage: Ginny and I laughing as we held hands and walked barefoot across a sandy beach; Ginny and I splashing in a crystal blue ocean – Ginny falling into my arms for a kiss; Ginny and I staring deeply into each other's eyes as the sun set behind our heads. That sort of thing. Unfortunately this wasn't Hollywood, USA, this was Birmingham, UK, so our montage wasn't quite so glamorous.

Montage Moment 1

It's Monday morning and I wake up with no Ginny beside me. There's a note next to the bed saying that she's got up early to buy us breakfast before she goes to work. I roll over on to my front, dangle an arm over the edge of the bed and brush against something. I pick up the object – a shoe-box. I know what it is immediately because I've seen her get some old photos of Gershwin out of it. I take the opportunity to look through them. Straight away I come across photos of Ginny and me that I haven't seen since the day she collected them from Boots. In these photos we are seventeen. I think about how young seventeen really is. She comes back. I hide the box and we kiss.

Montage Moment 2

It's early evening on Tuesday. Ginny and I are sitting on the doorstep looking out on to the back garden even though it's raining and the garden is a jungle of weeds. She is feeding me a whole packet of Revels one by one, just as I fed her a small bunch of seedless grapes only moments before. We are being that sickeningly together. I decide that when we get to the end of the packet we are going to have a talk – The Talk. The one about us. And the future. And what we actually think we are achieving by doing this. Stuff we both know we need to know. I look into the packet and can see that there are only three left.

'Do you know how cute you are?' she says.

The honeycomb centre one.

'You are cute, you know. Unbearably so,' she continues.

The milk chocolate one shaped like a flying saucer.

'I think I might actually be . . .' she begins, then hesitates.

The orange one.

'You think you might actually be what?' I ask, still chewing. She shrugs, kisses me and says, 'I think nothing.'

Montage Moment 3

We're in the city centre in the late afternoon on Wednesday. Ginny's come here straight after work and we are wandering around aimlessly because that's what we did virtually every day during long, hot, post-exam summers. We wander into a shop that sells pictures and picture frames and look through some black and white prints. I point out one of Louis Armstrong that I like. He's standing next to Ella Fitzgerald and looking so happy that he must have been on the verge of exploding.

'I'll buy it for you,' says Ginny.

'No, there's no need.'

'I think there is,' she says, ignoring me.

Five minutes later I'm walking around with the print and frame, and I don't know what it is I'm feeling but I am feeling something quite incredible.

Montage Moment 4

It's Thursday evening and Ginny and I are over at Gershwin and Zoë's for dinner. I expect us to modify our behaviour – to keep it our secret for a little while longer but we don't. Ginny sits next to me the whole time squeezed right up against me, staring at me as if she really is interested in every word that comes out of my mouth, no matter how inane. I suspect I am doing the same. Gershwin and Zoë are really cool about it. They don't bat an eyelid, even though I can see that Zoë is dying to interrogate us. A couple of times during the evening I catch Zoë looking at me with a question in her eyes, but it's not really a question she's asking so much as a silent comment she wants to be confirmed. 'You're in love, aren't you?'

Montage Moment 5

It's Friday night around eleven o'clock and we've just got back to the house after a night out at the Kings Arms.

We're drunk but not ridiculously so and our breath smells of chips and curry sauce. All the way home I have been feeling subdued. I don't know how to say what I want to say. I turn on the TV and watch it silently wrapped in my own thoughts while Ginny makes popcorn for no other reason than that today I bought her a popcorn-maker because she said she'd always wanted one.

'What are you doing?' she asks, entering the room with a small dustbin-sized container filled with enough popcorn to supply the local multiplex.

'Thinking,' I return.

'Is that what you're doing?' she says, with gentle sarcasm. 'I thought you were just watching . . .' she looks at the TV '. . . reruns of *Magnum PI*.'

I smile. 'I know that's what it looks like I'm doing but I'm actually doing stuff. It's all in my head. I'm doing a very good job in my head. Just not anywhere else.'

She walks across the room, places the vat of popcorn in front of the TV, sits down and puts her arms around me.

'Everything's going to be all right, you know,' she says.

'Is it?'

'Of course.'

'How?'

'Because I said so.'

eighty-four

'Er . . . look . . . Ginny,' I began, unsteadily, to make the point that had been five long days coming, 'I . . . er . . . know this is difficult but I think we need to talk.'

The two of us were sitting in All Bar One in Brindley Place, nursing a bit of a hangover, eating a fried breakfast, consuming orange juice by the litre (as if vitamin C were sufficient antidote to the aforementioned hangover) and I was determined that we were going to talk about the thing between us that we just weren't talking about. After six days of rolling it round in my head I hadn't come up with a single solution of my own.

'I know, I know,' said Ginny, after a long moment of reflection. 'You're right. I've been avoiding it like the plague. It's not that I don't want to talk about things, Matt, I promise you. It's just that . . .'

'You're afraid that if we talk about it suddenly it will come to an end?'

'Exactly. But even so, you're right, we've got to talk.'

Silence.

'You first,' she said. 'You're so much better at this talking thing than I am.'

I wished for a moment that Elaine could have heard that. 'Okay. It's like this . . .' My voice faded.

Silence.

'Maybe I should have a go,' suggested Ginny.

'Be my guest,' I replied generously.

'Well, the thing is . . .' Long pause. Followed by a sigh. Followed by a long pause. 'This is impossible, isn't it?'

I took a sip of orange juice to combat a sudden case of hangover-head explosion. 'The conversation or the situation?'

'Both.'

'Look,' I said, squinting – the hangover-head explosion was still attempting to shake my foundations, 'I'll understand if this is just a fling, you know. I'm a big boy now. I'm nearly thirty. I won't fall apart if it's like that . . .'

'It's not like that,' said Ginny. 'It's nothing like that. In a lot of ways I wish it *was* like that because it would be so much easier. I have no idea what's going on here, Matt, I really don't. If you were to ask me how I felt about Ian, I'd probably tell you that I love him – which is true – but I also know that it's never going to work out with him and what I've got with him now just isn't worth having. I'm tired of all the lies and the deception. I want my life back the way it used to be. So, the way I see it, even if nothing more happens between you and me, even if we finish now and decide to be just friends, I'll have no regrets at all because this . . .' she gestured to the table, which I assumed represented the concept of 'us' '. . . will help me get over him. I suppose what I'm trying to say is that it's nice to be reminded that it's not all set in stone – it's nice to know that nice things do happen every now and again out of the blue.'

'So, are you saying that you want this to be it?'

'No.' She leant forward and kissed me. 'Of course not. I'm saying that, yes, I'd like this to be more than a fling but if it can't be then I accept that.'

'I couldn't.'

'What?'

'Accept that this is just a fling.'

Ginny looked over at me and smiled. 'Me neither.'

'But you just said . . .'

'Keep up with the action, Matt,' she said. 'I was lying. All that "I'll have no regrets at all because this will help me get over him" stuff was a load of rubbish, total fabrication, girls' lies, in case you didn't feel the same way. But I am glad you feel the same way because if you didn't the last thing you need before your thirtieth birthday is to be quaking in the knowledge that an ex-girlfriend/not girlfriend from your schooldays has totally fallen for you.'

'Totally?'

'Incontrovertibly.'

'So you'd like to make a go of it?'

'Me and you?' There was a brief, barely perceptible pause. 'Yeah, of course.'

'You don't sound that enthusiastic,' I replied, reacting to the barely perceptible pause.

'How can I be, when everything seems to be stacked against us? You're leaving to go to Australia, there's Ian . . .'

'Well, the first thing's easily remedied. I won't go to Australia.'

Ginny looked shocked. I couldn't work out whether this was a good shocked or the bad kind. When she began her next sentence with the words 'Listen, Matt . . .' I decided it was the bad kind. I suspected I'd come on a little too strong.

'You don't want me to stay,' I said defensively.

She reached across the table and took my hand. 'Of course I'd love you to stay . . .'

'Then that's all there is to it,' I said, taking the proverbial bull by the horns. 'We've made more progress in the last six days than we have in the last ten years. This feels right, Ginny.'

'I know and I agree, but six days is still six days, Matt. And that's way too much pressure to put on any relationship.'

'It would be under normal circumstances, Ginny, but these aren't normal circumstances, are they?' I was unsure whether to proceed with my next sentence. 'Do you remember the pact we made at Gershwin's wedding?' Ginny opened her mouth, and I could tell by the expression on her face that she was about to pretend not to recall the conversation.

'I'd had a lot to drink,' she said laughing. 'But, yeah, I do remember. We said that if we were both single by the time we turned thirty we'd get together.' She looked embarrassed. 'But we said all that when we were twenty-four, Matt. That feels like almost a lifetime ago.'

'I'm not saying that we should make a go of it because of some stupid pact, I'm saying we should make a go of it because, even then, we knew exactly what we know now and have probably known since the day we first saw each other: we are meant to be together. Think about it. This has been going on since we were seventeen. We've tried everything to avoid being together – going out with other people, moving cities, moving countries, even – and look where we are. Right back here where it all began.' I kissed her. 'We don't have to rush anything. We can take our time and see how it goes. But if you think that I can come back home feeling like I have no direction, have all this happen and still walk away, you don't know me at all.'

'Do you mean that?'

'Of course I mean it. I've never meant anything more. If you want I can phone work today and tell them I'm not going to Australia.'

'No, wait. At least until I've spoken to Ian. Once it's all over with him I'll be able to think straight. I'll do it tomorrow,' she said quietly. 'Definitely tomorrow. But for now let's just have a nice day.'

'And do what?' I asked.

She knocked back the last of her orange juice and stood up. 'Let's go shopping.'

eighty-five

It was two hours later and we were standing in the same men's clothes shop I'd visited during my first week in Birmingham. The goatee boy DJ was still doing his stuff in the corner, the stick-insect shop assistant with the sneer was still sneering, and I was still attempting to hold true to my dark blue/black clothing rule. Ginny, however, was having none of it.

'So you're telling me,' she began, as she rifled through a rack of T-shirts on my behalf, 'that all the clothes you have bought since you turned twenty-six have been dark blue or black?'

'Every single thing,' I said proudly.

'Socks?'

'Yes.'

'Boxer shorts?'

'Always.'

'Shirts?'

'I do have a few white shirts but I only ever wear them when I've got to meet a big client otherwise it's—'

'—dark blue or black.'

I could see from Ginny's face that she couldn't believe what she was hearing. We moved on from the T-shirt rail to a rail of 'casual' trousers.

'What about these?' she said, showing me a pair of green combat-style trousers.

'No, they're green.'

She moved on to a pair of burgundy velvet trousers. 'And these.'

'*Burgundy?*' I responded. 'Are you joking?'

Ginny still couldn't quite believe this. She moved across to a row of suits and picked out a a three-button light grey one. 'Come on, Matt, even this can't offend your sensibilities. I could really fancy you in this suit.'

'Light grey? I'd spend my life tripping backwards and forwards from the dry-cleaners. Not in a million years, my dear.'

'You know this is weird, don't you?'

'I've told you,' I said. 'I can't help myself. I know exactly what I like. If it's Indian food, I like Chicken Tikka Masala. If it's music, I like female singer-songwriters, and if it's clothing then it's dark blue/black.' I turned and looked right into her eyes. 'And if it's women then it's you.'

She laughed and kissed me even though the shop was now quite busy.

'Steady on,' I said.

'Never mind steady on. There's plenty more where that came from. It's been a long time since I've had the pleasure of gratuitous public displays of emotions so excuse me while I make the most of it.' She kissed me again then looked me in the eyes intensely. 'Why does this feel so right?'

'Because you've been in denial and I've shown you the way,' I said, suddenly filled with self-assurance. It felt good to be here, in public, with this beautiful woman. It felt good that every man in that shop, no matter how pretentiously dressed, would know that Ginny was my girlfriend. 'You've been scared of knowing what you want because you think life should be some sort of adventure where you just run around making the same mistakes again and again, never learning from them. That to you is exciting. Whereas for me exciting is knowing exactly what something's going to be like and knowing that once I've got it, as long as it's well maintained, it will always hold the same delight for me that it had the first time I encountered it. In fact, sometimes it can get better. I don't like the new. The new makes me nervous. I like the old. The tried and tested.'

'Mmm,' said Ginny, grinning. 'And I take it from this that I am both "old" and "tried and tested"?' She laughed. '*Very* appealing.'

'I don't expect you to understand because you're not me. But the thing about my favourite things in life is that I never get bored with them. Never. Because every time I look at my favourite things, or hear them or whatever, I experience something new, discover some small detail about them that I'd never noticed before, and that only makes them more fascinating.'

Ginny laughed so loudly that a group of lads in their late teens looked over at her. One of them was holding a bright orange T-shirt in his hand and Ginny pointed and mouthed, 'Fashion disaster,' at him and carried on laughing. It was like she was drunk or something. I was considering getting very embarrassed.

'What's wrong with you?'

'I'm happy. I can't believe I'm about to say this but that whole spiel you went into about why you only wear blue/black? Well, I think you've convinced me.'

'To stick with what you know?'

'I wouldn't go that far but you have convinced me of something.'

'What?'

'That you would look terrible in those velvet trousers.'

eighty-six

To: mattb@c-tec.national.com
From: crazedelaine@hotpr.com
re: **Your last 2 e-mails**

Dear Matt

   I think we've been through enough together for us to be 'honest' with each other. As you so rightly pointed out in your last e-mail, 'Honesty is everything,' and it's true. When I think of you, when I think of everything we had, that's what I remember most – that we could always talk about everything . . . eventually, at least. I say this as a preliminary to telling you how I took your 'news' – I cried. And what's worse is that I cried more than the day you left. I've tried to work out why. I was up all night thinking about it. It's not like I want us to get back together. I don't. It's not even that I'm jealous – I am genuinely pleased for you. In the end I kind of worked out that the reason has something to do with what you said in one of your early e-mails when you talked about all the things you dreamt of being when you were a kid. You said turning thirty was forcing you to face the fact that some things will never be. Well, I guess your moving on is my turning thirty. I know when we were together I never gave you any indication that I thought about the future – or rather our future. But I did. I used to love imagining us having kids (six at least – not v. practical huh?) and figuring out what they'd look like, and which one of us they'd take after character-wise. I used to daydream about us moving out of NY to Philadelphia, to my grandparents' old house. I used to think about us growing old together – you getting grumpier and me getting more 'out there' as the years went on. I even used to think about us dying together (I'd go first because I'd hate to be on my own and you'd follow me a week later because you'd miss me so much). Even though I always knew it was over between us I guess I still hadn't said goodbye to all my daydreams, and you and Ginny getting together made me face facts. I suppose that if I'm being well and truly honest (and I think I should be) I have to say that this wouldn't have been half as bad if it had just been some random girl that you'd gotten together with like my random bar guy. Some pretty but vacant Transitional Girl who would be totally unsuitable for you. But you seem to have struck gold first time. Or maybe that should be second time???? I am sooooo rambling now. If you want my advice (and I'm not sure that you do), if Ginny's the one for you then you should go for it – forget about Australia. It's hard enough finding whatever it is we're all looking for to ignore it when it lands in your lap. Whatever you do I want you to be happy. Really I do.

Love always,

Elaine xxx

PS I guess you won't be wanting your birthday present now. It was going to be kind of a surprise: I was going to come and see you for a week before your birthday. (You would've been proud of me. I actually SAVED up the money for the flight.) But I suspect ex-girlfriends and current girlfriends don't mix too well! I'll get you something else and spend the money on a holiday to the Caribbean. I've never been and it'll be a great excuse to show off my tattoo (which incidentally has gone septic – hmmmm, nice).

eighty-seven

I immediately e-mailed Elaine back to let her know that I wanted her to come and visit and wouldn't take no for an answer. She wasn't convinced at first that it was a good idea but I insisted and assured her everything would be okay provided she still felt more like ironing my clothes than ripping them off. To me Elaine wasn't just an ex-girlfriend, or a friend – this might seem a little idealistic – she was just like family.

eighty-eight

It was the Saturday evening that followed my afternoon shopping spree with Ginny. I was on my way to Gershwin and Zoë's wearing a bright red Stüssy hooded top that Ginny had bought for me that very afternoon. She wasn't with me. When we had come back to the house she told me that she wanted to spend some time on her own to get her head around the whole idea of splitting up with Ian. I understood, so I'd called Gershwin and Zoë to see what they were doing and ended up being invited to their house for a takeaway and a video.

'Here's a cup of coffee,' said a hyperactive Zoë, dragging me into their living room. 'Charlotte's asleep,' she said, pointing to the ceiling. 'Gershwin's over there,' she said, indicating her husband, who was sitting in an armchair looking puzzled. 'And what we want to know . . .' She stopped as she caught Gershwin's eye and wilted temporarily.

'I'm not that bothered about what's going on,' said Gershwin. 'I'm used to it, Zoë.'

'Okay,' said Zoë 'What *I* want to know is what is going on with you and Ginny. I need to know the details and I need to know them now!'

It was a nice feeling, having a love-life that was worthy of gossip, and it was even better to have Zoë showing an interest in it because her enthusiasm was making the whole thing seem more glamorous than it really was. If I had told Gershwin he would have down-played the whole thing and said, 'Oh,' and maybe raised his eyebrows, but Zoë made it seem like the top story on a news bulletin.

'What's going on with me and Ginny?' I said, clarifying the evening's topic of debate needlessly.

'Yes.' Zoë nodded enthusiastically. 'I want to know everything.'

I contemplated not telling her, just for a laugh, but she was having none of it.

'Come on,' she said, baring her teeth. 'Spill the beans.'

'I have no idea what's going on,' I explained. 'I don't think it's got a name yet. It's all been a bit of a—'

'Enough's enough,' interrupted Gershwin. 'Much against my better judgement I'm interested now in what's going on too. So come on, out with the details. When, how and most of all *why*?'

'The when part is easy enough,' I began. 'It was last Sunday evening after everyone left to go home. The how is a little bit trickier, though . . . I don't really know how the how part happened . . . I suppose at a push you could say it was a moment of spontaneity, but I wouldn't stake my life on it. And the why . . . Well, the why is one that I'm still working on. I think it's because she's the one.'

'Which one?' asked Zoë.

'The love of my life, the woman I've never forgotten . . . the one I'm going to be with when I turn thirty.'

Zoë looked incredulous. I could tell she just wasn't getting her head around any of this. 'So let me get this straight. You've decided that she's the one, even though she's got a boyfriend and you're moving countries in three weeks' time.'

'Good point,' said Gershwin laughing. 'Well made, dear

wife.' Zoë glared at him. 'Look, babe, you shouldn't be *that* surprised,' he explained. 'They've been doing this sort of thing since they were seventeen. It's just a habit.' He paused. 'Although I must say six days on the trot is something of a record for you two.'

'It is,' I confirmed cheerfully. 'It is. There was a brief spell when we were twenty-two when it was all systems go for two weekends on the trot but . . . yes, I think this is a world record.'

'Anyway,' continued Gershwin, 'they'll say all this stuff, then tomorrow they'll split up. She'll carry on with Ian and he'll carry on with Australia and everything will carry on as normal until the next time their paths cross.'

'Thank you for your cynicism, Gershwin,' I said, with a grin. 'And under normal circumstances I would, without a doubt, agree with you, were it not for the fact that by this time tomorrow Ginny will be seeing the person formally known as her boyfriend to give him a well-prepared dear John speech.'

'She's getting rid of Ian?' said Gershwin incredulously. 'But I like Ian. He was really funny on my birthday. Zoë's friends Davina and Tom have been going on about him for ages.'

'Cheers,' I replied curtly.

'Come on, Matt. You must agree that he's ideal boyfriend material. Much better than you, mate.'

Zoë looked at me curiously. 'As I haven't known you since you were eleven I'll refrain from disparaging you too much, Matt, but even I can see the holes in that plan. I mean, what about Australia, for instance?'

'I haven't worked out all the details yet but I'm not going. I can get a job here in England easily enough. I might not be on as much money as I was in the States or if I'd gone to Australia but it'll be enough.'

'And you'd live where, exactly?'

'I don't know.' I shrugged. 'Wherever. We haven't really sorted that out either.'

'And yet Ginny's splitting up with Ian?' said Zoë. She paused. 'He's married, isn't he?'

I attempted to deny this.

'Don't lie, Matt,' said Zoë determinedly. Her voice and manner changed. Everything about her suddenly became sharp and anxious. 'It all adds up now. They don't live together. He turned up late to meet her at the pub on Gershwin's birthday. Gershwin told me they see each other irregularly, which seems strange considering how long they've been together. He didn't mind when you moved into Ginny's. He pulled out of that party in London at the last minute.'

'Is Zoë right?' asked Gershwin. 'Is Ian married?'

'Yeah,' I confessed, 'he is.' And, starting from the beginning, I told them everything I knew. In a way I was relieved that this was coming out into the open. Gershwin and Zoë listened carefully but as I continued speaking I could see that Zoë was becoming more and more upset.

'Has he got any children?' asked Zoë, when I'd finished.

'Yeah.' I nodded. 'A little boy.'

No one reacted to that.

The atmosphere was immediately uncomfortable. I tried to change the subject and Gershwin got the film he had rented out of its box and slotted it into the video. We'd barely got past the credits when Zoë, who hadn't said a word since my revelation, left the room abruptly. Gershwin went after her and was gone for over a quarter of an hour. When he came back downstairs, he grabbed his coat, handed me mine and we left the house, heading in the direction of the Kings Arms.

eighty-nine

'I suppose you're wondering what was wrong with Zoë?'

I nodded.

'And how she guessed Ian was married?'

I nodded again.

'She's sensitive to it I suppose,' said Gershwin, his voice drained of emotion. 'Because about three years ago I had an affair too.'

I couldn't believe what I was hearing. I'd been best man at his wedding. I'd seen how happy they were.

'I promise you, Matt,' he continued, 'I never stopped loving Zoë, not for a second. I know this is no excuse but I just started doubting myself. I had no confidence in myself and no idea where I was going. I hated work more than anything. Zoë kept telling me I should leave and do something I really wanted as soon as she went back to work. She kept telling me that we'd manage somehow, but I couldn't see it – especially when it was easier just to put up with it than do something about it. I took the easy way out. I got on well with Kay – one of the senior administrators at work – and confided in her. We began an affair. It lasted about six months.'

'Did Zoë find out about it?'

'No, I almost wish she had – it would've been easier. I ended it. I couldn't stand the guilt. I couldn't stand not liking myself. Zoë and Charlotte are my family and I let them down, Matt. Zoë's never once given me an excuse not to love her. Even now I can't believe I'd ever do anything that would mean I'd risk losing them. I ended it all with Kay and told Zoë everything. I know I could have got away without telling her but she deserved better than that.'

'What happened then?' I said, stunned.

'We split up.'

'You and Zoë split up? How come you didn't tell me any of this?'

'You were in London at the time. We barely saw each other and when we did it never seemed like the right time. It wasn't your fault. It was just the way things were.'

'Look,' I began, 'I'm sorry. I'm sorry you were going through all that and I wasn't there for you.'

'It's okay,' he said, and gave me a smile that acknowledged what I was trying to say, in spite of my difficulty in expressing it. 'I ended up moving back in with my mum and dad for about five months,' he continued. 'It was awful, Matt. Zoë was crying all the time, the doctor had her on anti-depressants, I almost destroyed her. I can't bring myself to think what effect this was having on Charlotte. I thought we were going to lose everything . . .' He cleared his throat. 'I wouldn't have blamed her for a second if she'd wanted a divorce. But all the time we were going through it she kept telling me how much she loved me. And she did, Matt. She really did. It was hard, sometimes almost impossible, but we worked through it. She saved us. She saved me.'

'So things are okay now?'

Gershwin shrugged. 'Yes and no. Sometimes it's like it never happened and others it's like it happened yesterday.'

'I don't know what to say,' I began. 'I really don't.'

'There's nothing to say. I got myself into a mess. It was all my fault I let myself down.'

ninety

'Listen, Matt,' said Gershwin, at about a quarter to ten, 'it's getting late and I think I ought to be getting home.'

'Yeah, of course,' I replied, putting on my jacket. 'Home.'

'Right, then,' said Gershwin, once we were outside. 'I'm off.' He looked at me. 'Thanks.'

'What for?'

'For being a mate,' he said.

'Same to you,' I said. 'Are you going to be okay?'

'Yeah, of course,' he said confidently. 'But never mind me, are you all right? I know I've been treating this thing between you and Ginny as a bit of a joke, but I do know how much she means to you. So, well, what I suppose I'm trying to say is good luck for tomorrow. I hope it all goes well for you.'

'Cheers,' I replied. 'But, whatever happens, I know I'll be all right.'

ninety-one

On the way back to Ginny's my head was still spinning with Gershwin's revelation. I'd tried to remind myself that it was ridiculous to be shocked when the history of civilisation is littered with examples of events that nobody had thought would ever happen. But I really had been surprised to discover that Gershwin had cheated on Zoë, that Ginny was in a relationship with a married man, that Elliot had died . . . yet stuff happens whether you like it or not and the older you get the more stuff happens. As a life lesson it seemed a little obvious, really – childish, almost.

By the time I reached Ginny's I felt as if I hadn't been living in the real world at all. I'd gone through life with all these expectations – fulfilling job with decent pay, good friends, a nice house, a relationship that didn't suck – but what were they except fantasies that only turn into reality for a tiny minority of people? Growing up with Gershwin, Ginny, Elliot, Bev, Katrina and Pete, I'd always believed that our lives would go pretty much in the same directions, that we'd all achieve the same things, that we'd always be equal. But life didn't happen that way. Everything was random: Ginny's mum dying, Pete's divorce, Katrina's career never getting off the ground, Bev finding out that she couldn't have kids,

Gershwin's unhappiness with his life. Our experiences were not universal: we had to face every trial on our own. And when I looked at my own life, when I looked at Ginny and me, I understood at last why, time and time again, we kept getting back together. It was nostalgia – as simple as that. We were trying to hang on to the way things used to be because we didn't like the way the world really was. And the thing neither of us had realised was that even the past was no longer what it had been. If the news of Gershwin's affair proved anything it was this: that none of us were the same people we had all been back then. We'd all gone so far down our separate paths, we'd all experienced such different things, we'd all grown so much apart that there was no way we could be the same. Ginny was about to change her life for me but she was putting her trust in a version of me that only existed in her head. I wasn't the same person she had known all that time ago.

ninety-two

It was a little after eleven when I reached Ginny's. Though she looked worn out she was still awake, curled up on the sofa with Larry and Sanders, watching TV with the sound turned down so low it was barely audible.

'Hiya,' she said.

'Hiya,' I replied, from the doorway. I walked over and kissed her. I had no idea how I was going to say what I had to say. 'What are you doing still up? You look whacked out.'

'Cheers.'

'You know what I mean.'

She laughed. 'Yeah, I am tired but I wanted to wait up for you.'

I sat down next to her. Larry and Sanders leapt off her lap on to the floor and disappeared into the kitchen. I wondered briefly whether cats had a sixth sense for when trouble was brewing.

'I missed you tonight,' said Ginny, wrapping her arms round my waist and pulling me closer to her.

I looked at her and kissed her again, and for that brief moment I was convinced I was wrong. She was right for me. She was the one. Sitting here with her, with her body so close to mine, feeling so comfortable, how could this possibly be wrong?

'How were Gershwin and Zoë?' she asked.

Hearing their names brought me crashing down to earth. 'Fine,' I lied.

'What did you get up to?'

'Nothing much.'

'Was Charlotte about?'

'She was in bed.'

'Have you eaten? I could make you something if you want.'

'We ate.'

There was a long silence, then Ginny removed her arms from my waist and sat up properly on the sofa.

'Are you going to tell me what's going on?' she said quietly.

I glanced at her but didn't say a word. She looked beautiful. She really did. I couldn't believe I wanted to split up with her at all. And yet here I was using the oldest trick in the book on her – the sullen bastard boyfriend – to bring everything to an end. I just couldn't believe it.

'There's nothing wrong,' I snapped.

'Yeah, and it looks like it.'

I shrugged and remained silent.

'I'm waiting, Matt.'

'For what?'

'For you to tell me what's wrong with you. We had a really nice day today. We got on so well. You were all right when you left this evening. What's changed?'

I closed my eyes and sighed, as I tried to summon the strength to do what I had to do.

I reminded myself why this wasn't going to work.

I reminded myself why I didn't have the right to interfere in her life like this.

I reminded myself that she deserved better and why I couldn't give it.

And then I finally said what I had to say. 'Listen,' I began, purposefully avoiding her gaze. I couldn't look at her while I was saying this. I didn't have that kind of strength. 'I don't think this is going to work between us.'

'Why?' she asked, carefully. 'What's changed your mind?'

'I don't know . . . It's because . . . because I'm not thinking straight . . . because I haven't got the right to mess up your life like this . . . because this isn't about you and me here and now, this is about nostalgia . . . security, if you like. You know this as well as I do, Ginny. You must do. How can we be thinking straight, making all sorts of decisions that affect our future after six days? I can't ask you to split up with Ian just because we've had some mad fling. You should split up with him because you want to. We're not teenagers any more. We can't do things like that.'

'You're right, of course,' said Ginny eventually. Her voice was quiet, controlled and direct. 'It never was going to work.'

'No,' I replied quietly. 'I'm not what's missing from your life.'

Silence.

'I'm sorry,' I said. 'I really am sorry.'

'I'm sorry too,' she said, standing up. 'But even so I think you'd better go.' She added, 'For good this time.'

It was all over in a matter of minutes. As I disappeared upstairs to my room and hers to collect my stuff, the same depressing numbness that had descended over me when I'd split up with Elaine returned. I didn't worry about it this time. I didn't panic that I was losing my soul. Instead I accepted my new-found power not to fall apart. *I'll be okay*, I told myself. *Whatever happens. I'll be okay.*

ninety-three

Much to my parents' surprise I moved back in with them and two weeks passed without event. Ginny didn't try to contact me mainly I suspect because I hadn't given her a reason to, and while I'd contemplated calling her or going to see her hundreds of times, I always resisted it. In the short time I'd been back in Birmingham I'd managed to renew our friendship, fall in love with her, make her fall in love with me, mess up what she had had with Ian (not that it wasn't already as messed up as it was possible to be) and split up with her. Now, the best thing I could do, I reasoned, was stay out of her life. So I did and life went back to what it had been when I first arrived in Birmingham nearly three months ago. I moved back into my old bedroom, my parents drove me regularly to the point of clinical insanity, and I made the odd trip to the supermarket on my mother's behalf at times of the day when I was sure that Ginny would be at work. Former schoolmates spotted: Adele Farley (then, the girl most likely to show you her pants for the price of a packet of crisps; now, assistant manager of a building society and mother of two) and Bridget Gibbons (then, the girl most likely to sell you a copy of *Socialist Worker* in the playground; now, a part-time Labour Party fundraiser). I also saw quite a lot of Gershwin and Zoë during that time too. At first it was difficult because I couldn't get out of my head the image of them splitting up. But the more I saw of them, the more I became aware of not only how right they were for each other but also how, despite all that had happened, they were still in love. And this, more than anything else, made me feel okay.

When it came to the arrangements about my birthday, things became more complicated. Without Ginny, the idea of Bev, Katrina and Pete coming from far and wide to Birmingham seemed pointless. So, despite Gershwin's protests, I asked him to call Bev and the others and cancel whatever surprise they had planned. Like Gershwin in preparation for his own birthday, I rejected all manner of celebratory suggestions: a weekend in London (Gershwin's) and quad-biking in South Wales (Zoë's) in favour of the Kings Arms. I didn't want a fuss. I didn't want loads of people celebrating with me either. I just wanted it over and done with.

With regard to the rest of my life I'd like to say that my thirty-people powered stoicism worked all the way through those two weeks away from Ginny. I'd like to be able to say that I kept control at all times and took on the chin the relative pain of possibly having lost the love of my life for ever and I did, up to a point. But there were times, usually late at night, when I'd allow myself the indulgence of thinking about her and I'd realise that while I was okay on the outside, on the inside I was undoubtedly falling apart.

I felt lost without her.

I really did.

The only thing that saved me was the arrival of Elaine.

ninety-four

'Matt!' screamed Elaine, at the top of her voice the moment she saw me. 'Over here!'

All the other passengers coming through into the arrivals lounge looked at her as if she was delightfully mad. As soon as she was past the barrier she abandoned her luggage trolley and launched herself at me, showering me with kisses.

'Now that's what I call a hello,' I said, as her onslaught finally ended.

Suddenly she looked self-conscious. 'I guess that was inappropriate behaviour for an ex-girlfriend to engage in with her recently fixed-up ex-boyfriend.'

'No,' I replied. 'Not at all.'

'So what is it?' she continued, awkwardly. 'I promise you, I'm not going to be the needy ex-girlfriend for the whole of this trip.' She laughed. 'I'll just be the needy ex-girlfriend for the first five minutes of meeting you.' She looked at her watch then hugged me again. 'Well,' she said, looking up at me, 'I've got at least another two minutes left.'

'Look,' I began, 'it's great to see you. I promise it is. It's just that, well, I haven't told you everything.'

Elaine screwed up her face in anticipation. 'Ginny's not

here, is she? I haven't, like, just got off on the worst foot in the history of getting off feet, have I?'

I hadn't told Elaine about what had happened with Ginny for what I considered several good reasons. First, I didn't want her to think that her coming to England was part of the reason we'd finished; second, I just wasn't interested in talking about it – even to her; and third, I suspected that if I did go into any detail about the split she'd work out for herself what a fool I'd been.

'No. Look,' I said, 'she's not here because . . . well . . . we're not together any more.'

'But it's only been, like, three weeks or something, hasn't it?'

'It happened a while ago. Six days after it began, to be exact. I'm sorry I just didn't get round to telling you.' I wondered which of my excuses to offer her. 'I was kind of ignoring it.'

'Six days, Matt,' said Elaine. 'I thought this woman was the love of your life. Your perfect woman and all that.'

'I think that was the problem,' I admitted. 'Any time you give things a label as big as that you're bound to screw up.'

Elaine looked at me searchingly. 'What did you break up over?'

'Nothing, really. I just had a moment of thirty-people inspired clarity and realised I was chasing a dream that would never work in reality. I told her I didn't think it would work, she agreed, then told me I should move out.'

'And let me guess what happened next,' said Elaine. 'You went all quiet like you do in these situations and eventually said, "Okay", casually, as if someone had just asked if you fancied a root beer. Then you packed your bags and left.' She grinned, pleased with herself. 'How right was I?' I smiled weakly and didn't answer. 'You don't think you can salvage this?'

'No. It's definitely over.'

'But I thought you were prepared to forget your new job for her?'

'It was all talk,' I replied. 'That's what Ginny and I did really well.' I paused. 'Anyway, let's not discuss this any more – it's depressing me.' I took Elaine's hand. 'I have my ex-girlfriend Elaine with me who is now nothing more than a platonic friend . . .'

'. . . which is true.'

'I have a thirtieth birthday happening in less than a week.'

'That's true too.'

'You've never been to England before, let alone Birmingham.'

'But I have seen *EastEnders*.'

'So I suggest that we enjoy what little time we have before you have to leave.'

ninety-five

Over the next five days Elaine and I had a brilliant time. She was installed in my sister's old room and made to feel at home. Very much so, in fact. As she was my mum and dad's guest as well as mine, they insisted on taking us to all the places we had visited on my arrival back home, which meant that we went to Stratford-upon-Avon again (where Elaine kept insisting that she pose with my parents for pictures in front of any 'ye olde worlde thing' they had going so she could show people at work), we went to the botanical gardens (where my dad just couldn't resist bringing up that mynah bird again) and we even got all the way to the Malverns without so much as a cross word.

It was all Elaine's doing. My parents loved her. She even turned her refusal to have anything to do with the kitchen into a strength. My mum kept going on about how modern women didn't have time to cook and it was probably my fault that we'd split up because, on the evidence of my messy room, I had never done any housework.

Gershwin and Zoë adored Elaine too. We went round there for dinner on the second night, and after just half an hour she was laughing and joking with Zoë like they were old mates. Even Charlotte, with whom I thought I'd built up something of a rapport, bonded instantly with Elaine.

Later in the week I showed Elaine all the buildings that had been key to my development: my old primary school, and the exact spot in the playground where I had broken my arm playing football; the Kings Arms and its flock wallpaper; even Safeway and its booze aisle. She didn't get annoyed when after only five minutes in the supermarket I bumped into yet more former schoolmates: Jez Morris (then, the boy most likely to fail all his exams; now, a part-time actor and model) and Mel Langer (then, the girl most likely to be an actress; now, a TV researcher).

'Do you know,' began Elaine, as we walked out of Safeway loaded with shopping for my mum, 'you have a nice set-up here?'

'I wouldn't call bumping into a few people I know in a supermarket the pinnacle of my career.'

'I'm not just talking about that.'

'I know.'

'But think about this: when I go out in New York I never see anyone I know.'

'You would if you went back to Brooklyn.'

'But I wouldn't go back to Brooklyn. That's my point.' She paused. 'Actually, I have no idea why you left here in the first place. You seem to love it so much.'

'Do you know what?' I said, as we reached the chip shop on the high street. 'I have no idea either. But it's what you do when you get older, you pack up and move along.'

ninety-six

On the eve of my thirtieth birthday Elaine and I went out for a meal with my parents. This time my mum and dad allowed me to pay for it without a fight. My dad must have noticed the look of surprise on my face because he said, 'You're all but thirty now. You can start paying your own bloody way a bit.' We got home just after ten o'clock. My parents went to bed, leaving me and Elaine to watch late-night TV although we soon fell asleep on the sofa. When I woke up, Elaine was lying on my chest fast asleep. It felt just like old times.

'Elaine,' I whispered, trying to rouse her gently. 'Elaine.'

She opened her eyes and yawned. 'We fell asleep.'

'I know. Is this a sign of getting old? When I was a kid my dad was always falling asleep in front of the TV.'

'No, I don't think *we*'re getting old. I don't know what your excuse is but I'm claiming jet-lag,' she muttered.

'Whatever,' I said. 'I'm going to bed.'

'What time is it?'

I looked at the display on my parents' video. 'Ten past one.'

She wrinkled her forehead in an exaggerated display of thinking. 'I think it's your birthday already.'

'What? In the sense that it's now technically Saturday?'

She stretched and sat up properly. 'No, in the sense that you were born at twelve forty-five a.m. You've been thirty for the past twenty-five minutes.'

'I wasn't born at twelve forty-five a.m.,' I said indignantly.

'So when were you born?'

'I don't know.'

'So how do you know that you weren't born at twelve forty-five a.m.?'

She'd got me on that one. 'Well, how do you know?'

'Because the woman who gave birth to you told me.'

I considered what she was saying for a moment. 'So I'm thirty?'

Elaine laughed and kissed my cheek. 'Happy birthday.' She paused and looked right into my eyes. 'Matt?'

'Yeah.'

'Do you mind if I sleep with you tonight?'

I flashed her my most disconcerted look. 'Where's all this come from?'

Elaine sighed heavily. 'Not "sleep with you" sleep with you, but sleep as in two people being unconscious in the same bed at the same time.'

'What for?' I asked, carefully.

'Because . . .' She looked away from me as she spoke. I don't think I'd ever seen Elaine embarrassed before. '. . . because it's the thing I miss most.'

I couldn't say no and I didn't want to. So we brushed our teeth in the bathroom together just like we used to, got undressed (she insisted on wearing the pyjamas my mum had given me so I slept in my boxer shorts) and climbed into my single bed. Within ten minutes Elaine was out like a light leaving me to grapple with the fact that I was now thirty. Rather than thinking *per se*, I turned the whole thing into a question and answer session with my soul that went a little like this:

Question: Do I have any regrets?

Answer: I suppose the question also translates as, did I spend my twenties wisely or did I throw them away doing nothing very much? For the most part, like Edith Piaf, I have no regrets about the way I spent my twenties. If I had them again would I do it all differently? I strongly doubt it. I suppose another regret is the whole 'letting my body go a bit' thing. I think if I could have gone back to my early twenties I'd say something along the lines of eat more, drink more while your metabolism's running high because in ten years' time people of your age now will be laughing at you when you try to buy new clothes. Also – this is becoming a long list for someone who a moment ago had no regrets – I wish, perhaps, that I'd been nicer to my parents. For all my moaning about them, I suspect that they were a lot smarter than I gave them credit for. But to get back to the point – something which has increased in difficulty with my age – do I have any other regrets? Yes, plenty: lending Stephen Cooper my mint condition copy of *Meat is Murder*, which I never saw again; my twenty-four-hour romance with Liz Ward-Smith that began when I told her I loved her and finished fourteen hours later; not learning to speak French (I don't know why, I just feel I should have done it). The list is endless.

Question: What is my greatest regret?

Ginny.

Question: Do I feel as though I'm no longer young?

The short answer to this is no. But the truth is yes and no. At thirty I realise that people who are twenty will look at me and know immediately that I am not one of them. If I strike up a conversation with them they will not ask me which university I'm at, they will not ask me what type of music I'm into, because undoubtedly there will be little crossover between our two musical worlds, and they will not ask me where I go clubbing, because of the crossover thing. They probably won't want to be my friend either – who wants a constant reminder that old age, death and hair loss are just around the corner hanging out with them? And why would I want to hang out with people who would inevitably try to force me to have the exact same long-winded, half-arsed philosophical conversations about life I had ten years ago? This, like all the other things, is stuff I am going to have to accept. And I know that I can live with it.

Question: Who or what would make me feel younger?

Ginny.

Question: Do I feel as though I am any older?

The answer to this is once again, 'Yes, but . . .' On a darker note I am aware that life doesn't always turn out the way you think it will, which is something to which I'd never paid much attention in my twenties, and on a lighter note I also acknowledge that the Remington hygienic hair trimmer will become a part of my future. (Can anyone tell me the evolutionary purpose of suddenly possessing nasal hairs that insist on growing just that little bit too long?) However, I am still light years away from weddings and 2.4 children but am also aware that a mortgage must surely be around the corner. In short, I have no desire to be needlessly young again but that doesn't mean I've got to start acting like my life is over. That said, I have no desire to be some sort of forty-something bloke, with a convertible, a flash pad in London and a continuous stream of eighteen-year-old girlfriends and no plans to ever settle down. That would only depress me.

Question:

Who or what would I like to spend the rest of my life with to save me from becoming some sort of trendy fortysomething bloke, with a convertible, a flash pad in London, and a continuous stream of eighteen-year-old girlfriends and no plans to ever settle down?

Ginny.

My Thirtieth Birthday

Date: March 31st
Days left until thirtieth birthday: 0
State of mind: ?

ninety-seven

'Morning, birthday boy!'

I opened my eyes with a start to see Elaine's beaming face barely an inch away from my own. 'Morning, nutter.' I sighed. 'Is this any way to wake a man on his thirtieth birthday? In my condition I could've had a heart-attack or something.' I rubbed my eyes. 'What time is it?'

'Six a.m.,' she said guiltily, showing me the alarm clock on the floor.

'Why have you woken me up at six o'clock in the morning?' I asked incredulously. 'Not even you can be that jet-lagged.'

'I was too excited,' she said, still beaming.

I looked at her and smiled. I was glad she was here. If anyone in the world could make this day okay, it was her.

'I want to give you your presents now,' she continued, ''cause I'm going to have to sneak back to my room in a minute before your mom finds out that I didn't sleep in my own bed.'

'Good point,' I said. 'It would only confuse her.' I reviewed the last couple of sentences. 'Presents?' I repeated. 'You've got me presents? I thought my present was supposed to be you visiting me for my birthday.'

Elaine looked sheepish. 'I couldn't help myself. I didn't

spend a fortune but I wanted to get you some things you'd really like.' She picked up a large carrier-bag that had miraculously appeared by the side of the bed and handed it to me. Inside were a number of tastefully wrapped parcels.

'Are these all for me?'

'No,' she said, grinning widely. 'I'm just torturing you for the sheer pleasure of it.'

'What are they?'

She sighed heavily in mock exasperation. 'Do you think I spent hours fiddling about with wrapping-paper just to tell you what's in them? Open them and find out yourself.'

Ten seconds and a flurry of tasteful gift-wrapping later I found out. A *Planet of the Apes* action figure of General Ursus ('It looked so cute in the store with its little gun and ape face that I knew you had to have it'); a tape of the self-help book *The Road Less Travelled* ('I figured it might suit your current frame of mind'); a few CDs ('I showed the guy in Tower Records a list of all those wailing, whining female singer-songwriters you like and he suggested that you might like these') and finally a photograph taken by Sara of the two of us lying on the Sofa from Hell eating a huge pack of tortilla chips ('I think we look happy in that photo. Like real friends. That's what we should always remember').

'I don't know what to say,' I said, putting my arm around her. 'Not only are they the first thirtieth birthday presents I've had but they will undoubtedly be the best.' I kissed her fondly. 'Thank you. They're brilliant.'

'You're welcome,' said Elaine. She kissed me back and slipped out of bed. 'I think I'd better be going now.'

Watching her standing in front of me, her small frame swamped by my pyjamas, her painted toenails just visible under the hem of the bottoms she looked adorable. Absolutely perfect. Why didn't I fancy her any more? Why didn't she fancy *me* any more? The perverse nature of human attraction, I thought, is so . . . well , . . perverse.

'Ten dollars for your thoughts,' said Elaine. 'What were you thinking, dude?'

She pronounced the word 'dude' like Keanu Reeves in *Bill and Ted's Excellent Adventure*. She did a very good Keanu Reeves impression.

'When?' I said evasively.

'Just then, when I got out of bed.'

'I wasn't thinking anything.'

'Liar.'

'I wasn't.'

'Double liar.'

I laughed. 'Okay . . . you're right. I was thinking something.' I decided against telling her about wondering why I didn't fancy her and opted to tell her the thought that had followed it. 'I was thinking about how there's some guy out there who at some point in the future is going to fall in love with you. And I was thinking about how happy you'll make him.'

'Is he a nice guy?'

'The best.'

'And do I love him too?'

'You're besotted.'

'Does he like the tattoo at the top of my ass?'

'He adores it.'

'And you can tell all that just from looking at me in your pyjamas?'

I laughed. 'Of course I can.'

'You're not such a bad catch at all, Matthew Beckford,' said Elaine, leaving the room. 'Not at all.'

ninety-eight

It was now early evening and Elaine and I were sitting in the living room watching TV, waiting for Gershwin and Zoë to arrive for my birthday drink in the Kings Arms. I'd been officially thirty for just over eighteen hours now and so far it had been a good day. After breakfast (the most huge fried affair I'd had in my entire existence) my parents had given me their presents (socks/soap/underpants/chocolate) then Elaine and I had gone for a walk around King's Heath park. After that we went for lunch at an Italian place in town, came back to my parents' and sat in the garden with them during a lull in the household-maintenance schedule. Later that afternoon Elaine had made me take a long hard look at my face in the mirror to see if I thought my new birthday had altered my features – she did it every year on her birthday apparently (twenty and twenty-two had looked really good on her but twenty-one had 'really sucked').

'What do you think of your new birthday skin?' she'd asked, peering over my shoulder.

I took a long time to answer her, I was so engrossed in gazing at my own reflection. I rarely looked in the mirror. The occasional glance, of course, but never a long hard poring-over-the-pores stare. I hardly recognised myself.

'And I look like this all the time?' I asked, barely able to believe the evidence of my eyes.

'You sound disappointed.'

'I'm not disappointed, I'm just sort of surprised. You know how you always have an idea of what you look like even if you never look in the mirror?' Elaine nodded. 'Well, mine's nothing like the real thing.'

'I think you're very handsome,' said Elaine.

'Thanks,' I replied. 'You're not too bad yourself, but I wasn't digging for compliments. I'm not saying I'm ugly – I'm just shocked that I've been walking round all this time with no idea what I looked like.'

The front-door bell rang.

'That'll be Zoë and Gershwin,' I said, getting up.

'Happy birthday,' screamed Zoë, coming into the living room. She kissed me and attempted to give me a bear hug.

'Thanks,' I replied.

'Same again,' said Gershwin, shaking my hand, then added, 'With knobs on. Are you all ready for your big night out at the Kings Arms?'

'Are you having a go at my choice of activity for my own birthday?' I asked him.

'I am indeed,' he replied. 'It's not too late to change your mind, you know.'

'I don't want to change my mind. You had your birthday in the Kings Arms, why can't I have mine there too?'

'It's a well-documented fact that I'm a miserable sod. But you, Matt, are actually quite gregarious.'

'I am not.'

'You are. Or, at least, you were at school.'

I laughed. 'Yeah, well, that was a long time ago, wasn't it?'

'Too long,' said Gershwin, chuckling to himself. 'Far too long.' He smiled at Elaine. 'How has he been today?'

'He's been fine, actually. I thought he might go into a bit of a birthday blues slump around mid-afternoon but he fought through it.'

'Come on,' said Zoë, looking at her watch. 'Let's go. We're wasting valuable drinking time.'

We couldn't leave without Gershwin and Zoë saying hello to my parents – they always liked to stop and chat with my friends, especially those who had given their parents grandchildren – and once that was all over the three of us made our way outside. Zoë headed immediately to her car, which confused me.

'Are you driving?' I asked.

Zoë nodded. 'Yeah, why not?'

'But what about "We're wasting valuable drinking time"?'

'I'll leave it in the car park and Gershwin and I will get a taxi back.'

I turned to Gershwin. 'Tell your wife that drinking on my birthday is compulsory so I don't want her turning round to me to say, "Oh, I've changed my mind about the taxi – I'll have an orange juice."'

Gershwin laughed. 'I'll make sure she drinks, okay?'

'I don't understand why you even brought the car,' I said, getting into the back seat with Elaine. 'I mean, you only live about fifteen minutes away.'

'It was cold when we came out,' said Zoë as she started the engine. 'Now, will you stop moaning?'

I moved to open my mouth but Elaine cut me short. 'Not another word,' she said calmly. 'Just sit back and enjoy the ride.'

ninety-nine

'Right,' said Gershwin, after we'd driven round for nearly ten minutes. 'Here we are.' Zoë stopped the car and I looked out of the window. We were in some nondescript cul-de-sac just off King's Heath high street.

'What are we doing here?' I asked.

Gershwin ignored me. 'Have you got the blindfold?' he asked Elaine.

'Sure,' she replied, and pulled a scarf from her bag.

'What's going on?' I asked.

'Duh!' said Elaine, chuckling. 'We're surprising you.'

I looked to Gershwin to clarify what I was hearing.

'Bad luck,' he said. 'We didn't cancel your birthday surprise because, well, honestly, sometimes you have no idea what's good for you. So be a good boy and let Elaine blindfold you.'

'But where are we going?'

'What is it with you today and dumb-ass questions?' said Elaine. 'It's a surprise and we're not going to tell you until we're ready to surprise you. That's how surprises work. Now, let yourself be surprised.'

Blindfolded I was guided out of the car and along a pavement for quite some way. Eventually we reached some steps, walked across what felt like grass and on to what felt like a tarmac path. Finally I was led up some more steps, across a long concrete floor and then inside a building. Although muffled by the blindfold across my ears I could hear music. I strained hard to work out the song. It was the opening bars to 'Holiday' by Madonna. Now I really was confused.

Listening to the clicking of my heels on a hard-surfaced floor I was led towards the sound of Madonna. When she eventually became so loud that it sounded like I was in a nightclub we ground to a halt. I could hear voices, making the occasional shout or scream. I had no idea where I was but I was certain it wasn't the Kings Arms.

'You can unblindfold him now, Elaine,' said Gershwin.

She took off the scarf as ordered and I opened my eyes. Not only was I standing in the main assembly hall of my old secondary school; not only was I surrounded by Katrina, Pete, Bev and a person who I assumed was her husband; not only was there a full-on mobile DJ who was now playing Harold Faltymeyer's 'Axel F', but scattered around the room, in large groups talking, in smaller groups dancing, and in huge groups queuing at an impromptu bar set up in the corner of the room, were a couple of hundred former King's Heath Comprehensive pupils from my year at school. Faces I recognised immediately because I'd seen them in Safeway, and faces I hadn't seen since the day they'd left school at sixteen. Representatives from the entire school spectrum as I remembered it were here: teacher's pets, thugs, geeks, weirdoes, loners, losers, dope-smokers, manic depressives, popular A crowd, popular B crowd, popular C crowd, golden girls, beautiful boys, brain-boxes, sporty types, petty criminals, weeds, headcases and finally, of course, a fair sprinkling of regular people too – anyone and everyone.

'Don't worry,' said Gershwin, laughing. 'This isn't your

birthday party. It's a school reunion. But happy birthday, anyway.'

'So how did this happen?' I asked. 'How did this all get sorted? Did you stand in Safeway with a megaphone and wait for everyone who ever came to school here to come through?'

Gershwin smiled. 'I haven't done anything. Well, very little.'

'So who did?'

'Think about it, Matt,' said Bev.

I thought about it. 'You're saying Ginny did this?'

Bev nodded. 'After you organised that get-together for everyone, Ginny came up with the idea to have a proper school reunion. What with everyone in our year at school having either turned thirty or about to turn thirty, it seemed like a good point to see what we were *all* up to.'

Katrina took up the story. 'So she organised a reunion to coincide with your birthday, thereby killing two birds with one stone. Okay, so I booked the DJ to play the music of our youth, and Bev, Pete and Katrina helped sort out the food but it was Ginny who did all the tricky bits. She booked the assembly hall to give it that school-disco feel, she rummaged through all the old school files and got everyone's address and sent the letters out.'

'So where is Ginny?' I asked, scanning the room. 'Is she here?'

'No,' said Pete, 'I'm afraid not, mate. She said she wanted you to have a happy birthday but that there was no way she would be coming tonight. She wouldn't tell me why exactly. I suspect you know, though.'

I exchanged glances with Elaine.

'Look, Matt,' said Gershwin, attempting to cheer me up, 'there's nothing you can do about this thing with you and Ginny. What's done is done. This is your thirtieth birthday, mate. This is a once-in-a-lifetime reunion of the people who were there when you had the best days of your life.' He laughed as the strains of Culture Club's 'Do You Really Want To Hurt Me?' filled the air.

'I love this song,' said Elaine, grabbing my hand and attempting to pull me on to the dance-floor. 'Come and dance. Loosen up a little!'

'I will,' I said, not in the least bit loosely. 'In a bit. I've got to make a quick call.'

So as Elaine herded everyone on to the dance-floor I made my excuses and left. I tore outside, found a telephone box and called Ginny. My heart was racing as I listened to the ringing tone thinking that at any moment she'd pick up the phone and I could talk to her. But that moment never arrived. Her answering-machine was on. I wondered if she was screening her calls. I left a short, heartfelt message: 'I'm sorry.' With that, I hung up and made my way back to the reunion.

one hundred

The rest of the evening went by in a blur as, encouraged by Gershwin and Pete, I drank plastic cup after plastic cup of wine, beer and even Thunderbird. At ease with myself, thanks to the alcohol, I entered into conversation after conversation of the I-can't-believe-it's-you variety, the I-can't-believe-how-bald-you-are variety, and the I-can't-believe-you're-not-in-prison-yet variety. It was fantastic seeing all those people after all that time, even people I had actively disliked at school, like Penny Taylor (then, the girl most likely to start a fight with me; now, a magazine designer in London) and John Green (then, the boy most likely to throw a pair of compasses at your head for a laugh; now, a car mechanic in Coventry). Elaine seemed to be enjoying herself too. She'd made friends with Katrina, Bev and her husband and, on a couple of occasions, I'd spotted her encouraging them to dance as maniacally as she was to such illustrious eighties hits as Blondie's 'Atomic', Musical Youth's 'Pass The Dutchie' and Jan Hammer's 'Theme To Miami Vice'.

I was on my way back from the toilets – thankfully we were allowed to use the staff ones – when I bumped into Katrina coming out of the ladies'.

'Are you enjoying yourself at last?' she asked.

'Yeah,' I replied. 'You?'

'Definitely.'

It occurred to me as we were walking back to the hall that I hadn't asked how her burgeoning relationship with Pete was going. She hadn't mentioned it all evening although they seemed to be reasonably friendly towards each other. I asked her directly.

'Do you remember how the Pete we used to know was a work-shy, egotistical, science-fiction-obsessed loser?'

'I wouldn't have described him exactly like that but I know what you're getting at.'

'Well, he's nothing like that now. I'd always suspected it was the arrogance of youth and I was right. This new Pete is so lovely and adorable I could weep real tears. Since the get-together at the weekend either I've gone up to Manchester or he's come down to Stoke. We're like schoolkids or some-thing, laughing, joking, phoning each other up three times a day just to say nothing. Okay, I'll admit he's not perfect – that geeky sci-fi obsession is too much to deal with sometimes, especially when he spends hours trying to prove to me just why the last three episodes of *Babylon Five* were the best three hours in television history – but this has got to be the best relationship I've had in, well, years.'

'Congratulations, I'm really pleased for you.'

'Well, we wouldn't have got together if it hadn't been for you.'

'I don't know what to say to that,' I said. 'I hope you're not trying to blame me or anything.'

'I told you, it's the best relationship I've had in a long time.'

'So you're sure it's a relationship?'

'What do you mean?'

'I mean, you know, you feel like it's going somewhere, that

it's got some sort of direction . . . I suppose what I'm trying to say is, well, it's not just nostalgia, is it? Are you and Pete together because you like who each other is right now or is it because of who you used to be? Obviously I'm not saying it *is* like that. But I couldn't escape the feeling that sometimes that was all Ginny and I were about.'

'I take it this has to do with her non-appearance tonight?'

I shrugged noncommittally.

'Matt, you think too much. Getting together with Pete had nothing to do with old times. I didn't even fancy him back then! Okay, maybe just a little bit. But the point is, he's so lovely, we get on great and we're friends. I'm not going to reject him just 'cause he's part of my history too. That's madness.' Katrina gave me a look of intense exasperation, and disappeared.

All alone again, the music reduced to a far-away rumble I decided to take a walk around the darkened empty corridors of the school. Bizarrely, I was compelled to visit the boys' toilets, if only to remind myself how truly disgusting they'd been back then. I was surprised, and not a little horrified, to discover that they were exactly as I remembered them: graffiti on the doors, mysterious burn marks on the walls and, above my head, twenty or thirty years' worth of once wet toilet paper pellets encrusted on the ceiling. However, elsewhere there had been a lot of changes. I discovered that the old English block on the third floor was now apparently the geography block. The old geography block on the second floor was now the new business studies block. And the history block was now the maths block and where the old religious education/music room had disappeared to was anybody's guess. I finished my tour of the school at the doors of the art department and searched out Miss Pascoe's room. The door was locked so I peered inside through the reinforced-glass window. There was just enough light to make out some of Ginny's students' work: paintings, friezes and papier-mâché models. It looked exactly the same as when I was there.

Just as I made up my mind to go back to the party I heard the heavy doors to the main corridor open. I turned to look behind me and there was Ginny, standing in the shadows.

'I got your message,' she said.

'You were in?'

She nodded. 'I was going to pick up the phone but . . . I didn't.'

'So you haven't forgiven me, then?'

She peered into the room I'd been looking at. It was clear that she didn't want to answer this question quite yet. 'I guess the school's changed a lot since you were last here,' she said.

'Yeah, it has,' I replied. 'Everything's shifted around.'

'Except the art room,' she said, smiling.

'Do you ever wish that we were all back here?'

'I am.'

'No, I mean all back here again at school or in the sixth form. They were good days, you know.'

'They were.' She nodded.

There was a long silence, broken only by the sound of a group of people passing the door on their way upstairs. They were obviously doing the tour of the school, just as I had.

'How did you know I'd be here?'

'Katrina saw you go wandering off. My next stop after here was the gym.'

'I hadn't thought of going there.' I considered what to say next. I wanted to get this sorted one way or the other *now*. 'How's Ian?' I asked.

'I don't know,' she replied. 'I'm not seeing him any more.'

'What happened?'

'You know what happened, Matt. You happened.'

'I'm sorry,' I said. 'I'm sorry about everything. I'm sorry if I hurt you. I didn't mean to. When I said to you that I wanted to be with you, that I was prepared to stay here and try to make whatever we had work, I meant it.'

'I meant it too.'

'The thing is, when I thought about us, I could never work out why we were together. I don't mean it like that. I mean – well, we're obviously attracted to each other.'

Ginny smiled. 'Obviously.'

'But every time we get together it never seems to work out.'

'True.'

'I really did think this time would be different. But I don't know . . . I think after I learnt about Elliot dying and all that, it just changed the way I looked at things. I suddenly knew that I couldn't take anything for granted any more.'

'I know,' she said. 'I felt like that when Mum died.'

'The thing is whatever it is about you that I like, well I don't want to take it for granted any more. But at the same time I don't want to spoil it either. I'm tired of being scared, Ginny. I want to give us a go.'

'You don't,' said Ginny. 'Not really. You just think you do. You think that us getting together will be the answer to everything. And if I'm honest that's exactly what I've been thinking too. It would be so easy for us to get together, Matt, because I really do love you. But you know as well as I do that it'll never work because at the back of our minds there would always be this shred of doubt that we're only together because we're scared of being on our own.'

Even though at that very moment I wanted more than anything for us to be together I had to agree that Ginny was right. I was scared of being alone. 'What do we do then?' I asked eventually.

'We stay friends,' she replied.

'But don't you think it's kind of sad that we've never got it together properly?' I asked. 'Don't you think it's sad that we'll never know for sure whether us getting together would've been the best thing ever . . .'

'Or a complete nightmare.' She smiled. 'You're forgetting one thing.'

'What?'

'The thing we do know.'

'Which is?'

'That we make good friends.' She paused. 'Shall we get back to the party?'

'Yeah of course,' I replied.

'Matt?'

'Yeah?'

'This is going to sound strange but . . .'

'What?'

'Katrina told me your ex-girlfriend Elaine is here.'

'And?'

'I'd like to meet her.'

'Why?'

She smiled and shrugged. 'I'm just curious that's all.'

Exactly One Year Later

To: crazedelaine@hotpr.com
From: mattb@c-tec.com
Re: **My thirty-first birthday**

Dear Elaine

First off thanks for the card and present – your Happy Birthday Snoopy card was v. tasteful and the self-assembly wine rack that accompanied it has pride of place in my kitchen. Life here in Australia is cool. My apartment is fantastic. (And so ultra-tidy that I scare myself. I went to bed last night leaving a Chinese takeaway foil container on a table in the living room and I had to get up ten minutes later to put it in the bin. That's how freaky I am.) As for my love-life, which you so coyly enquired about ('So, come on, tell me, Matt? Who's blowing your bagpipes?') I'm afraid to say it's been a bit quiet. I was seeing a girl at work for a while but I don't know, she was nice and everything. But she didn't have . . . that thing. So I suppose I'll have to keep on looking. Glad to hear, however, that the single life for you is still as eventful as ever. To be truthful I didn't like the sound of Harry in advertising (too full of himself) or Woody the musician (a thirty-two-year-old who thinks he's twenty-two – how sad) but I liked that last guy, Carl, he had some good points (and reminded me a little of me) and you were way too hard on him.

You asked how Gershwin, Zoë and Charlotte are, and the news is

they're all fine. Gershwin has finally packed in his job and is going to university in October to be a mature student and study history. Why history? I have no idea. But they've got quite a bit of money saved up so they'll be fine. Charlotte's cool too. She's loving school and doing very well but apparently she misses my ability to make farty noises on the back of my hand. Katrina and Pete, who you met on my birthday, called me recently to say they've got engaged. Katrina was apparently dead set against it but Pete managed to persuade her it was a good idea. I heard via Katrina that Bev is okay too – which reminds me I must give her a call soon. And finally Ginny. She's changed schools now and this one is apparently a lot less hectic. She's still single although there was a brief thing with a guy at her new school (thankfully this one wasn't attached) but that's all over now. In fact, she called me yesterday to wish me happy birthday and to say that now she's single again she's thinking about coming over to visit me over Easter to see if I can fix her up with any good-looking Australian guys. I told her I'll see what I can do. And that – as they say – is the news.
Take it easy,

Love always

Matt xxx

PS In your last e-mail you asked for some advice culled from my experience of the front line of thirtydom that might be useful to you as you turn twenty-five. I racked my brain for ages and the best I could come up with was this:

1) Don't take anything for granted because when it's gone it's always too late.

2) Look after your mates – and they will look after you.

3) The only thing in life that gets easier the older you get is the ability to fall asleep in the middle of a conversation.

4) Never move back in with your parents – it's always a bad idea.

5) And, finally, don't go to the pub unless there's somewhere to sit down. But basically it's all just common sense.

TURNING FORTY

The hilarious follow-up to TURNING THIRTY

How to turn forty:
1. Set yourself a personal challenge.
2. Clear wardrobe of all age-inappropriate clothing.
3. Relax.

How not to turn forty:
Have a complete meltdown.

'Wise, witty and wonderful . . . a triumph!'
Jenny Colgan

'As sad, funny, touching and unpredictable as real life. Mike
Gayle at his absolute best.'
Lisa Jewell

'Honest, poignant and very, very funny.'
Sun

HODDER